THE CREATOR
AND
THE PROMISE

THE CREATOR
AND
JOSEPH A. LUNINI, SR.
THE PROMISE

THE JOURNEY BEGINS

TATE PUBLISHING & *Enterprises*

Published by Tate Publishing & Enterprises, LLC
127 E. Trade Center Terrace | Mustang, Oklahoma 73064 USA
1.888.361.9473 | www.tatepublishing.com

Tate Publishing is committed to excellence in the publishing industry. The company reflects the philosophy established by the founders, based on Psalm 68:11,
"The Lord gave the word and great was the company of those who published it."

Book design copyright © 2011 by Tate Publishing, LLC. All rights reserved.
Cover design by Kristen Verser
Interior design by Lynly D. Grider

Published in the United States of America

ISBN: 978-1-61777-567-3
1. Fiction, Fantasy, General   2. Fiction, Religious
11.05.05

DEDICATION

This book is dedicated to an unknown hand that guided me in the writing of this book, and also to my wife and granddaughter who inspired me with their love and all of my family who believed in what I was writing.

ACKNOWLEDGMENTS

I would like to thank Tate Publishing for their belief in what I have written, so that others would be able to read and wonder. I would also like to thank many of my family members who inspired most of the characters in my book. As I was writing, I could see their different personalities.

PROLOGUE

Long before the universe was formed, there was a spirit that longed for life to walk upon the planets that it would create, placing them into the blackness of space and filling that emptiness with life.

Gathering the particles from the energy that was released when the universe was born, it formed the first world; that world sparkled with such brilliance that if someone could see it, they would marvel at its beauty.

Life was placed upon its surface. All would live in perfect harmony; for this was a place where there would be no wants or emptiness. It was complete in every sense.

As other worlds obtained life, another spirit that was evil lay sleeping, it contained a flaw so small that, in the beginning, no one noticed; it waited in silence for the right moment to take a breath and live.

Slowly, like a cancer, it began to grow and spread, causing the life on this enchanted planet to change. This evil that had come from a single cell spread at an unbelievable rate, spreading its blackness of discontent through all those who lived upon that world.

A council of twelve was formed to try and stop this evil, but it was already too late, for three of those twelve had already been tempted and had crossed over to evil's side.

This began the struggle between good and evil, causing the planet to split into two worlds. This blackness moved throughout the universe, swallowing souls of all who lived there. It hid in the look of innocence but in truth, these evil beings were hideous creatures, called the Gara.

Good tried to stop this from happening, but evil grew too strong, forcing the remaining beauty from the world, and loneliness surrounded the darkness. It was insulated from all the others. After thousands of years, evil arrived upon the earth to spread its destruction and hatred over the people, moving with intense speed. The world was tossed in a place where all aspects of evil flourished, causing us to hate others for their beliefs or appearance. Greed, diseases, and all sorts of evil plagued mankind causing dissent among all the nations of the world.

All appeared lost, but when the first planet had been formed, an unknown force had prepared a book; the title of that book was *The Book of Forever*, and it foretold all that was to come.

On a page in this book it was written that three would rise up from this plague to overcome one, bringing light to the darkness that covered the earth. The struggle wouldn't be easy, as the battle raged not only on our planet, but also in the whole universe.

Sacrifices would become part of these three people's lives: a grandmother, grandfather, and most importantly, their ten-year-old granddaughter. She would rise above all others to push away this darkness.

Death and destruction would seem to be the norm; victory was almost in their grasp, only to be ripped away. The struggle would go forth until...

CHAPTER ONE

I watched as the four of them walked up the small path to the top of the hill where the one unknown figure stood, and inside, I wondered what was going to happen to her. Suddenly a bright light appeared and then—

"Come on, sleepy head. It's time to rise and shine. It's Saturday, and I know you want to sleep in, but the basement is waiting to be straightened up," I heard Sue say through my dreams.

I struggled not to open my eyes. I wanted to see what happened next with the four people and the figure, but then she reached down and touched me, shaking my arm and laughing.

"Dear husband of mine, I know it is the last thing you want to do, but you promised that today would be the day. So come on. Get up, lazy bones."

My mind finally gave in to reality, leaving behind the answer to what I was dreaming. Maybe someday I would find that answer.

Rolling onto my back and blinking my eyes several times, I tried to see clearly. I was like a child that was trying to get Mr. Sandman out of his eyes. Slowly I tried to get the energy to rise from my bed.

"At last," I mumbled as everything became clear. My wife was still laughing as she let go of my arm. She turned and walked out of the bedroom, still talking about the basement. She knew that even after all the years of living here—twenty plus years—there was something about being down in the basement that unnerved me.

I had lived in this house all my childhood, and I still carried the same fears from then till now. . When I graduated college, I wanted to do something great for this world, but before my plans came to be, my parents disappeared without a trace. Many searches had been done, but they were never found, and our house stood empty for a couple of years. Then I met Sue. As they would say, it was love at first sight. So I changed my plans from what I thought would lead to greatness and married her, which I believe brought far more to my life than any other thing would have.

I looked at the clock on the night stand, and I was startled to see that Sue had let me sleep this late. But I knew she was aware of my apprehensions about the basement. Sue never asked me about it, never even acknowledged that she knew my fear. By the time I finally forced my body from the bed and into my crummy work clothes, it was past noon. I had spent two hours getting up and dressed. Going over to the window, I looked out and for a brief moment, I felt as if someone was watching me, but I couldn't see anyone.

It was a warm afternoon, and I wanted to stay inside where the air conditioning kept the house nice and cool, except for down there, but I had made a promise to myself that I would start this task of cleaning up the basement.

But then I found myself saying, "Man, I don't want to do this."

Finally I was able to overcome my fears as I walked over to the basement door.

Going down the stairs to the basement, I walked over to a partial brick wall that also contained the crawlspace under a part of my house. It was dirty and covered with thick cobwebs, and the light from behind cast strange shadows over it that appeared to *move*.

I remembered back to when I was a child; this was that place where you imagined the boogeyman hid and was waiting to drag you into the depths of—

A shiver came over me. *Oh stop it,* I thought. *You're a grown man.* I tried not to look over my shoulder.

Taking care of a fifty-year-old house was a pain; there was always something new to fix. This was Saturday, and all I really wanted to do was to finish this job, go upstairs, watch television, have something cold to drink, and relax.

Moving my shovel across the ground, I heard a clank. The shovel hit something.

"All right now, what's going on?" I said to myself. "It's probably an old brick or a piece of trash. I need to put up some more lights in this section of the basement." I hated this job more and more. Lately everything I did was routine. I loved my family, yet deep inside, there was something else I knew my family was destined to do.

Taking the shovel, I tried again to move whatever was buried there. Again, it hit something hard.

"What could be there that is so hard and heavy?" I said out loud, as I got madder. I didn't want to do this crazy job anyway. A shiver ran through me. Shaking it off, I still could feel something cold in the air moving around me.

When I tried to move the shovel again, it still wouldn't budge. It felt as if something was holding it. I was getting madder; I pushed the shovel as hard as I could. Finally, to my surprise, it gave way, almost making me lose my balance. I felt as though there was something attached to the blade of the shovel, but the darkness shadowed the end of it.

What the heck is going on? I thought, trying to lift the shovel. It finally moved, and I could see that a small box was attached to it. The box had an eerie glow to it and I sensed it calling my name. I tried to drop the shovel, but it wouldn't leave my hands. I tried to move my legs, but I found that they wouldn't move either. My skin bristled; my stomach became a knot, and sweat began to run down my face.

My breathing had become labored; my heart beat like someone was pounding on a bass drum. Fear gripped me like a vice. Every part of my body felt cold.

I had become trapped between my childhood fears and my own curiosity, yet I wanted to know what was happening.

I felt lost in a swirling dark void of space and time. Even though I felt cold, more sweat began to slowly run down my face, dripping off into the unknown—to some place where I thought my feet should be. I looked down for a moment, but they weren't there.

My mind was being pulled in two directions, one of fear and the other of wanting to know what was happening to me. Maybe it was a dream. I looked again at the box that was attached to my shovel. No, it was real; there was a voice that was calling my name, and it was becoming louder. *God help me!* I tried to shout, but my mind wouldn't form the words. I was totally engulfed in fear. I tried to brace myself for the worst. This was it; the boogie-man was real, and he was going to drag me off.

Then something flashed in my mind. Everything stopped. What had been darkness became light; fear faded into calm. I could move my legs. Everything returned to normal, yet it also felt strangely different. Something was about to happen. I could feel it inside me.

My mind became calm. I felt myself wanting to know more about the box. Looking at it, I saw that there was nothing special about it, a plain, gray box. As I pulled the shovel toward me, the box moved with it. There was no fear in me. The box now lay within my reach. Somehow I knew this was predestined to happen. No questions and no doubts. Reaching over, I picked it up. Slowly I turned it around and over. What I was doing felt like the right thing to do. On one side of it, I could see what looked like a handprint. As my hand passed over it, something slowly pulled my hand into the print. Watching, I saw that it fit the impression perfectly, and it was held firmly in place.

In my mind I felt someone speaking to me. It wasn't with a voice, but through thoughts, "*I am the Creator. You have been chosen to change the world and beyond,*" the voice said.

The Creator... to change the world... my mind began asking what was going on, not really a question but somehow deep inside I already knew the answer. I didn't know how or why; I just knew.

The voice in my mind continued. *You have been given this task. It is written in* The Book of Forever, *even before time began. You will do for all and not for one. All things will come to pass when it is done this way. Remember, three will overcome one, not the reverse.*

In my hands the box began to disappear. In an instant it was gone. It was replaced by a ring. Nothing fancy, just a band of silver. Slowly taking it in my left hand, I placed it on the forth finger of my right hand. Looking at the ring, I thought now a journey was to start—a long and troubled one. *What in the heck do I mean, I'm going to take a journey?*

I wasn't sure of the meaning of it all. Whatever I did must be for everyone, not only for one, but for my family as well. I wondered, *Is this ring magic? Like the genie in the bottle?* I decided to give it a try.

"Give me a million dollars," I said. Looking around, there was nothing; it was still the dirty, old basement. My wish hadn't been granted. I was really confused. Now I had a box, which is now a ring, and a journey. What was all this about?

But it was like the voice had said, it had to be for all, not for one. Walking down to the hall that was at the other end of the basement, to a room which had once been used to store coal for the old furnace, I stopped for some reason. I closed my eyes for a few seconds. Opening them, I looked down at the floor.

Something strange was happening; where the floor had been, there were now steps leading down. Standing there, I knew I had to take the next step. Slowly I went down; there were no thoughts of fear inside me. At the bottom, I entered a large, brightly lit room. My fear was completely gone.

Hearing a soft hum above me, I was aware that the floor over my head had closed. At the same time on the other end of the room, a door opened. A man entered. He was of normal height, thin in stature. Slowly he walked over to me. He reached out his hand, and as I put out my hand, he took it firmly in his. Still there was no fear in me. I felt in my heart this was right. A voice in my mind affirmed what I felt.

Looking into his eyes, I asked, "You are not the Creator?" How did I already know the answer? This was the first time that I had met him, and looking up, why did I say the Creator?

"*No,*" he replied. "*The Creator of all has sent me to lead you through the journey you are about to take. I am The Keeper; my name is Daniel.*" He said this not with words, but with thoughts. "*I have come to help you keep the Promise. Once you start on this journey, you will be given powers that are above all others. Your journey will contain great joy and great sorrows. You will always have your heart and mind leading you. I know this all seems beyond your capabilities, but someday you will understand it. The promise will then become clear to you. The powers that you will be given will expand as time goes by.*"

I tried to understand what he was telling me. I would have powers? There would be triumphs and tragedies? But if I have faith and love, in the end, all will overcome one. What was this about? I could feel something creeping over me. It felt cold, a feeling I didn't like; yet as I looked over my shoulder, I saw something, but it was gone before I could see it fully.

The Keeper tried to ease the fear in my mind. He was able to read my thoughts. "*You will unite the world in peace and eliminate poverty, hate, and prejudice. This will take you far from this world, and to other worlds in the future, but this is where you will start. Evil will try to destroy you any way it can.*"

I really didn't understand these words. I needed time to think. My head felt like it was going to explode. How could I even begin to believe his words, considering the fact that I just met him? Everything was too rushed, but the cold feeling around me was growing stronger.

"I have to talk to my wife first; all of our children are in college. Our youngest daughter has had a lot of problems in her life, so we're raising her child, our granddaughter. This has to be a family decision," I said. Looking deeper into his eyes, I asked myself, "What am I getting my family into? This is not happening." Closing my eyes for a moment, I said to myself, *I need time to think. Who is this being who calls himself The Keeper? Is he good or evil, and where did he come from?*"

"The Creator, your Creator, sent me here because you were chosen from the moment that first living cell was born. You and your family are to lead this struggle," The Keeper said.

Then in my mind I heard, *"Go now. We have little time. You will need to contact your two daughters and your son. Their safety is in jeopardy. All of you will be taken from here to a safer place."* And with that, he turned and walked back to the door and was gone, like nothing had ever happened.

As I turned and went back up the stairs, not looking behind me, I felt that old fear. *Don't look back, or I'll get you*, it said, as a cold shiver ran up my spine.

Was The Keeper part of my childhood fear, or was there something more in his words that I would have to learn to trust? Had I already entered the struggle, could it be that the coldness that I felt was the evil that he talked about? Was The Keeper truly the messenger of good?

Many questions flashed through my mind. *Uniting the world? Ridding it of all the things that crippled it? What does it mean, people going into other worlds? Evil that wanted to kill us? Leave and go to a safer place? This can't be real.* Then, looking at the ring on my finger, I realized that it was real. I still wasn't sure about anything. How could I tell my wife and granddaughter this story? It would mean that their lives would change forever. We had been chosen. I didn't know why. I had to trust what he told me. Taking a deep breath, it had to be done.

Walking into the kitchen, I saw my wife, Sue, and granddaughter, Skylar, playing a game. Standing there, all I could do was watch them. I tried to speak, but the words wouldn't come out.

My wife looked at me with concern. "Joe, are you all right? Did you hurt yourself?"

"N—No," I stammered. "I—" was all I could get out. My eyes filled with tears.

"Grandpa." Skylar looked up with a frown on her face. "Did you hurt yourself?"

My wife jumped up from the table and hurried over, putting her arms around me.

She again asked, "Are you all right? What's wrong? Please tell me."

As I looked into her eyes, I took a deep breath. "I have something to tell you, but I really don't know where to start. How do you tell a story that you don't completely believe it yourself?"

"I don't care what it is, but please tell me." She held me closer, and as she held me, I could feel her body tremble.

"Something happened downstairs that, if someone had told me about it, I would think that they were nuts. But honest to Pete, it did happen, and I know I'm not crazy. You have to believe me."

"Joe, tell me," Sue pleaded.

"Let's sit down first," I said, taking her arms from around me and pulling her over to the table.

Sitting down, I slowly started to speak, hoping she would understand. I held out my right hand. "Sue, see this ring on my finger? I found it in the basement; it wasn't a ring at first, but a box."

"A box?" she asked, surprised. "You're telling us you found a box, then a ring?"

"Please, let me finish," I said, trying to make her believe what happened to me was true.

Sitting there, she didn't move or ask another question. When I had finished, I could see there was a different look on her face. Sue's eyes had become brighter. A small smile was on her lips.

"Why are you smiling?" I asked, puzzled. "If someone, even a person I loved, told me a story like the one I have told you now, I would probably think they had lost all their marbles."

She didn't seem that way.

"You do believe me then?" I asked, hoping what I was seeing in her face was belief.

Reaching out and touching my face, she said, "For a long time I have been having dreams where I am on a boat sailing to an unknown place. Along the way I see great beauty and also horrible destruction and people in anguish. Then out of a mist, three figures appear, and with a move of their hands, the ruins are turned to beauty—such beauty that I sometimes I would wake up crying, wishing everything could be that beautiful."

"You believe me then?" I asked.

"Yes. I think my dreams were a foretelling of the future, but I couldn't tell you. Something in my heart told me to wait for the right time. I know that time is now," she said, holding my hand tightly.

"Grandma and Grandpa," Skylar chimed in with a giggle. "I have had dreams too."

"You have?" I asked as I looked at her.

"Yes, Grandpa, in my dreams I see people dressed in blue with flowing capes of yellow. One of them speaks to me, saying, 'Child of life, you are to carry the hopes of many near and far.' He reaches out and touches my heart. It makes me feel so happy. I sometimes don't want to wake up," she said, bouncing up and down in her chair.

He also taught me how to speak in another language, one that people won't understand, but it will give me great power over the coldness. Whatever that means, he said in time I would understand. In another part of my dreams I was told that the language I would speak was spoken by the one who created all, and it has not been spoken until now.

Now I knew it was true. The three of us stood up and held each other in a warm embrace, and I wondered what the future held for us. Still I tried to understand and most of all, believe.

"We have to call the children." They were all in college, but to me they were still little—our two daughters, Marsha and Nancy, and our son, John.

They were all special, each in their own way. John was a strong and caring person. He was always there to help no matter what the problem was, even to the point of trying to save any living creature, from the time he was a toddler. Now he was completing his dream of being a doctor, finishing his last year of med school.

And then there was Nancy. She always wanted to be someone else, dressing in her mother's clothes or dressing up to be a part of nature. No one could ever know what she would be next. She would pretend to be a tree or a rock, maybe even another person. She had finished college and now was attending liberal arts school. Sometimes the things we do as a child foretell what is in our future.

Last was Marsha, the smartest of the three. At least that is what she thought, but it was probably true. Our troubled child, she was always trying to be older, wanting to be the center of everything. She was willing to try the unknown. She had attended several different colleges, only to drop out before attaining her degree. Now I was sure that she had found a college that held her interest. It was a school that dealt in long-forgotten religious beliefs. Marsha was now twenty-eight. Time was running out for her to settle on a career, and maybe this would fulfill her words that would always be in my mind: "One more time, Dad. Please, please!"

Sue and I looked at each other; there was agreement in both of us. Walking over, she picked up the phone and started to call each one of them. *Would she tell them what I had told her and Skylar? What words would she say?* I wondered. But a mother has a way of making her children listen. She was able to reach both John and Nancy, but not Marsha.

I hoped Marsha had overcome many problems in her life. From trouble in school and also with the police, would it never end? But she was the mother of Skylar, a joy in our life.

I listened as Sue first told John and then Nancy that there was a problem and she needed them to come home as soon as possible. It wouldn't take them long. The college they attended was a little over an hour away. But what about Marsha? How were we to reach her? Sue still couldn't reach her. Time was crucial. If we were in danger, time couldn't be wasted.

As we waited in the living room, talking to each other, time seemed to go on and on. We finally heard a car pull in the driveway. Getting up and going to the window, I looked out. It was John and Nancy. They ran from the car, bursting into the house, both talking at the same time.

Holding up my hand, I tried to quiet them. Finally they stopped talking.

"I need both of you to listen. What I am going to tell you will be hard to believe. I didn't believe it myself at first. But your mother and I have never lied to you, have we?" I asked, looking for belief in their eyes.

They looked at each other and then back to us. "No," they responded. They both had a look of concern on their faces.

I had them sit down and then slowly, I told them what had happened. When I finished, they looked at me as if all the wind was taken out of them.

"Dad, do you really mean it? This isn't some kind of a joke or something, is it?" John asked.

Shaking my head and wishing that it was, I said, "No, John. It's not a joke. This has really happened. We have to leave now. I don't know how much time we have left."

"What about college and our friends? Do we have to leave now?" Nancy asked.

I knew that this was tearing their lives apart, but it had to be done.

"I'm afraid so, Nancy. There isn't much time. Those are the things you will have to put on hold for now. It'll be hard, I know, but it must be done. If the person called The Keeper is right. We are in danger by staying here," I answered her.

The air in the room had become cold. Everyone felt it, and all of us looked around, trying to find out where the cold was coming from.

"What about Marsha?" John asked. "We can't go without her."

"I know, John, but we can't find her. We have called all of her friends. No one has seen or heard from her in days. We have no other choice. I hope she will be safe," Sue said as deep sadness choked her voice.

"We have to believe in what we are doing. I know in my heart that it is right. God, forgive us. I really don't know where she is," I said as my own voice cracked.

I walked over to John and put my arm around his shoulder. I knew that Marsha and John had been close growing up, but lately something had come between them. I didn't know what their problems had been. But as a parent I worried. There was something pulling at me.

"It's time for us to leave," I said. Looking around, I could sense something was wrong. I wanted to scream for us to run, but I had to stay calm. I signaled for them to follow me.

We went to the door that led to the basement stairs. I started down. Everyone followed, saying nothing. Once in the basement, we went to the coal room. Standing side by side and looking down, we watched as the floor moved aside and exposed another flight of stairs in front of us, leading down. John and Nancy's faces turned white as they watched what was happening. Out of the corner of my eye, I saw something. I knew we had to hurry. Motioning to all of them, we hurried down the stairs.

As before, a door opened on the other side of the room. The Keeper appeared through it. He came toward us, not so much by walking, but as if he floated. Maybe I thought it looked that way.

Once close to us, he spoke, "Welcome to the first day of a new life." Taking the hands of our son and daughter, he whispered to them. Their faces looked relieved but still puzzled at the same time.

He then addressed Sue and Skylar.

"The two of you, now with Joe, complete the circle. It is a great pleasure to meet you. We must start. Follow me, please," he said as he turned.

His movements were hurried. I felt something cold trying to move over me, and I sensed that the cold contained evil.

We followed him to the door he had come through. Once on the other side of it, we found ourselves in a smaller room. There was a large door on the opposite side of it. The Keeper stopped in front of it, and as we came up close behind him, we stopped.

I watched as he raised his arm toward it; the door slid to one side. Turning to us, he motioned for us to go through it. We walked past him, finding what looked to be some kind of vehicle. There were six seats inside it. Without being told, each of us went to a seat and sat down; The Keeper sat in the last seat. I wondered why there were only six seats. Had The Keeper known that Marsha wouldn't be with us?

The vehicle started to move forward, gaining speed as it moved. Faster and then faster it went. I felt myself being pressed back into my seat. The pressure was intense. I couldn't move any part of my body; my mind was the only thing functioning. Fear began to creep into it. Then I felt something calming enter my mind.

My body began to relax. Closing my eyes, the calming effect completely poured over me. I could feel myself starting to drift into a deep sleep. Deeper I went, with no thoughts. Only sleep was important now.

Something woke me from the slumber. First I wanted to resist it. My eyes fought to remain closed, but they wouldn't. Light slowly entered them. I was now fully awake. I felt as if I had slept for hours. This was the most restful sleep I had ever had.

Sensing that we were not moving, I rose from my seat. The Keeper wasn't with us. Everyone else was still here. As the rest of them woke, we looked at each other. Where were we? At that moment the doors opened in front of us and The Keeper entered. Without saying a word, I knew he wanted us to go with him. I motioned for everyone to come. Rising from our seats, we followed him out the door.

We found ourselves in another brightly lit room. Now for the first time, we were met by other people. I looked down at Skylar. She smiled up at me. Her dreams were true. These people were dressed in blue, as she had seen in her dream.

One of the people dressed in blue came over to us. It was a woman.

"We have places ready for you to freshen up. John and Nancy, will you please follow me?" she said, at the same time pointing to some stairs that went down.

They turned to look at me. I nodded yes; it was okay to follow her. That left the three of us there with The Keeper and the other people I didn't know, but I had no fears about them.

Turning to him, I was about to ask a question, but he answered with his mind before I could ask it. *This is a safe place. There are many things for you to learn and do before you can start*, he said.

How did he know what I was going to ask? Could he read minds?

"Yes," he replied. This time he spoke.

"You have the ability to read minds. If that is so, did you also come into Sue and Skylar's dreams?" I asked.

"The answer you already know. Not only their dreams, but yours as well, for as long as you can remember, we were preparing you for this day," he said.

"Why did you wait until now to come to us?" Sue asked.

"We had hoped that your world would change so that you wouldn't have to go through what is about to happen, but it is written in *The Book of Forever* that the three of you would be brought forth when it was time. That time is now," he said.

Again I could feel something in my mind; it wasn't my thoughts, but The Keeper's thoughts.

"The Promise is starting. One of the gifts has already been given to the three of you. Your minds can penetrate others. No mind will be able to keep you out. But for now, this will only happen when you are close to them. In time, it will expand to far distances," he said, looking deep into my eyes.

His look penetrated deep into my soul. It was searching for something. I didn't know what he was trying to find. After what felt like an eternity, he turned, saying, "Come with me, please."

He started walking down a hallway that was brightly lit. We followed him. At the end of it, there was a set of double doors. As we approached they opened, as if by magic. Entering, I stopped, and what I saw could only be described in one word: *fantastic*. It appeared to be a chapel.

On both sides stood people dressed in blue, with long, flowing yellow capes. Colors of all kinds appeared on the walls. In front of the chapel stood two white columns, one to the left and the other on the right of what appeared to be an entrance. They were immense, but what I saw now between them took my breath away. A wall of water fell gently between them. It contained all the colors of a rainbow and more. The water made no sound as it fell into the basin of water below. The pool was the clearest color I had ever seen, but at the same time, a light blue color emanated from it.

The Keeper turned to us. Speaking softly, he said these words, "You are now ready to receive the gifts of eternal life. Once you enter the waters, your bodies will stop aging, except for you, Skylar. You will age normally until you decide to stop. At that time you will have to come back to the Pool of Life. What all three of you will receive today is the power of your bodies not to be destroyed by anything or

JOSEPH A. LUNINI, SR.

anyone. Each of you will also develop certain other powers. These are unique to each of you. They will become known to you when they are needed. Death can only come by your own choice."

The Keeper stood to the side. Looking at each other, our eyes locked together. I felt our hearts also touch. This was the moment. Taking Sue and Skylar's hands in mine, one on each side of me, I could feel the warmth flowing between us. Each of us took a deep breath and moved slowly into the water. We were engulfed in a feeling of something that no words could describe. It felt as if our bodies were now lifted toward the warmth of never-ending love.

I could hear words being spoken to us, hearing not with our ears but with our minds. *You have given yourselves to the world that awaits you. There will be times of joy and also times of grief. Mistakes will be made, but by making those mistakes, you will learn. Remember, I will be with you always. Your powers will grow as you learn. Evil will disguise itself. Hold each other in your hearts. Remember, three will always overcome one. Now go out into the world; it awaits your coming. You are the power that can defeat the evil and save mankind.*

As we came from the changing waters, The Keeper was waiting for us. Lowering his head before us, he spoke. "The powers that the Creator has blessed you with are great. Nothing can destroy you. Your minds will make it so that time and space can be controlled by you, and by simply thinking of a place, you will be there. The war against evil will not be seen by others at first. It will not be like wars before. The struggle against the enemy will go unnoticed in the beginning. One thing you cannot control is another mind. Everyone must have free will, but those that choose evil will have to be dealt with. When it is most dark, seek the Creator. For then his powers will lift you up. Remember; keep the Promise as it is written in *The Book of Forever.* What you do is for all, not for one."

Looking at The Keeper, I asked, "Why do you bow your head to us?"

"Your names are now written in *The Book of Forever*," he answered.

"Our names are to be recorded?" I asked.

Nodding in response to this, he stood close to me. Touching my shoulders, he spoke, "Your name will be Josaphat, a name that means a great leader of the people. Fairness and caring will be your legacy."

Taking his hands from my shoulders, he moved before my wife, placing his hands on her shoulders, speaking to her. "Your name will be Susanna. You are the lily of the world; the heart and mind you possess will help the worlds become a place of great beauty. By doing this you will minister love and beauty to all, especially to your husband."

He now moved and stood before our granddaughter. Looking down, his hands came to rest on her shoulders. She looked up to his face. The Keeper smiled, speaking to her, "Child, you are so young. You have taken on a task that would be hard for people much older than you to try. But I feel in my soul that your heart is willing, even at your age of ten years. You are older than the years you have lived, and so Skylar, your name shall be Joan. Your name means 'a leader of the oppressed.' You will carry their burdens in your heart, not stopping until they are free of all that makes their lives a struggle. A child will lead the way; you are that child."

Time stopped after he spoke. Afterward John and Nancy joined the three of us. They were not allowed to see the transformation that we had gone through.

CHAPTER TWO

After he had spoken to us for a few moments, everything went dark. Slowly light appeared around us, and then I found that we were now in a different room. I had to ask where Marsha was. But before I could ask him, he turned to me and said, "We are not sure. We went to the places she had lived, but there was no sign of her. In fact, we found nothing. As of now, there is no record anywhere that she ever existed."

"She is our daughter. We know she is out there somewhere," Sue said to The Keeper. Firmness was in her voice, but there was no anger in her. There was something in her voice that I couldn't put my finger on. Was there something that she knew?

"We know she is out there someplace. There is a reason why she cannot be found. No one is sure why," he replied. Reaching over, he touched her arm. "All things will be answered in time, but now you all need to rest. Tomorrow will be the next step. You will have to show power in the face of evil. This will start the process of uniting the world. Remember, three will always overcome one."

Another person came up to us at that moment, saying, "Would you please come with me."

Turning, Sue, Skylar, and I walked back down the hall with her. John and Nancy followed, not knowing what to expect. None of us knew.

As before, on both sides, people were standing. Passing between them, they all put their heads down. This felt strange; they were showing great respect to us. I felt honored, as I knew Sue and Skylar were, but it didn't seem right. We hadn't done anything yet to deserve it.

"You have." I heard the words. *"Giving up your lives, your homes, friends, and family is a great sacrifice."*

Looking around, I couldn't see who said those words. Maybe it was only in my mind. Or was someone trying to make me understand all this? Who or what I didn't know.

She led us to two doors.

"This room is for you, Joan," she said, opening the door. "The other room is for both of you." Opening the door to what was to be our room and lowering her head, she turned and left us.

I thought that Skylar wouldn't want to be by herself, but to my surprise, she looked at us, saying, "Good night," and went into her room, closing the door behind her.

She truly is older than her age, I thought. Yes, I knew in my heart that she would have to be.

Taking Sue by the hand, we started to enter our room. But out of the corner of my eye, I could see four people dressed in blue coming toward us. They were carrying something in their hands.

Closing the door, I wondered what they were doing. If we are safe, they didn't need to be here. Then I felt a calmness come over me. It was all right. I was tired, even though we had slept on the way here a short time ago.

Sue and I changed and settled into our bed. It felt strange. My mind began to wander. In less than twenty-four hours, my life and my family members' lives had been turned upside down. What were we doing? Why had I agreed to this? Everything was starting to swirl faster and faster. I felt like my mind was on the edge of erupting into thousands of splinters, but just as I thought it would happen, Sue laid her arm across me.

"Joe, everything will be all right," she said.

I turned and listened to her voice. Those few words pulled my mind back from the edge of a cliff. That area of fear that had tried to grip my sanity closed, and at the same time, peace drifted over me. Feeling the bliss of contentment confirmed what I already knew deep in my subconscious—everything was meant to be as it was.

Somehow I knew that even before my birth, it was foretold.

Everything is written before each one of us is born. We are destined to do certain deeds; we come from ashes, and we, at some time, will return to ashes. What happens in between has already been foretold. We can't change our destiny; only sometimes that path can be altered.

Looking at Sue, taking her in my arms and holding her close, sleep finally engulfed me in a sweet calmness. As I felt myself drift into sleep, a voice moved through my mind, speaking softly. I felt the words more than heard them. *Love, faith, and belief are your allies; but above all, remember I am always with you.*

The light crept slowly across my mind. Morning had arrived. *Sleep was slow to come*, I thought, but instead it was over in a minute. Opening my eyes, I knew it was time. What had been foretold in the past had arrived. We were reborn, for thousands of years' time had waited for this moment. Today was the first day of a new beginning.

Then, our granddaughter came running into our room.

"Grandpa and Grandma, time to get out of bed. Come on, sleepy heads. Get out of bed!" she said, jumping on our bed. She landed with the force of an earthquake.

"Come on!" She continued jumping up and down, rocking the whole bed.

"All right," Sue said, grabbing her and pulling her down on the bed, kissing her face all over. "Let us get dressed."

Skylar jumped off the bed and ran to the door. Opening it, she was gone in a flash.

"Wait for us!" I hollered, but it was too late. She was gone. Getting out of bed, we dressed and left our room. In the hall we were met by the young lady who had brought us here last night.

"Your granddaughter has already eaten. She is now wandering around and looking at everything." She laughed.

That fast? I thought. "What's your name?" Sue asked.

"Lori," she answered, as a beautiful smile crossed her face. Turning, she pointed down the hallway.

We followed her down the hall and into the dining area. The Keeper was there to meet us. Lowering his head, he asked, "Did you have restful sleep?"

"Yes. Once sleep came, it was very restful," I answered.

"Are you hungry?" he asked, pointing to a table that appeared to go on forever. There were dozens of different kinds of food.

I could feel the emptiness in my stomach, not having anything to eat for a long time.

"Very much," I answered. Taking Sue's hand, we walked over to the table. At that moment John and Nancy came into the room. After hugging each other, we sat down and ate until I thought my stomach would bust. Talking afterwards, I explained to them what had happened. I wanted them to know everything.

After speaking for a long time, I hoped that their questions were answered. They would be involved in this too, at some time.

Looking around, I saw The Keeper come back into the room. I hadn't realized he had left. He walked over and greeted everyone. Then he joined us at the table.

"What you have gone through so far seems like a lot, I know, but you must know it is only the beginning," he said.

Speaking to John and Nancy, he said, "You both can stay here, if you want. We will try to protect you, but there is no guarantee. I'm saying this so you will know the dangers. Our enemies will do whatever it takes to stop us. I can't give you the powers that these three have." He pointed to Sue, Skylar, and me. "You will be needed in time. What you will be asked to do is important; remember that."

Standing up, my son spoke. His voice had firmness to it. "What I'm going to say I know is for both of us," he said, looking down at Nancy. Turning back to The Keeper, he continued. "Our parents and Skylar have given up their own lives to help. They have always been there for us. So you can't ask us to do any less. Whatever needs to be done, no matter what, we will do it."

Both of them came over to us, embracing for a moment. There was only one thought. This could be the last time we would be together for a long time or maybe for forever. Somehow, I wouldn't let that happen.

"Thank you," The Keeper said, touching both of them on the shoulders. "I knew you would feel that way, but I needed to hear those words from you. Now we are ready."

The Keeper pointed to a table in the center of the room. A light rose from it, and in the middle of it, the earth appeared. It looked beautiful—a blue marble spinning against a black background.

Walking over to the table, he spoke, "There are people here on earth and far away who want to corrupt and control everything. They use poverty, disease, hatred, and prejudice to win. By dividing, they can control. Our mission is to unite and destroy all evil that is here and far away."

Looking and listening, I could feel something forming a picture in my mind. The earth was in front of my eyes, but I could see something else. It was the future, but there was fog covering the meaning of it. I tried harder to get a clear view of what it was. It wouldn't clear; maybe I wasn't supposed to see into the future at this time.

"Where do we start?" I asked.

Turning to me, The Keeper said, "We will start in the United States. Several of our agents have infiltrated the White House.

The president is a good person. Her concern for all of the people is heartfelt.

"The agent who is there is named Ann; I believe the president will be able to help us once we can explain what we can do to help the country."

"How do we get inside the White House to meet with her?" I asked. "We can't just walk in."

"Remember what the Creator said about your being able to, with a thought, go to any place you want to?" The Keeper asked. "Our plan is for you to meet Ann there. Josaphat, you and Joan will go. Susanna, you will stay here for now."

This was the plan, and it was to start now. Skylar and I walked to the far side the room. I have to admit there was a small amount of fear in me. Looking at Skylar, I couldn't sense any fear in her.

Now was the time; there was no walking away. We both closed our eyes; in an instant we were there. We had moved as if time didn't exist. Opening my eyes, I found that we were in the Oval Office. Ann was there to meet us.

Looking around, still a little nervous, I asked her, *"Are there any security devices here?"*

"Yes, but we are invisible to them. I don't know if you have realized it or not, but you have been using your mind to communicate with me, not your voice."

I was taken aback for a minute. She was right. We hadn't been talking. Each step I would learn something new. Sensing that someone was coming into the room, I turned to the door. It opened, and in walked the president. There were two people with her. Watching them was strange. We could see and hear them, but they couldn't see or hear us.

She talked with them for a few minutes, and then they left. I was a little leery of appearing before the president for fear of scaring her, but before I could stop her, Skylar became visible to the president, saying "Good morning, Madam President." Skylar didn't move. She had a large, caring smile on her face.

It startled the president for a few seconds, but she regained her composure quickly. As she stood up, I could sense fear in her, but that wasn't going to control her. She was the president. Slowly that fear was replaced by calmness.

Looking down at Skylar, she asked calmly, "Who are you, child, and how did you get in here?"

"My name is Joan. I have come here because we are in need of your help," she said.

"You said 'we'; are there others here with you?" the president asked, as she looked around the room.

"Yes, I'm here with my grandfather and Ann. They are invisible. We didn't want to frighten you too much," Skylar said with a laugh in her voice. A child's outlook at things was sometimes funny.

"They're here in this room with you?" she asked, turning and looking around.

Skylar nodded her head, saying, "They're right beside you."

The president turned to look at both of us as we became visible. There wasn't any fear in her eyes.

"You must be Ann, and of course, you are Joan's grandfather," she said, extending her hand to both of us. "I'm a good judge of character. If I wasn't, the alarm would have been sounded," she said as she raised her hand. I could see a small button on the desk.

"Thank you, Madam President, for not doing that," I said.

"Will all of you please have a seat and explain to me why you are here and why you need my help?" she said, sitting back down, gesturing to some chairs. "My name is Josaphat, and that this is Ann, and you have already met Joan," I said, touching Skylar on the head. "Until two days ago, I was an ordinary working person, living in the Midwest with my wife and raising Joan." For the next few minutes, I tried to explain what had happened. When I had finished, she sat there looking at us. I could see uncertainty on her face.

Finally she asked, "A few people? How in the world do you think that only a few people can undo what no one for thousands of years has been able to do?"

The president looked troubled and at the same time there was a hint of something in her voice that was seeking to know whether we were saviors or simply a bunch of nut cases.

"Let me show you some of the powers we have. Take my hand, Madam President," I said. "Joan, you and Ann stay here."

Standing, she slowly reached out and took hold of my hand. Talking softly to her, "Madam President, please close your eyes."

She looked frightened, but she did as I asked. In an instant we were at the United Nations building. No one could see us. She looked around. "How is this possible?" she asked.

"This is one of the powers that we have been given," I answered.

"If this is true about your powers, then by seeing them, I believe maybe there is a possibility that there is hope," she said.

Turning to her, I once again said, "Close your eyes." In that moment we were back at the White House.

The president looked at her watch. No time had elapsed.

"This is unbelievable," she said, holding out her arm. "If your powers are this great, we need to start right away to change the world. I have always hoped there would be a way I could do something to make this a better place."

"We have to plan how we will move forward," I said to her. "Your help and the help of others will be needed. This will be a long and tedious road. You need to gather your most trusted people, tell them what you know, but no one else should know that we exist. This has to be kept under wraps. Our enemy has eyes and ears everywhere. They control many people. Some of them are in high places. I will contact you again as soon as possible. Now we must leave. Good luck, Madam President," I said, hoping that she truly believed us."

As Skylar and I closed our eyes, I heard her say, "Thank you. I will do whatever needs to be done."

We instantly returned to our base. As we opened our eyes, Skylar and I were met by The Keeper.

"Did everything go all right?" he asked.

"The president will work with us; I think that she can see the good in what we want to do. With her on our side, we have a great ally," I answered.

"This is only the beginning. We will need a lot more people helping us. We will have to plan and be ready for evil to strike at us, from afar, as well as near," he said.

Looking puzzled, I stepped closer to him.

"Attacks far and near? Near I understand, but afar, what do you mean?" I asked.

"The evil that is on earth was planted there before the beginning of man from a galaxy far from this solar system," he answered.

"They have come from…" I hesitated. "From… space?" I asked.

"Yes, they are a race of beings that have traveled throughout the universe, slowly creeping into the population of each planet, taking control of it. They will not stop until this planet is under their control," he answered.

"Why were we chosen to stop them?" I asked.

"As was told in *The Book of Forever*, it is written that three will overcome one. You are the three who were chosen," he answered.

Looking at Skylar, I turned to him, saying, "She is only a child."

"Yes, she is only a child, but her heart will be able to carry the power of enough love to help save the world," he answered.

I hoped that combining her power with ours was going to be enough, but I knew we couldn't stop them alone. Even with the help of some of the world leaders, I didn't think we would be strong enough to defeat this unknown evil.

The Keeper had been reading my mind. Turning to me, he said, "We have people here to help; we know that the aliens are like an octopus. The head controls the arms. Destroy it, and the arms will also be destroyed."

Turning, he signaled for us to follow him.

Leaving the room, we headed down another long hallway; at the end of it, there was a large door. Going through, we entered a room filled with hundreds of people. They were all dressed in blue, but a darker shade. At their sides, there was something strapped to their waists. Somehow I knew that it was a weapon.

As they watched us enter, they stood very quiet, heads lowered for a brief second. Then in unison I could hear, *Long live the three*, not out loud, but more as a whisper.

The Keeper stopped in front of them. We were close behind him. Raising his hands, the whispering stopped. Speaking softly, he began, "We have started on the path of ridding this world and other worlds of this plague that has held it in an iron grip."

A cheer rose up from the mass of people gathered there, one that made our hearts jump, filling us with hope.

Continuing, The Keeper went on. "This fight will not be known to many for a long time, but what happens now will inspire more and more to join us. At the darkest moments will be our greatest triumphs."

Again cheers rose up, now louder than before. The Keeper signaled for us to move to the front, and as we moved in front of him, I knew in my heart and mind what to say.

"We all have been chosen for this; none have refused, even with the knowledge that we may give the highest price. But what we give will rid the world of this evil. This is not just for us but also for our ancestors who have died at the hands of it and also for our children and grandchildren, so they may live in peace."

The room was totally quiet. The only thing that could be heard was the beating of our hearts. Slowly, everyone began to leave. We turned, and with The Keeper, went to meet our destiny. Now there was no turning back.

"They must know that we are going to try and stop this evil," I said, looking at him as we entered the main room.

"That is why those people we just left are willing to give up everything, even life itself, to stop them," he answered.

At that moment my son and daughter came into the room. Approaching us, John spoke, "Dad, we are here to help you any way that you need."

Putting my arms around both of them, I said, "In time, you will each be called upon to help, but this is not the time or place where your help is needed."

I could see the hurt in their eyes. But this wasn't the time for them to help.

In my heart I knew the time would come when they would be called upon. There was something heavy weighing on my soul. It was as if I could almost see the future. Tears formed in my eyes.

Sue put her arms around me, speaking softly.

"Joe, I can feel the pain in you. We have agreed to take this path; the future is something we can't control. What happened was foretold a long time ago, but it is the right path."

I knew she was right; still it was hard not knowing what lay ahead.

The Keeper spoke to us.

"It is hard to make such a sacrifice. You made a choice, not knowing when you did this that when you gained something that you would also lose something that is close to you at the same time. That is a hard choice to make, but there is one thing you can still do. We can take you back, cancel out everything you have been through; everything will seem like a dream."

I heard his words, but they were just that—words. There was nothing I could do; we couldn't go back in time, no matter what. Looking at him, I knew my answer. I didn't have to say it. We had to continue; it was predestined long before we were born.

"What is our next step?" I asked.

"You must rest. You will go back to the White House. The aliens know you exist. They are moving to stop us. All of their undercover people are on the move. Your old house has been burned; several people have been killed. They will try to get to the president. Someone close to her is a traitor. Our people can protect her for a while, but not for long. You will need to go back there tomorrow," he answered.

Going to our rooms, we rested and talked for hours. Skylar didn't join us. It was her choice to make, not ours.

On waking the next morning, it was decided that I would go with some of our people to the White House.

Sue and I spent a few final minutes together. Finally it was time for me to leave. Standing by the others, I closed my eyes, and in a flash, I was back at the White House. We now stood in the Oval Office.

The president was talking to several people; I could feel that they were close to her, advisors and friends. She was trying to convince them.

"I know it's hard to believe, but it's a fact. There is a group of people who have certain powers that are greater than anything we have ever seen. With their help we can win."

Watching, I could see she was having a hard time convincing them. It was time for us to act. Slowly, we became visible.

One of them jumped up, screaming, "How did you get in here?" He started shouting, "Someone call security!"

"Larry, stop. These are the people I was telling you about," the president said as she took his arm.

Larry stopped and turned half-way back to her, saying, "Madam President, how can you believe them? They magically show up. I know it's impressive to move from place to place with your mind as you say, but how do we know that they are not some of the aliens that want to destroy us?"

"Have I ever steered you in the wrong direction, Larry? I know deep inside that what they are telling us is the truth, and if so, we have to listen to them," she said. Her voice was commanding, but also reassuring.

"Listen to me, all of you. The aliens know we exist, and they fear that the balance of power between good and evil is shifting against them. We have to be ready for anything. We believe that they will move against you, Madam President," I said.

"If this is the case the president needs to be guarded more than ever. We need to beef up security," Larry said.

"We will use our people, not others who we aren't sure whether evil has taken control of them or not," I said.

"We have brought some of our allies here to help guard you," I said to her. "These two people will help." I pointed to two of my companions.

Larry started to say something but then stopped. I could feel his thoughts. There was fear for the president, not for himself, but I also felt something else. There was a closeness he felt for her, not as the president, but as a woman.

"What do we do?" she asked.

"You need to keep to your schedule. Get the leaders of your closest allies to meet here. You will need their help as this struggle moves forward. Our biggest problem is time. The longer it takes, the more power they gain," I said.

At that moment as I was speaking, The Keeper appeared. The president and her staff were startled, moving back. I could feel the fear in them.

"Don't be afraid. I'm here to help," he said.

"This is my friend. He is the one who will help lead us," I said, touching his shoulder. Some of the fear in their eyes started to ease.

"We don't have the time to get all of your allies here. The aliens are moving faster than we anticipated; I have generated a list of people we can rely on for help to fight against the aliens. Evil is buried deep inside some of them. Good is forgotten in their hearts," he said, handing me a small book.

Taking it, I opened to the first page. There were several names listed. Somehow I knew what to do next. Closing my eyes, I said each name; one by one they appeared in the room with us. You could almost say it was funny, but the look on their faces was pure fear.

They were scared, trying to scream, but no words would form. Turning, they tried to run, but their legs wouldn't move. It was if they were fixed in time. The evil that was around each of them was a glowing light of eerie blackness.

The Keeper went to each one, and closing his eyes, he touched them above their heart; as he did that, some simply disappeared. Others fell to their knees, crying like children would.

Turning to me, he said, "This was the first of many confrontations with evil. This was easy, but as our mission moves forward, it will become harder. Evil will rise up to challenge us. Some will fail. But where they fail, others will rise up and take their places. It will be a long and difficult process."

He suddenly stopped and turned back to me, "It has begun. Evil has started to move. Madam President, our people will keep you safe, we will bring others here to help protect you. They will become known to you when the time comes."

"What about these people that you have brought here? Won't they be missed?" the president asked.

"That was only their souls that were brought here. Their bodies remained there. It will be as if, by some unknown act, they died," The Keeper said.

"But won't that be strange, that several world leaders all died at the same time?" Larry asked.

"Yes, but it's a risk we must take," I found myself saying.

Something gripped me as I said those words—fear. A dark shadow had crossed over me. Taking The Keeper's arm, I said, not quite sure what was happening, "It's not right. There's something that is evil, and it's moving around us. It's not directed at the president, but at us." It felt like it was trying to swallow me.

"Yes, I feel it too. Evil has penetrated here. Your being is in very great danger, even with the powers the Creator has given you. They know your weaknesses, your family and your fears, and they will use them against you. We must leave at once." He spoke with a tone I had not heard or felt before.

"You will be safe, Madam President, for now. We will contact you very soon. But we must leave now," I said. Closing my eyes, I was back at our base. When I opened my eyes, I saw Sue and Skylar running into the room. I could see the fear in their faces.

"Where is everyone?" I asked, as fear now gripped me. But somewhere deep inside I already knew the answer.

The Keeper spun me around. "They are in the hands of Lati. They are in great danger. Evil has come and taken them far away. They will all be destroyed, for they will not give into evil."

Looking at him, I said, "I feel that they all will be killed, if we don't find them before it's too late."

"No, they will not be hurt right away. Lati will try and use them later against us, and then it will happen," he answered.

"How did Sue and Skylar escape them?" I asked.

"The power that they possess kept them safe," he answered.

"What can we do to help?" Sue asked, holding Skylar against her, not wanting to let go of her for fear of what evil was capable of doing.

"We will continue with our plans. If we don't, I believe they will kill our people now, not wait," The Keeper answered.

"How did they find this place? I thought it was safe. If not, there is no way I would have left my family here," I said, walking away from The Keeper; stopping, I sat down next to the wall.

Walking over to me, he put his hand on my shoulder.

"We have several things to be thankful for. Our group of warriors had left before the aliens came. Susanna and Joan are safe, but most of all, remember you have the power to find the ones that are missing."

Turning and looking up at him, I said, "How? I have met most of them only the one time."

"To find them, you need to visualize their faces in your mind. Remember each one of them is calling out for your help. But there is someone among them who is a traitor. Your son and daughter are also there," he answered.

Sue and Skylar came over to me. Sue knelt down by me, looking into my eyes with a love that was never ending.

"You have to find them, no matter who is the traitor. But most of all, bring our children home," she said, almost begging me as her eyes filled with tears.

A force began to build in me—something powerful. Shaking my head, I raised from the floor as my mind reached out and blended with Sue's. I knew that she could feel the strength and resolve in me

Standing up, she lightly kissed my cheek. Tears brimming in her eyes, turning, she walked away, taking Skylar's arm; they left the room. I used my mind to search, looking for something; there it was, and in a moment, I was gone.

CHAPTER THREE

Opening my eyes, I was in a building, but I wasn't sure where. It was abandoned; the walls were covered with graffiti, and the floors were littered with debris. The windows were broken out.

I started walking down a long hallway; there were rooms on each side. I thought that maybe this was a school, but where was it located? Opening several doors, they all contained nothing but more broken windows, walls that had long been forgotten, and floors covered with trash. It looked as if no one had been here for a long time.

Why was I here? Was it to find the traitor? Who was the traitor? Could it be one of my children, or someone else? *Let it be the latter*, I felt myself pleading from my heart.

There was something trying to slip into my mind. I felt uneasy. Darkness was also creeping around me. I tried to fight it off. I had to keep myself under control; I couldn't let it win, or all could be lost.

Something cold, filled with evil, was trying to take control of my being. Its icy fingers were pulling at my very soul. I had to save my mind from it. There were shadows moving around me; inside, they were trying to destroy me. It was taking every fiber of my soul to fight them off.

A fire slowly started to build in me. As it grew, the fear I felt was being replaced with hatred so strong that my body began to shake with rage. Thrusting my arms forward, I began to spin around. My mind released a rage in the form of a blinding light.

This light searched the shadows, and in a brilliant flash, there were screams, and then nothing. Again I could feel more evil shadows rush at me. Their power was intense. My body and mind braced for it. My powers matched theirs in intensity. What was in me? I felt like nothing could control it, not even myself.

The evil I was facing came at me wave after wave. The power that was held in me was too strong. Each time, it was easier to destroy them. There had to be hundreds of the evil beings moving constantly toward me. But it made no difference. Finally all that was left were their screams and then only silence.

It felt like they kept coming for hours but in reality, it was only minutes. At last, it stopped. I could sense nothing now—no evil, not even my son or daughter. In the attack they had been moved to an unknown place. Searching with my mind, I found nothing. Had I failed? My children were still lost. I had been given powers, but now it appeared that all of my powers had become useless.

It was the same when my parents disappeared. Everyone searched for them, but with no results. It was the same—here one moment then nothing. Could they both be tied together somehow? Had evil known about us long ago? Maybe I would find a clue to where they disappeared when I was finally able to find John and Nancy. *Maybe.*

The only thing I could do was go back empty-handed. How could the world be saved when I couldn't even save my own children? Why was I brought here? Standing there alone, I slowly closed my eyes.

Dreading it, I opened my eyes. I was back at the remains of our base. Sue and Skylar ran over to me, as both of them asked at the same time, "Did you find them?" The two of them looked around, asking, "Where are they?"

Taking them in my arms, I could feel Sue's body shaking, and all I could say was, "They were there, but before I could help them, they were gone. My mind searched, but nothing. I don't know where they are." Looking at her, all I could say was, "I'm sorry." Rage built inside me for what I had done—getting them involved.

At that moment The Keeper came over to us saying, "I felt them taken before you arrived. The traitor could be one of them. Evil has tried to take their souls; it will use that power, if it can, to try and destroy all three of you."

Grabbing his arm, Sue screamed, "How do we save them? I thought you could see or find anything? Why not now? What have we let ourselves become involved in? All I want is my family back." Tears were streaming down her cheeks.

All I could think to say was, "I'm so sorry, Sue. I knew that there would be dangers, but I put it in the back of my mind. I wanted to be a hero. If I had known that this was going to happen, we would have gone back home when we had the chance. Never would I have become part of this had I known that our children would become pawns," I said.

The Keeper interrupted. "Evil is striking at your weakest point, your love for your children. In the beginning I told you there would be suffering, and that is how it must be. I'm sorry, but we still have to move forward. This is their only chance to end it now, by making you doubt what you have been given. It's also the world's only chance. There is one person among you who can help us to overcome them, and that is Joan."

I took Skylar's hand. Looking at her young face, I saw great strength in her; it was the rock that we had to build on.

Before I could speak, she spoke to me with authority, "Grandfather, I know what has to be done. They are part of me too, as they are a part of you. It must be me."

Looking down at her, I knew that she was the one who had the power at this moment to help.

"Child, what I'm asking you to do I have no right to ask, but I know you are the only one who can. I'm putting your life in great danger, but inside me, I knew it would be this way," I said, tenderly stroking her hair.

Again she tried to reassure me. "Grandfather, it will be all right. As you were predestined for what lies ahead, I also have been."

"You and Joan must combine together so that your powers will overcome the mind blockage they are using against us," The Keeper said, speaking to both of us. Turning, he signaled for the two of us to follow him.

Sue turned away from me, not wanting us to see the tears or the fear in her face. No good-byes were to be said. She knew that both of us would return to her and hopefully with our children.

The three of us went to a small room. In the center of the room, there were two chairs facing each other. Skylar and I sat down; taking our hands in his, The Keeper spoke.

"Strength together is the only way to overcome their power. Remember this—they will try to separate you. Keep your minds as one. If they can part the two of you, victory will be theirs. Fight them with every ounce of strength that you have. Remember this—the Creator will be with you," he said, letting go of our hands.

Sitting back in the chairs, Skylar and I held each other's hands. Closing our eyes, we locked our minds. We were joined together like two different rods of steel that were melted and poured into one.

Drifting through areas of dark, then light, and back again, each time we went into darkness, we could feel the presence of something evil. It tried to pull us into it. This was pure evil, an evil that was strong and consumed everything around it.

We had to fight it. Our minds had to stay together. *Don't let it pull us apart*, my mind spoke to Skylar. *John and Nancy depend on us. Not only them, but the only chance the world has of breaking free from the hands of evil that holds it in its icy grip.*

Out of the darkness, I saw one of my daughters calling out to us, pleading, "Help me, Father! I'm scared, and I hurt so much."

Reaching out her arms to me, again she yelled, "Please, Father! Grab my hands and pull me out."

I felt the urge to reach out to help her. My hands moved toward her, but Skylar wouldn't let go of them. Why wouldn't she let go of me? My daughter needed my help.

"No!" she shouted, pulling hard on my hand. "She's not real, Grandfather, it's a trick to try and separate us. Don't let go of me!" Her small hand felt like vice; she was holding on to my hand so hard that it went numb.

Something began to move in my subconscious; words started to take hold of me. A low voice, almost not really there, was saying, "*Evil is everywhere. It will take many shapes. Remember, all will prevail over one. I am with you forever; my strength is your support.*"

My mind started to clear; the image was being removed from my eyes. Looking at the figure of my daughter, I knew at once that this was not her.

"No!" I shouted. "You are not my daughter. Evil has possessed you. I will destroy you!"

Focusing all my energy toward it, light shot out from me—not from my raised arm, but from my mind. The darkness around her burst into light, and if I had made a mistake and it was truly her, God, please forgive me.

The force of the energy that my mind brought forth in that instant blinded me for a second. When I looked to where she had stood, there was nothing. She was gone.

"Grandfather," Skylar shouted. "Over there!" I directed my thoughts in a different direction.

Out of the darkness, several beings came rushing at us, followed by many more. They were all around us. I could feel their thoughts pushing at my mind. We had to fight against them. Forcing our minds tighter, I shouted at Skylar.

"Concentrate harder!" Standing our ground, our minds locked together as one, even tighter.

The battle was in full force. Our minds were being hammered by their mental assault, which was overpowering us. There were too many for us battle alone. They were pushing deeper, trying to split us. I could feel we were losing. Looking down at Skylar, her face was bathed in sweat. With every cell in me, I tried to hammer our minds tightly back into one. This was our only hope.

More and more shadows rushed over us, like the ocean pounding relentlessly against rocks. Could we withstand it? Doubt tried to crawl into me. I could taste my own sweat now as it cascaded down my face in rivulets. How could we hold on? There were too many. Had the risk been too great? Was this to be the end? Were we to be stopped almost before we started?

There simply wasn't enough power to defend ourselves, let alone defeat them, but my thoughts tried to reach out to Skylar. All I could muster was "I'm sorry." Something called me back from the edge of submission.

"Grandfather!" Skylar was shouting and pointing as she pulled on my hands. "Over there! Over there! The Keeper!"

Was she imagining it? If she was, then so was I. There was something moving through the darkness. It was him. Light moved with him, casting the shadows aside like paper being blown in the wind.

He took the two of us in his arms at the same time, like a father carefully lifting up a child.

"Don't despair. We have come." I felt the warmth of his words as they began to rush through us.

I looked at Skylar, and then at The Keeper, a small spark in me became a raging fire. The three of us turned to face the winds of evil. Walking side by side holding hands, our power became as bright as the sun.

I kept thinking about the words we had been told: "All will overcome one."

Our strength at that moment increased tenfold. The power of the Creator was with us, as it had always been.

"Seek, and you shall find." Words I remembered from a passage in one of my favorite books I had read long ago.

We were now one, pulled from the ashes to be whole. Darkness and shadows moved back; light pushed against the evil. It tried to run, but there was no hiding place to be found. The power of the Promise was too strong. In a matter of seconds, it was over. Darkness no longer engulfed us. The battle was won. There would be many more before the war was won. We had learned a valuable lesson. Next time we would be stronger, more aware of the power of evil. Maybe this would bring us closer to finding our children.

A picture flashed across my eyes as I looked at The Keeper.

"Where is Sue?" I asked. Fear was starting to rise in me again.

"She's safe; the helpers are protecting her. Time is short. We must get back to them," he answered, as he turned to face us.

We closed our eyes, and in an instant we were back. I knew we were not really safe here either. Someone or something had betrayed us. Was it my daughter Marsha or was it someone else? I didn't know. But if it wasn't her, they wanted it to look like she was the one who betrayed us. It angered me to see how evil could possess anyone if their heart was weak.

Evil is a seductress; she will promise you anything, but once you accept that gift, free will is lost. You become an addict, having no power. You're its slave to do its bidding until the time comes when you are no longer useful, and then it destroys you.

Turning to The Keeper, I said, "We have to leave this place. We've been here before, and it tried to destroy us. After what has happened, they know that some of us survived the attack. It's not safe in this place." Then Sue came running over to us.

"The Creator has already made a safe place for us. We will leave right away," The Keeper said.

"What about our children? We can't abandon them," Sue pleaded.

"Sue, they will not be left alone for long, but we must get to a safer place. If we are taken here, there will be no hope for any of us," I said.

In a heartbeat we were moved from a place of danger to a place of safety, but the fear inside me wouldn't let go. I was torn between the fear of losing them and the hope that what we were doing was right. Only time would tell.

Opening my eyes, I was surprised to find we were standing in a wooded glen. We stood there quietly listening. We could feel and hear the wind move around us and through the trees. It almost sounded like someone whispering to us. Slowly, I could understand its words. *Be not afraid.*

For a brief moment, everything that had been inside my mind was gone. I felt nothing but calmness; no heaviness was in my heart.

The Creator was with us. We could feel a power flowing over us. With this I knew we could destroy evil. There was also the Promise; it would be kept deep in our hearts forever.

The Keeper appeared beside us, saying, "Come, you must rest," pointing to a cabin ahead. It was nestled between giant redwood trees, a picture of peace.

Walking over to it, I asked, "What about the president? If they can breach our security, what about her safety? How can we rest after what has happened?"

"They don't want to expose themselves to the world yet. But to be safe, we have sent more of our people to help guard her. But you must rest," he answered.

Once inside the cabin, I had to agree. Rest was what we needed. Lying down, my mind was too tired to think. Waves of calmness drifted over me. Looking at Sue lying next to me and Skylar on her bed, both had drifted into a peaceful slumber. I was following them. Trying to fight sleep, it was one confrontation that I was relieved to lose. As I fell asleep I heard these words in my thoughts, *"You have done well; now sleep."*

I opened my eyes as the light of morning crept over me; it was as if time meant nothing. As I slowly moved, I felt my wife still lying beside me. Listening to the quietness of my surroundings, the only thing I could hear was her soft breathing. It was a sound so peaceful, everything was like a dream. If it only was for a brief moment, I almost forgot everything that had happened.

Skylar came over to our bed and excitedly spoke to us. "Come on, sleepy heads. Rise and shine. Come on, it's time to get up," pulling on the blankets.

"Okay, okay," I said, trying to get my body to move.

Sue started to move, saying, "If only we had that much energy."

Taking Sue's hand in mine, we looked at each other, smiles crossing our faces for a few seconds. Time was forgotten, if only for this moment.

After a shower and a shave, I felt human again. Next, a good breakfast was what we needed to fuel up and keep our bodies moving. After eating, leaning back from the table, I glanced out the window at the beauty of nature. Why couldn't everything be like this? *Maybe someday,* I thought, *a day that will be long in coming, like a winter's night, waiting for the first light of the morning sun...*

Without turning, I felt The Keeper come into the room. Joining us at the table, he said, "We need to find your children before they are poisoned by evil."

Looking at him, I asked, "How do we help them if we don't even know where they are?"

"We know that your son and daughter have been taken to different places," he answered.

"Do you know where they have been taken?" Sue asked, her voice showing strength but also worry.

The Keeper answered, "We haven't located Nancy. Our people are searching for her, but we have been able to find your son. He's less than two-hundred miles from here."

"That seems a little strange for him to be that close. Do you think they know where we are and are using John as bait to get us to come after him?" I asked.

"It's possible. I feel it's a gamble that has to be taken, but we will need Joan's help," The Keeper answered.

"Why have you chosen Joan? Why can't you find Nancy another way?" Sue said.

"I can't answer why. All I know is that Joan is the one who will be able to find her," he answered.

Skylar stood up and walked around to me, putting her arms around my neck. She looked into my eyes. Her voice was firm as she spoke. "Grandfather, you know as well as I do that everything that happened had to be that way. It was designed and written before anything ever existed. You and Grandmother are my life, but my life doesn't belong to any of us. I have been chosen for this, and it can't be changed. Now I must take my journey."

I watched Skylar follow The Keeper out of the room, and then I turned to Sue.

"I share your fears for her, but we have to have faith in this. She has been chosen, like you and me," I said.

I wondered if my words were empty. Had I let her go into the hands of evil? My faith had to be in the knowledge that the Creator was her protector. He would keep her safe; he would fulfill the Promise.

Something was taking control of my mind. It wasn't evil. Closing my eyes and squeezing Sue's hand, I let it control me. Leaving this place, I watched myself follow Skylar. I felt that she could sense that I was with her.

I moved past her. Somehow I knew where my son, John, was. The alien beings that held him captive weren't anything I could describe without feeling ill. They were pure evil.

Skylar and The Keeper appeared before the evil beings. Once they saw Skylar, some of them charged at her. She couldn't react to them in time. Her body was tossed backward, hitting hard against the wall. She tried to scramble to her feet, but they wouldn't let her up.

The Keeper quickly moved to her. I could feel the rage in him. Seeing him, the beings tried to flee, but there was nowhere to run. In an instant they screamed and disappeared.

More and more came out of the shadows. The darkness made it impossible to know their numbers.

Their numbers were like trying to count the grains of sand in the desert. The Keeper was being pushed back by the overwhelming number of them.

I tried to help, but I couldn't move. Even my mind was not under my control. The more I fought, the stronger its control over me became. All I could do was watch helplessly.

Then in the midst of ever-growing darkness, a light started to grow, filled with millions of sparkling diamonds. At its center, Skylar rose to her feet; her face contained a look of power, no longer at their mercy. I could hear words coming from her.

"*Ro-Ki. Ro-Ki. Ly-Sa-Fou.*" (Destroy them. Destroy them. Bring forth light.) As she said those words, her body began to float like The Keeper when I first met him. The words were unfamiliar to me, but I knew they gave power to Skylar.

She drifted through the darkness. The shadows started to move, backing away from her. In my mind I could hear their silent screams and feel their agony.

The Keeper joined her, watching in amazement as both of them floated into the darkness. I could feel the control over me being removed; my mind and body were now under my own control once again.

I saw John. He was in front of Skylar. The shadows parted around him, and he ran to her. Not stopping, Skylar signaled for him to get behind her.

Somehow the Creator had brought me here. I didn't know why. Seeing that I was there, he ran into my open arms. Holding him close, I could feel the fear still in him. Turning, we watched Skylar and The Keeper stop in front of a wall for only a second. Then it shattered into millions of pieces.

Behind it was a large creature that rose up to meet them.

Skylar shouted, "*RO-GARA.*" (Destroy Gara.) It started to shake, as well as everything around it. Again she shouted, "*RO-GARA.*" (Destroy Gara.) In that moment, it exploded, covering everything with a green slime, except for Skylar and The Keeper.

When it was over, they turned and came back to us as if nothing had happened. Skylar, John, and I hugged each other, never wanting to let go.

The Keeper joined us, saying, "We have destroyed one of their cells. The creature was the head and mind that controlled the evil in this region. When it was destroyed, the evil that it controlled also died. This area is now free from it. The people need our help; they will need someone to stay here. For now the work will be done in secret."

Looking at each other, not knowing who he meant, I felt something pass between John and Skylar. I knew deep inside my heart who The Keeper was talking about.

John spoke.

"Dad, I know that person is me. You told me my time would come when I would be called upon to help. This is the time."

"John, what can you do?" I asked.

Before John could answer, The Keeper answered for him.

"He has been given the power of healing by the Creator. When he was taken by them, it had already been written that he was the one who would be called the healer of all."

While The Keeper was speaking, something was happening to John. His stature changed; he was no longer a young man. Something shone around him, an aura of soft color. Holding out his hands, I could see warmth radiating from them.

Skylar took hold of his hands, saying, "You have been chosen. The work you do will go unnoticed, but it will never be forgotten. Millions will be saved by you; suffering will be your companion. Life will be long and hard. Your name is written in *The Book of Forever*. Thank you, John."

I was facing a parent's worst fears—having him and losing him to the unknown. His life wasn't in our hands, but the hands of the Creator.

"Dad," John said, bringing me back from my thoughts. "I feel that there is someone near us who is alive."

"Alien?" I asked.

"No, it's one of our people who's in great agony. We must find and help her," he said, turning and walking away from us.

We had to run to keep up with him. Stopping every few seconds, his mind was searching for her, following the faint beating of a heart, heard only by him. Going through one tunnel after another, finally he stopped. Turning his head, he looked at a large mound of broken pieces of concrete piled up in one corner. He quickly went over to it. We followed behind him as we moved around the mound. John stopped; his face became pale. Now we saw what he did. Lying on the ground was a young woman. She was covered in blood, and her breathing was labored.

John knelt down, taking her in his arms and holding her close. He could feel her life slowly slipping away, and he knew in his heart that he couldn't stop it. She looked up at him, her eyes locking on his. Struggling to speak, the words were labored. He could barely hear them. He listened closely, more with his heart than his ears.

"Thank you," she said, taking her hand and lightly touching his face—a touch that bound them together. "Please, there is a picture in my front pocket." She let her hand drop from his face, trying to pull the picture from it. Her hand moved, but she couldn't pull the picture out. There was no strength left in her. Tears formed in her blue eyes. "Please," again came slowly from her lips.

John reached out and took the picture from her pocket. He turned the picture toward her. I caught a glimpse of the picture. In it there were two small children, a girl and a boy. Both were about four years old, twins. They were beautiful. He lowered the picture to her, watching as she used the last bit of strength that she had. She took the picture from his hand and put it to her lips, one last kiss, and good-bye for now. Her eyes slowly closed. She breathed one last time. Silence filled the air around us.

John slowly laid her back down, and taking her arms, he crossed them over her chest. Leaning down, his lips lightly touched her forehead. As he turned to us, we saw tears streaming down his face. Composing himself, he cleared his throat, "This isn't supposed to happen. Two beautiful children are now left alone. They are so young to lose their mother." By a twist of fate this mother had been placed in harm's way. Was it fate or simply an accident of chance that she was in that exact location when the wall came crashing down on her after the explosion?

The Keeper approached him. "John this is the way of evil; we can change it someday. Remember that, at a future time, this mother and her children will be together again in the arms of someone greater than us."

Turning back to where she lay, we watched in amazement as the area above us turned blue like the sky. Her spirit began to rise from her lifeless body, floating up into the blue. What looked like a hand reached out gently and lifted her. A smile was on her face—no more tears, only peace.

In my heart I knew that it was time for John to leave and start his journey. Holding each other, I knew we would be together again, but it would be a very long time till then.

"It's time, John," The Keeper said.

John let go of us, turned, and faded from our sight.

CHAPTER FOUR

Returning to the cabin, Sue was waiting for us. She asked, "Where are the children? Did you find them?"

"Something happened, Sue. We found our son, and it's his time to help," I said.

The Keeper interrupted. "Susanna, please try to remember back when John and Nancy were told that there would be a time when they would be called upon to help. That time has come for him."

"What could he possibly help with? He is only nineteen years old. That's too young. John is only a child," she cried out.

"Susanna, deep inside, John is older than his years. Everyone has to face what he has been destined to do, and it can't be changed," he answered, taking her hand, trying to calm her.

Looking at both of us, Sue started to cry. I think she knew before we left that our return would be without either of them. This was something only a mother could know—the time when her children would be leaving home. The Keeper left us alone to heal our hearts. She didn't ask any more questions, for in her heart, she knew there would a time for us to be together again.

Night was upon us; our bodies grew very tired. Barely making it to our beds, we felt as if we had been drugged. Sleep overpowered us in seconds. I hoped this rest would help.

Opening my eyes, I felt as if days had passed. I took my watch from the nightstand and to my amazement saw that it had only been eight hours. I felt Sue stir beside me; from the other side of the door, I could hear Skylar talking to The Keeper. Sue and I got up dressed and joined them.

"We've learned that one of our people has betrayed us. They gave our location to the Gara," The Keeper said. "We believe it was Lori. While we searched for your son and daughter, Lori led the Gara to where the Waters of Life are located. Looking at him, I asked, "How did Susanna escape them during the attack?"

"She was able to go back to the safety of the cave where the Waters of Life are located. The power of it kept the evil from gaining access to her. They cannot cross into the water," he answered.

"Why did they attack there? The risk had to be large, and their losses had to be great. What did they hope to gain, besides taking our people as prisoners?" I asked.

"They needed to know what our power was capable of doing to them and who we had contacted," he answered.

"Did they find out about the president?" Sue asked.

"Yes, but we have sent more people to protect her," The Keeper answered.

"If we keep sending more and more personnel there to guard the president against their harming her, won't it start to make people wonder what is going on? And besides that, if we cannot make that place safe, what good will that do her?

"They have learned more about us, but we have also discovered more about them. We know if the three of you combine all your powers, you can destroy them in time. We also have to see if, by using your mind and powers, the three of you could find out where they are hiding."

"If Lori was the traitor," The Keeper said, "we have to move fast to save your daughter Nancy. We cannot stay here; the Gara are waiting for us to re-enter the struggle. You three have to return."

The president was in real danger; I knew she was the main person who could help us save the world. She was respected by almost every nation on earth.

The power of evil could pull her into their grasp, and all could be lost if we didn't get to her in time.

Once again I took hold of Skylar and Sue's hands. As I felt my mind enter their minds, I knew it was time, and closing our eyes, I prepared for another confrontation. We moved through time and distance, and in a heartbeat we were back at the White House.

As we opened our eyes, we found that we were in a room next to the president's office, and we could hear screams coming from the Oval Office. Using our minds, we again jumped into her office. The president was under attack by several large creatures ... the Gara.

The president's guards were fighting hard to save her, but they were no match and were giving up their lives to save her. One after another, they fell like dominoes.

We had the element of surprise to our advantage. The Gara sensed we were among them, but it was too little too late. Directing the power of our minds' energy, a blinding, bright light flashed toward them. Their powers were too weak to stop us.

The power we had unleashed surprised even us. It was as if we had started out like a small spark of light but in a second, the strength of that spark was unstoppable; it contained the force of a bolt of lightning, one that had never been seen before. It was so much energy in this small space that the room shook from it force.

The president's remaining guards started to charge at us.

"Stop! They are here to help us!" she shouted. They stopped at her command, and slowly lowered their weapons at the same time.

"Thank God you came, whoever you are or whatever you are. In a few more minutes, I don't know what would have happened," one of her guards said.

The president fell back into her chair, letting out a small, unnoticed sob. Slowly she pulled herself together and sat straight. Now I could see determination in her eyes where only a moment ago there had been fear.

"They appeared out of nowhere. My people fought bravely, giving their lives to save me," she said, looking at the few guards who were still alive.

"They didn't only save you, but maybe the world, for you are an important part of saving mankind," I said as I walked over and put my hand on her shoulder. Who would ever have ever thought I would be doing such a thing?

"How could they get past our security?" she asked. "It was like they were invisible and walked right through with no one questioning them. How could that be?"

I looked into her eyes and spoke to her, not with my voice but with my thoughts. I didn't want anyone but her to know. "*Someone close to you has fallen under their control.*" As I finished, I could see fear in her eyes. There was also a determination to know who it was. "*We know who most of the traitors are,*" I continued. "*Some of our people who are called helpers are moving them at this time.*"

"I want to know who they are," she demanded in a voice filled with anger.

Slowly The Keeper became visible, and we watched as he reached into his pocket and pulled out a small brown book. Opening it, he handed the book to her, saying, "This was found on one of them."

Taking it, she silently began to read. Suddenly a look of intense anger came over her face, followed by surprise, then slowly hurt.

"This is impossible. It can't be true; Jim is my friend and my husband. It has to be wrong. We have known each other since we were children," she said with deep despair in her voice.

The president slumped against the desk; it was the only things that stopped her from collapsing to the floor. The Keeper walked over and gently took hold her of arms to help steady her.

"I know it's hard to understand this, but evil knows no bounds. It finds weakness in people, and with that, it possesses them by promising to give them untold power and riches," The Keeper said.

"I want to see him. Now!" she demanded. She turned to face her remaining guards. Anger raged through her body, and her mind threatened to explode.

The Keeper tried to calm her. "The time will come when you will be able to see him, but this is not the time," he said, hoping she would understand why it was not possible.

She turned and faced The Keeper, looking into his eyes, she nodded as if a quiet understanding in her had doused the flames of anger with calmness. Someplace deep inside, she understood.

"What will happen to them?" I asked.

Turning to me he answered, "They will be taken to a secret place known only to a few of us. In time you will know this place as well. All I can tell you is that this place is called Redemption."

"Will the president be safe, now that we have caught the traitors?" Sue asked, with concern in her voice.

The Keeper answered. "Yes, this area is now guarded by our most trusted people, and it has been anointed with the Promise. Evil can't cross into it. Once the Creator has marked it, evil has no power there, but we can only keep it safe for a short time. They will keep trying to break the Promise to reach her."

"Before that happens, we must move the president to a safer place," Sue said, as she moved toward him.

"She can't leave this place; she will have to stay here. No matter what happens. This is written in *The Book of Forever*," The Keeper answered, looking back at the president, knowing she understood him.

"I know it is my duty to stay here. The people need my protection; there is no walking away. I have no other choice. If evil wins here, it will spread like a plague," she said, with strength and determination in her voice.

This was her destiny. It had been written before time began. We had to believe in the Promise. None of us could turn back. Battles had been fought; evil had tested our strength. People had been lost to it. Places we thought were safe had been breached. New ones had been made. How long this would go on, I didn't know. Evil had to be brought to its knees. This path we were traveling was unknown and treacherous; there were pitfalls everywhere.

The Keeper's voice came into another part of my mind. His words penetrated it, forming a picture. I could see our powers secretly starting to drive the evil beings that controlled the minds of hundreds of people from the capital. It was like watching a movie. From the unknown to the powerful, evil was being forced out of them.

I wondered how it could control so many. We all had our minds. Evil beings had theirs. The evil was far more powerful than I thought.

There was a thought rising in the back of my mind. A picture flashed across it so quickly that I only had time to hope that what I saw was a mistake. Right before it faded I caught a glimpse of a final battle between good and evil. What I saw had to be wrong. The side I thought had won was changed by a future event. I could only hope that time would tell whether my quick glimpse of the future was right.

Shifting my thoughts to the present, I focused on one thing: we had to move fast. This area had been brought out of the darkness and into the light, but how long could we hold it?

Evil had been driven from the eastern states. We now controlled some parts east of the Mississippi River. Washington DC was ours for now. But we had to expand the area around it. The cell that controlled evil had to be close. I could feel it was strong. We had to find and destroy it.

The next few weeks became a blur. We were moving from one state to the next, battling the evil beings and still having to backtrack to the White House to make sure that the President was safe. We were winning, but we were also paying a high cost for our victories.

This didn't last for very long, and in a short time, everything came to a complete standstill. Then our enemy mounted a new offense against us, striking back at several areas at the same time. Washington DC was one of the worst; they had learned to attack us in different ways. We also adapted to this new strategy.

Slowly we started to control most of North America, some of Europe, most of Central America, but South America was a toss-up. The aliens had fortified their control; somehow we had to break their grip on it.

It was time was for Sue, Skylar, and me to use our combined energy to try and break their grip in South America. We had to leave the areas we controlled. This would leave the president protected by only a fraction of what forces there were now, but The Keeper would stay with her to help.

This time we would go together, but each of us would take a different country. Sue would go to Chile, Skylar would go to Argentina, and I would go into Brazil.

Standing together, holding hands, we closed our eyes. Everything was moving so fast that it all became a blur. Only this time we would each travel in different directions. I thought we should go as one. But I knew it had to be this way.

I could feel the three of us separating. Would the Promise be broken? I had to have faith in the Creator.

Skylar was the first. As she opened her eyes, she found she was standing in a deep, dark covering of trees; strange sounds bombarded her, and it took her a few seconds to sense that she was in danger. Swinging around, her mind penetrating the darkness of the evil that was there, she could feel it—the icy cold fingers of evil tried to move around her.

There was evil trying to crawl into her mind to control her thoughts; could she resist it? At the same time she sensed other words trying to move into her thoughts, words—strange and familiar words; at first she didn't understand their meaning, but at the same time they

JOSEPH A. LUNINI, SR.

were becoming easier to understand. It was a language older than time itself. Somehow her mind began to understand their meaning. It was like before when she first spoke this ancient language. It was now becoming as familiar to her as speaking with her grandparents.

"*RO. RO-KI. AMI-LY-SA-FOU.*" (Destroy. Destroy them. Darkness bring forth light.) After saying the words, the darkness moved back; light began to spread around her.

Dark figures started moving back into the retreating shadows. The light was chasing them deeper into the darkness. It was like a race; light pushed the shadows faster till nothing was there.

Suddenly her mind was invaded by something of great strength. She knew that it was more evil. She fought to keep up her attack, and at the same time she tried to fight the darkness that was trying to destroy her. Back and forth, back and forth, her mind swayed; sweat began running into her eyes. Taking her hand, she tried to wipe it away, but something prevented her from moving her arms, and then she found that she couldn't move any part of her body. Fear was trying to overpower her. As she struggled to fight it off, at the same time, she had to keep control of her mind at any cost. Losing control would mean defeat, and that was something she couldn't let happen.

She could feel that their attack was gaining power over her. She had to break its grip, but how? As she tried to think, it became harder to keep them out of her mind.

Let your eyes close and relax your mind, Joan, a voice spoke to her from some place hidden deep, where evil couldn't find it.

The thought of doing this scared her, *What if it's a trick?* She felt as if her body was standing on the edge of a cliff, looking down. She could see the dark waters crashing against the rocks; again and again it tore at them.

The voice was still there, saying, *Joan, believe in me. Let go child. Be not afraid, for I am always with you. Put yourself into my loving care; I will not let any harm come to you.*" the voice was stronger than before.

Taking one last look at the waters below, the decision was made. Skylar closed her eyes, letting her mind become empty. Taking a step forward and putting her faith in the voice, she went over the edge.

The waters rushed up to meet her. Opening her arms to it, she could feel the icy water embrace her, and then there was nothing.

In that moment of nothing between life and death, there is place that helps us to decide what road to take. If you have a chance to choose between them, what choice would you make?

"Good blessings on you, Joan." As she opened her eyes, she was greeted by a beautiful woman with a warm smile dressed in a long, flowing gown that sparkled in the warmth of what felt like and looked like a perfect summer day.

Taken aback for a moment, Skylar didn't know what to do.

"Do not fear, my child. I am here for you. Whatever questions you need to ask, there is an answer," the woman spoke softly, reaching out to her.

Realizing that she was lying on a soft carpet of the greenest grass she could possibly imagine, she jumped to her feet, looking around. There were trees of all sizes, many different kinds and colors of flowers. The sounds and fragrances dazzled her. This was the most beautiful place she had ever seen. It was almost too much for her young mind to understand. It was unbelievable. Where was she?

"Do you like it here?" the woman asked, looking into Skylar's eyes.

"Oh very much," Skylar answered, as she kept turning around. Every place she looked, there was something new and wonderful to see.

"My name is Diana," she said, bringing Skylar's attention back to her.

"I'm sorry, but everything is so beautiful. There is so much to see. It's all so wonderful," Skylar said, turning to Diana, still trying to look around.

"Yes. It is very beautiful here, isn't it?" But it was as if she was asking Joan something else.

Not quite understanding what had happened, Skylar was lost and confused. A few moments ago, she was struggling for existence, but now she was in this strange and beautiful place. How did she get here? Why was she here, and who had brought her here and most of all, who was Diana?

"I have read your mind, and I will answer those questions in time Joan, but for now, come walk with me. Time is short; you need to rest so your mind can make the decision," she said as she took Skylar by the hand.

"Where are we going?" Skylar asked, confused by Diana's words. What did she mean *decision*?

Joan, you have been given a second chance. That is why you have been brought here," Diana said.

"What is this place called?" Skylar asked, still trying to see everything like a child in a candy shop. After all, she was a child.

"It's called Everlasting," Diana answered.

"That's a funny name, and why do you call it Everlasting?" Skylar asked.

"Because it has no beginning and no end; it has and always will be here," Diana said with a smile as she continued. "Come, Joan. Let's have some fun. As I said before, time is short."

This puzzled Skylar. Still being a little girl, she lived to have fun. She had no thoughts of what had happened in the past.

Diana and Skylar ran up hills and back down, through streams, rolled in the grass, laid down, and looked at the clouds, naming each one, shouting, "Look, a dog—no, a horse! Over there, a rabbit. Wow, that's a lion! Oh, there are so many different ones." Skylar giggled.

Diana listened to Skylar's screams of happiness and smiled, but tears formed in her eyes. She had to look away; she didn't want Joan to see the tears.

After having fun for a long time, Diana again took Skylar's hand and not saying a word, the two of them walked quietly for a while. Finally they stopped by a large, clear pool of water where they sat down and Diana took off Skylar's shoes.

"Put your feet in," Diana said as she also put her feet into the cooling blue water. Diana had already taken her shoes off before she had removed Skylar's. It felt so good; she had never felt as calm as she did now. Both of them lay back on the soft grass. Diana stroked Skylar's hair as they turned to each other and taking a deep breath, Diana said, "As I said earlier, you have to make a decision."

"What decision do you want me to make, Diana? I don't understand," Skylar said with a puzzled look on her face.

Diana pulled her close, holding her tightly, laying her hand over Skylar's heart. She could feel it beating fast, as she began to speak.

"Joan, the Creator will give you a choice," Diana said.

"What kind of choice?" Skylar asked, as she tried to understand what Diana was saying, it was confusing.

"You are very special in the heart of the Creator, as you are in the hearts of your grandparents. Your name is written in *The Book of Forever*. But you are a child, and you shouldn't have to suffer in your young life. That is why you have been given the choice to stay here and not have to suffer pain anymore," she said.

"If I stay here, will I ever see my grandparents again?" she asked almost crying, fear in her voice.

"Child, I don't know if you will see them again if you stay here. If you do stay here, no harm would ever come to you," Diana said.

"If I don't leave here, will I grow up?" she asked, and she wondered if that sounded like a strange question.

"You will stay as you are now, never aging. Life will be full of happiness. No worries, nothing will ever make you sad," Diana answered.

"But if I don't ever see my grandparents, that would make me sad. I love them so very much. It would make me cry," she said.

"No, that wouldn't happen, for you wouldn't remember them; all you would know is here." Diana answered.

"What happens if I go back? Will I be hurt?" Skylar asked.

"Again, I don't know the answer, child. Only the Creator knows what the future holds for you," she answered.

Standing up, Skylar walked away from Diana. She picked up a small pebble, tossing it into the water; she watched the circles form around it as they moved out farther and farther. She thought if the water was me, and where the pebble landed, it would start a rippling movement away. But it all would come back to the center. No matter how far away I move, I am still a part of them.

Turning back to Diana, Skylar started to speak. "My life is with them. Whatever happens to me has to be with them. No matter what, it would be easy to stay here, but I can't. I have to go back."

"I knew that would be you answer. Your life is there with them. I'm sorry for what you must endure. You are well beyond the age of ten. Your heart and mind are that of a mature person, someone who cares for others before themselves," Diana said, rising and walking over to Skylar.

Taking Skylar in her arms one last time, she held her tightly, wishing that she could stop what was about to happen. But in her soul, she knew that it couldn't be changed. It has been written. This was Joan's fate. Tears again formed in her eyes as they cascaded down her cheeks falling softly onto Skylar. She could feel it was time; her tears flowed like millions of rain drops were falling.

At that moment Skylar began to fade from Diana's arms, and then she was gone. Back to meet her fate.

Skylar could feel herself being pushed back up from the dark water. Calmness fled from her; fear replaced it.

Her mind was all she controlled. Again she felt the icy fingers of evil creeping into her mind. They were winning. She grew weak; her mind was losing the struggle.

"Grandmother," she cried, as darkness closed around her.

She could feel the water rise over her head, surrendering her soul to the fate that Skylar felt had been foretold. At that moment her eyes began to close, and then she heard a voice saying her name: *Joan, I have not forsaken you. Lift up your hand to me.*

CHAPTER FIVE

Sue opened her eyes. She was standing in a rocky and hilly, desolate terrain. As she looked around, she felt that something wasn't right; she used her mind to move to another area that contained large boulders, as she hid among them she hoped that whatever it was wouldn't be able to locate her, for she knew that it was trying to destroy her.

At exactly the same moment she moved, a bright light flashed and exploded, ripping the spot apart where she had been standing. Then there was another and another bright flash, each tearing up sections of the ground tossing aside some of the boulders like they were feathers.

The explosion spread out in a pattern, destroying everything it touched farther and farther, as each one searched for something. The ground began to shake violently, and still more kept coming. Smoke began to cover everything in a veil of darkness. The only things that could be seen were the bright lights as each exploded.

It was as if they had a mind of their own. She knew the light was searching for her. It was getting closer.

She could feel fear starting to build in the pit of her stomach. Very soon it would find her. There was no place to hide.

All she wanted to do was to run before they found her. How did they know she was there? It was as if they had been waiting. Her mind screamed, *Run, before it's too late!*

"No," the word spilled from her lips. "I will not let them force me from here, and they will not win."

Her eyes frantically looked for a place to hide. Looking at the rocks beside her, she felt something trying to pull her into them. Sue tried to resist. Thinking that she would be crushed, she pushed away, but it wouldn't let her. It was as if her body wasn't under her own control.

In the back of her mind, something was saying it was all right. Let go. Don't fight. Finally she relaxed herself. Putting her hands out, she watched in amazement as they disappeared, then her arms, then her whole being entered slowly sliding into the rocks.

What she was seeing was unbelievable; she and the rocks were now one. Deeper into them she went. Fear was forgotten. Somehow she knew that this was one of the powers that had been given to her.

The rocks closed around her. Sue moved through them as though she were walking through water.

Stopping, she partially closed her mind, no breathing. Even her heart was still. Was she alive?

"Yes," she answered. For her belief in the Creator was strong.

The explosions suddenly stopped. There was nothing—no sound—no movement of anything; a deadly quiet surrounded her. Even time stopped.

Suddenly her eyes caught something coming toward her. It was on the outside of the rocks, and she wondered how she could see it from inside. Words came into Sue's mind, and as she listened she heard, *"All things are possible when your belief is strong."*

Looking carefully, she could make out that it was some kind of craft flying close to the ground. It made no sound. It was some kind of sphere with black and silver colorings marking it.

It slowly settled to the ground, a few yards from her. Did they know where she was?

A door opened on one side of it, and then a ramp moved out, touching ground. Several figures looked out the door, and then they moved down the ramp. They were holding something in their hands. Some kind of weapon maybe, she thought. This was her first true look at them. The beings she saw were hideous, and this sickened her stomach, but somehow she was able to control the bile as it rose into her throat.

They were at least eight feet tall with long arms that hung almost to the ground, skin that had a reddish cast to it and faces that were scarred and hideous to look at. This was evil in its purest form.

They moved slowly to the spot where she had first landed and then, they spread out searching for something: her.

Sue knew that they were looking for something that they had been sent to find and if they found her, she would be destroyed.

Sue knew that what they carried in their arms were weapons of some kind. They were about four feet long and black in color. Even though she had never seen this kind of weapon before, she knew what kind of power they contained. As they moved farther from the ship, she could tell by the look on their faces that they were determined to find her, and she could also sense fear in them, for if they failed at their task it would mean certain death for them.

But they couldn't find her. She wasn't there—nothing was. It was only the creatures and the boulders.

Searching for a long time, nothing could be found. They were arguing with each other over what they should do, and then they finally gave up and went back to their ship. She wondered what would happen next. How would this play out?

Suddenly she became aware of her chance to gain the upper hand as she swiftly moved out of the rocks, but it wasn't her body that came out of them, only a mist which moved toward the ship.

She could feel herself being pulled toward their ship. Would it be like the rocks? Would she become part of it? As she came closer to the ship, she was pulled faster, and then she let herself go and became a shadow as she entered the skin of the ship.

Everything stopped as before. She could see the beings inside the ship, watching as they settled into chairs, working several switches and levers. There was no noise, except the hum of the engine. The ship rose from the ground, then it shot forward at an incredible rate of speed. She could feel no movement; it was as if it was standing still in this blackness of space—strange.

Where was it headed? *Maybe back to their base*, she thought. Hoping it was the main part that contained the head of the being that controlled the arms of evil that snaked into the souls of the living, and by being here, it would give her a chance to destroy the cell of evil that controlled this area. She knew that it wouldn't be easy, but it had to be done.

She watched the aliens move around inside the ship, knowing that they could be destroyed at any time with her mind. But she wanted more, not only them. This could be her only chance, and this was something she wanted to do.

Turning her sight to the outside of the ship, a large mountain loomed in front of the craft and it was heading directly toward it. Sue could feel the ship as it started to slow down and drop lower. Heading to an opening that appeared at the base of the mountain, the craft slowly moved through the opening.

Once inside, she could see that the craft was in a very large cavern. Looking around, she could see there were other crafts stored inside this hidden base.

Not knowing much about their security systems and her own powers, the only part of herself that she allowed herself to move was her eyes.

After landing, the doors of the craft opened, and the beings walked down the ramp and stood beside the ship. Several more creatures came into the area, moving over to the craft. They stopped, and the beings that exited the ship bowed before them, speaking in a strange language. She couldn't understand anything they were saying. The ones from the craft were frightened, for they moved back from the others; they were trying to explain that they had found nothing. She knew that they had searched the whole area where she had landed, but they hadn't been able to find her. She had become part of the rocks, and she knew there was no way they could see her.

Sue could tell that one of the new arrivals was the leader. He kept pointing at them. His tone was getting louder, indicating that nothing the others said could appease him.

They all began to plead, moving their long arms up and down, moving around, but never taking their eyes off him. He listened and then swung his arms, and they stopped talking.

Finally, as if hearing enough, he turned and nodded to the others that had come with him. All but two followed him out of the room. After they had gone through the door, Sue watched as the two that remained lifted what she took to be weapons and pointed them at the other aliens that had tried to find her. A bright light flashed.

In an instant they were gone; nothing could be found; they were completely disintegrated; the only things visible were dust particles floating in the air.

Sue was barely able to control herself and not scream. It took every fiber she could muster to stop, for a scream would give her location away, and that would mean an end to her quest.

Slowly, she was able to calm herself. What she had seen could only be described as barbaric. With no hesitation of any kind, they killed all of them. They were evil for sure.

The two remaining aliens turned and headed out of the room. Sue had to follow them. Moving out of the crafts skin and again becoming a mist, she floated to the wall.

She could feel herself being pulled into it. Sue watched as she became part of the wall. It felt weird, yet natural. As she moved inside the structure, she followed them closely. She made no sound; they didn't even know she was there, moving as silent as the dark.

They were going up a long corridor; at the end of it there was a door. Opening it, they went through, and she followed them in. They were now in a larger room, but she still remained part of the wall, unknown to them.

There were dozens of aliens inside, and each one carried a weapon like the ones she had seen earlier. As she watched, a door slowly opened on the far side of the room. The alien who she took to be their leader entered.

For a brief moment, she wanted to let herself scream. There were several humans among them, and—Oh, my God! One of them was her daughter, Marsha.

What is she doing here with them? Could it be true? Had Marsha turned evil, swayed by their promises of giving her anything she wanted? Had Sue overlooked something inside her? *What could have happened to turn Marsha against me?* she thought.

The alien that was standing close to where Sue was hidden suddenly turned in her direction and at the same time, she realized that maybe they could pick up her thoughts. She hadn't been controlling her mind since seeing Marsha.

Some of the other aliens turned in her direction. Had they also realized that she was there? They raised their weapons; she could feel their thoughts trying to locate her. She closed off her mind; she had to hope that it wasn't too late.

They walked up and down in front of her, trying to figure out if anything was in the room. They didn't know of the power that enabled her to become part of any surface, and she had become part of the wall right in front of them. This power was the only thing that could save her; if they found where she was hiding, with their combined power of their weapons, Sue wasn't sure if her strength could defeat them, let alone defend against them.

Now the leader joined them. He also walked along the wall, searching with his mind for what seemed an eternity. They stood there, finally after not locating anything, their searching stopped.

This was Sue's chance; she acted swiftly, letting herself drift down, bracing herself and pushing backwards from the wall, she found herself on the other side of it, becoming a mist once again.

Her next step was to be on the opposite side of the room and moving fast, she mind-jumped to the wall behind the aliens. Moving only her eyes, she watched them.

The aliens had stopped trying to figure it out. There was nothing there to be found. Sue had to act now—either let fear win, leave, or do what she knew had come to do.

Sue moved from the wall and into the room. None of the aliens had noticed her behind them, mustering all of her courage, feeling anger and hate boiling in her, replacing the fear that had tried to control her.

Letting the power that was in her slam into them, they were disintegrated one after another into millions of pieces. Some tried to turn around to fight, but it was useless.

The power Sue possessed was too strong for them to overcome. There was only one figure left, her daughter, but could she try to stop her. Looking at Marsha, Sue was confused. What should she do? For a brief moment, she felt in her heart that she should reach out to her.

"Mom," her daughter cried out.

In that moment Sue's heart ruled over her mind letting down her guard. It was in that split second that Marsha knew her chance had come. Marsha charged Sue, knocking her down.

Hitting her head hard on the ground, she lost consciousness for several seconds. Marsha knew that by herself, she couldn't defeat her mother and in that moment, she ran past Sue and through the door down the hall and into the landing bay where the aliens kept their ships. Entering one of them, she closed the door behind her. Sitting at the control, she reached forward and started it. Putting the craft in full thrust, it rose from the floor and in a burst of energy, it shot out of the hidden cave.

Moving rapidly, it was out of sight in a moment. Sue slowly regained consciousness. As she struggled to her feet, her head began to clear. Trying to think as she reached the wall, she steadied herself. Feeling the cold surface of the wall, it brought her mind into focus.

Marsha, her mind screamed. She spun around; now her mind was clear. She mind jumped to where the alien's crafts were stored, but she found nothing—no aliens, and no Marsha. She was gone. Using her mind, she, again, tried to search the area surrounding the caves, and again, she couldn't find anything.

Sue had destroyed part of the evil, but not everything, and the one person that could be the worst was her own daughter. She knew they would meet again, only it would be different. If she could do it, love would have to be forgotten, even though it was her daughter and Skylar's mother. Marsha would have to be dealt with somehow. Something had to be done, but Sue wasn't sure she could be the one to do it.

She had to find the head of the evil that controlled this complex and find out where it was hiding. She hoped her power would be strong enough to find and destroy it.

Closing her eyes, she mind-jumped back to where she had fought the aliens before Marsha had overpowered her. Opening her eyes, she let her mind search, but this time it was different—she was after the alien who controlled everything that was here.

A noise from behind startled her. She turned fast. A sigh of relief escaped her lips. It wasn't the aliens she saw but several dozen people dressed in blue—the helpers.

One of them stepped forward. Extending his hand to her, he said, "My name is Thomas. We are here to help."

Sue took his hand firmly in hers. "How did you know to come?" she asked.

"The Keeper sent us. He said to tell you to remember three will overcome one," he answered.

"We have to move fast. We must not let any of them here escape; too many have already fled," Sue said, as she turned and headed for a door on the far end of the room.

"Wait thirty seconds then rush in after me," Sue said, as she blended into the wall. The aliens didn't know her power of being able to mind-jump to any location, and closing her eyes, she passed through the wall and into the room, where the aliens were waiting to ambush her. She once again became a mist, a shadow, and she had the element surprise. When she opened her eyes she saw several aliens, and then everything turned to chaos.

Suddenly the door flew open and the helpers rushed in. At that moment she pushed herself from the wall behind the aliens. The evil ones were caught between her and the helpers. In one swift movement, it was all over. The aliens were destroyed. Nothing was left, only dust floating to the ground.

There wasn't time to celebrate, as more aliens came rushing into the other end of the room firing their weapons. It caught Sue and the helpers off guard, but only for a split second.

Again and again the aliens kept coming. Too many to count, but each time they were beaten back. As the helpers returned fire and combined with Sue's power, the remaining aliens realized they were no match and tried to retreat. Finally the last of the aliens that attacked Sue were destroyed.

Sue looked around. There had been many losses on her side. Many of the helpers lay at her feet. They had given their lives freely for all the others.

Stopping for a moment, Sue knew that they still had to move on. The aliens would fight to the end to save their leader, for it was him that controlled and gave life to them. Moving through the tunnels and from room to room, the battles grew more intense. Sue knew that they were getting closer. Finally everything came to a stop. There was nothing except a few helpers and herself, standing in front of a large door that was made of material that none of them recognized.

One of the helpers walked over to it. Before she could holler for him to stop, he put his hand out. In a flash of bright light, there was nothing left of him. It was like all the evil ones; there was only dust.

There had to be a force field of great power blocking the door. Raising their weapons, the helpers fired at the door. Nothing happened. The energy was absorbed into the barrier. Again they fired, but again nothing happened. The force that was protecting the door grew stronger.

What could they do now to break through it? She knew that on the other side was the target. It had to be destroyed; this was the evil that controlled this vast area.

Destroy the evil and then this place could be rebuilt. The people's lives could be made whole again. This is what we had undertaken. But now this door was stopping us. Sue concentrated her mind into one small point of power as she braced her body, and then directed it at the force field.

A flash as bright as the sun smashed into the door. This light forced Sue and the helpers to raise their hands as they tried to shade their eyes and for a brief moment, the force field gave but did not break. Again she forced her mind to respond, but the same thing happened—only this time it was more powerful. Sue was tossed back against some of the helpers, knocking them to the ground. She struggled to her feet; she could feel herself weakening. Should she try one more time, yes—it had to be done.

Before she could try again, Thomas came over to her. Touching her shoulder, he said, "It's not going to work. Their force field is too strong for you, even with us helping it's no use, and I don't think we should stay. More of the aliens are probably on their way here to help."

Turning to him, Sue almost called him a coward, but stopped before saying it. Looking into his eyes, she could see the fear. She needed to be strong. They couldn't leave.

"Thomas, have faith. I know things seem bad right now, but inside I have to believe that we were sent here for a reason. The Creator wouldn't let us be stopped. It's our fate," she said.

The words hung in the air. She had to be right. The path that they were on was the right one. It had to be.

Turning back, she wasn't sure what to do. Her mind didn't seem able to decide what to do next. Standing there, she felt alone, even with the helpers. The decision was hers to make.

In that moment Sue felt something moving over her mind. What was it? Was the feeling good or evil? Steadying herself she let it possess her.

Susanna. Words started to form—words only she could feel or hear. They continued. *You were given powers that have grown each day. In you there are different ones. Think with your mind. Let it be clear. You have no choice. Inside, you will know which one to use. Have no fear, for I am with you.*

Without turning, she spoke out loud, "Thomas, be ready. When I disappear, wait two minutes, and then fire your weapons at the door."

Thomas looked puzzled, but he knew he had to listen and do exactly what she said. The others also prepared to fire. Sue walked up to the force field, and closing her eyes, she raised her hands and reached forward. She watched as her hands slowly disappeared into it. *So far so good*, she thought.

Then the rest of her body entered. It felt strange. She could see every particle of energy. Her body fit between them. For a moment she stood there, watching in amazement.

She forced herself to focus back to what she had to do, her body moved through the field. Sue was now standing in front of the door. Slowly she became a part of the door. From inside the matter of the door she looked around the room. There in the center was the evil that she was looking for, and around it were several of the aliens, their weapons raised at the door. They didn't know that she was there; she had used her power to disable the force field.

At that moment there was a loud explosion. The door came apart; beams of light flashed into the room. Sue brought the power of her mind against the aliens. The aliens were destroyed in an instant; nothing was left in the room except it—the being that controlled the evil.

It lacked the power to put up a fight. Somehow this thing controlled people, making them do its bidding. That was its only power.

Sue could feel it trying to possess their minds. Evil was moving among the helpers. The evil was everywhere. Now was the time to act. Her mind focused on it. All the rage that had built up in her came to a peak.

Her mind unleashed the energy that had built up in her. A bright light flashed and hurtled itself at the evil being. In that instant it was destroyed. Pieces of it floated and fell to the ground. It was over that fast; the evil that had gripped the people in this area was gone.

Sue leaned against the wall, and tears fell from her eyes as great sobs racked her body. This was the feeling you got when you had destroyed other lives, even if those lives were evil.

Something deep inside her was calling for help. She tried to picture who it was. Where was it coming from?

Sue closed her eyes, letting her mind become connected to the cry. She felt the voice pull her to it. The sound became stronger. It was trying to reach deep inside her.

Something was familiar about it; the power of it grew, gripping her mind in its hold. It contained fear and strength at the same time.

Whose voice? her mind asked.

Skylar's was the reply.

But was that voice real? Did she let her mind make it Skylar's voice, or was it someone else? It didn't matter. She didn't have control … or was it that she didn't really want control?

The voice was pulling her toward it. If it wasn't Skylar, could it be her husband's voice that was calling to her? She didn't know for sure whose voice it was. There was something peaceful that took hold of her, answering the question of who.

You must go to Joan, the voice said, now stronger than ever. *She needs your help, but it may be too late. Later your husband will also need your help. The helpers will finish this. Go to her.*

Sue felt fear—not for herself, but for Skylar. Was it too late? How could the Creator let anything happen to her? Skylar was not only our child, but a child of the Creator.

Power grew inside her, along with rage. Closing her eyes, she could feel herself move rapidly. She had to help her granddaughter.

CHAPTER SIX

After I opened my eyes, I was startled to see where I was. There was nothing, only a stark and barren land. No trees, mountains, water, or life … it looked as if someone had stripped it of everything—nothing but sand, sand, and more sand.

I could feel the overpowering glare from the sun. My body melted under its intense heat. I felt alone, as I wondered why the Creator would send me to this desolate place; fear was trying to gain control of me. Somehow I had to get hold of myself. If I let fear control me as it has done many times before, then my defeat was possible. I knew evil was near as a cold, icy hand tried to reach into my soul. Even under this intense heat, my body felt cold.

Straining hard to bring back control, my mind began to clear; inside I could feel my fear subside. My mind started to focus and began to search the area around me. There was nothing. Straining now with all my powers, I pushed farther out, but I still couldn't find anything. Had I come to the wrong place? No, I knew deep inside that this was where I had to be.

Suddenly something flashed; it was on the edge of where my mind was searching. Again it happened—a flash, brighter this time. Again and again, it came. Each time it was stronger.

My mind tried to locate where it was coming from. Everything was starting to spin around me; my mind kept trying to focus on the flashes. But it was all moving too fast.

Whatever it was, it stayed one step ahead. It was always out of my search pattern. I kept trying, but my mind couldn't determine what it was or where it was coming from.

Then my searching stopped. There was something surrounding me.

It was so high my mind couldn't reach the top of it. I couldn't penetrate through it. Again I tried, but with the same results.

What is going on? I asked myself, as coldness surrounded me with its icy fingers. Darkness now followed, and everything stopped. Only the coldness, which had now become my companion, moved closer around me.

Suddenly a flash hit me with such force that I was tossed into the air, twisting every which way. Up, down, side to side till I didn't know which way was up, and then I landed on my back. My body twisted in pain; I wrapped my arms around myself as I tried to rid my body of this unbearable pain, but I didn't know where to start.

My mind was asking, "*What about the powers I have? Nothing can destroy me. But this was close to it. Maybe it would be better if I did die.*" "No!" I heard myself shout.

Then before I could move, another flash of light brought another spasm of intense agonizing pain that ripped into me and once again I was thrown up, down, back and forth, again crashing back to the ground. The pain was worse this time. I tried to crawl, but there was no place for me to hide and once again, I was hit by this unknown force.

Time after time, my body was being tossed around like a rag doll. How long could I withstand this? Again I thought that maybe it would be better for me if I died, but no, I had to fight this thing—this evil entity.

My mind couldn't focus on anything. Nothing was real anymore. Every part of my body was suffering with this horrible pain. How could I stop it? Somehow I had to figure a way out of this; I was determined not to give in to it.

What was happening to me? My power began to weaken and whatever this was that was attacking me was too strong. Maybe it was possible for me to separate my mind from all this pain.

Then something strange happened. My mind and body felt nothing—no pain—why? The lights passed through me without doing any harm, but how could this be?

Watching it felt strange. Was this real or not? What could be happening? I could feel words entering my mind, "*My son, I am with you. Be not afraid. Our power together is greater than that of the evil.*" I struggled to my feet, as my body and mind regained strength, I could now focus. Concentrating on this invisible force that was surrounding me, I felt the power in me growing stronger, once again letting it build until there was no way to control the energy that my body possessed.

That energy of great power was unleashed at the invisible force surrounding me, ripping a large opening exposing what I had been sent to destroy. Again and again my mind unleashed a greater power and in a matter of seconds, most of what I found to be a wall was destroyed, leaving a pile of rubble in its place.

My fear was replaced by strength and a new faith, and with this strength, I mind-jumped through one of the openings. On the other side were several aliens and my sudden appearance startled them. They tried to raise their weapons in my direction but before they could fire, my mind directed the power inside of me and sent a bright flash at them, blasting them into dust particles. They were gone in an instant, but I could see more of them moving toward me. They were trying to blend the power of their minds into one force before I could prepare myself for their attack.

Bracing myself, I felt my mind form a shield around me. I had now discovered a new power that was given to me and this amazed me. This made me realize why I had been hurt before by the alien's weapons. You have to suffer yourself so that you can truly understand the pain that these people endure every day from this evil, and even as bad as I felt, it was in some cases only the tip of the arrow, for others had suffered more.

Watching the aliens, I wondered how any higher being could let something evil like this exist. My mind answered its own question as soon as I had asked it: *You have to suffer in some form and then be cleansed of that suffering so that you can become pure in spirit and heart.*

The energy of their combined strength bouncing off my shield brought me back from my thoughts. They tried again, but with the same results as before. I could be hurt but couldn't be pushed away from my chosen path.

With the power of my mind, the aliens were gone; nothing was left, as the dust simply floated in the air. It was as if they had never been there. The power in my mind was growing. Had I truly suffered? Was my soul cleansed of all doubts? Was I truly ready to move forward? *Yes,* the answer came from my heart, not from my mind. *But you still have a lack of faith and this will make what you have to do harder.*

I turned and closed my eyes. I could see with my mind a large formation of rocks in front of me. There was no apparent entrance, but in my mind I could see one; it was buried and hidden behind them.

Walking up to the rocks, I used my mind to move several of them aside to form an opening. Without opening my eyes, everything was clear to me as I went in. I knew it was there, but there was nothing but darkness. My body was now giving off a light of its own. More of the unknown power I possessed became known to me.

As I went deeper into the cave, I discovered it was empty. Slowly at first, I continued moving, and then my body moved at a faster pace. I came to another wall. Again, stopping, I used my mind to search over the surface. Looking for a weak point, I found it wasn't solid in the center. From floor to ceiling there was a crack. Using the energy from my mind, I separated the wall into two sections, one to the left and the other to the right. Moving again, I found myself in a large room. The wall slowly closed behind me. I didn't have to look back to see if it had closed, for I could see it in my mind.

Before, if something like this had happened, fear would have crept into me, but now I felt nothing. My whole being was different; I had changed inside. I was no longer afraid of this path that I had been chosen for, but would my faith be as strong.

Walking around the room, I carefully looked at the surface of the walls. Something was written on them. I took and wiped my hand across it. Layers of dust that must have been there for as unknown time fell to the ground.

I watched in amazement at the dust and dirt, which, if I was to make an educated guess, I would have to say that it had been here for centuries. Amazingly it removed itself, and the writing that had been hidden under it began to glow. It also changed from some unknown language that I didn't understand to English. I couldn't begin to figure out how I knew, but then, I thought, *Oh, yes, I know.*

The room was now totally dark except for the writing, which grew brighter. My body was drawn to the center of the room where a chair had mysteriously appeared. With understanding in my mind, I went over and sat down.

The words written on the wall began to speak as if being read by someone. I closed my eyes as I listened and saw in my mind a figure of some kind. There was total silence except for the voice in my mind.

Falling into a trancelike state, my mind was no longer in the room. Everything started to rush past me. Faster and faster it moved; my mind was suddenly splintered into millions of particles, racing like shooting stars. Wait, it wasn't in my mind. It was millions of shooting stars flashing by me. I was no longer in the room. I was someplace else.

Suddenly it all stopped. I could see my body standing in the blackness of the universe. There were lights appearing around me—stars—too many to count and around the stars—small dots of different colors, planets. To me, it was as if something or someone was placing each one in a certain spot.

It started to grow larger as the seconds went by, and some of the colors of light began to fade and then disappear. My mind was drawn to a certain section of them. Moving my mind closer to them, I could see that they were truly planets. Like earth, they had beings living on some of them that looked like us. Everything looked like earth. Others contained different creatures. Their homes weren't like ours. But inside they had the same wants and needs as us. With all living things we are different on the outside, even though we are still the same on the inside.

As I watched these worlds, they developed from living in caves to buildings, moving past that to unbelievable structures. Traveling went from walking to machines that could carry us faster than the speed of light.

These people traveled to other worlds, always in peace and friendship, sharing all they had with whoever they encountered. No war, no hate, always harmony, reaching hundreds of worlds over a span of thousands of years. These worlds united in a common goal, understanding that each was different, but also the same.

I could feel the wonder in each one as they moved through the universe; always uniting in peace.

Suddenly there was a horrible change. These peace-loving people were being driven back; worlds slowly began to turn dark and ugly. Peace was changed to hatred. Living as one now splintered into many.

A dark mass now moved through their lives. Whatever it touched was turned into evil, finally reaching back to where they had started.

Somehow the evil stopped short of the small section of planets that I had first observed. These handfuls of planets resisted the evil. Slowly the dark mass of evil faded back, being pushed by good.

Through time these two battled each other until a change occurred. Evil stopped destroying from outside, but started destroying from within. Good tried to stop it from happening but each time, evil won. Something was missing for good to overcome evil; it needed … yes, the Promise. All would overcome one with the coming of the anointed ones, the three that would save all.

Now a different voice spoke, one that was familiar to me.

"You were alone, but now you are not." In that moment of learning, everything changed, and I found myself lying on the ground. Light was exploding around me, shaking my soul and once again pushed me away from what I had been chosen to do.

It had to be the aliens; they were once again trying to destroy me. Somewhere in my mind, this had all happened before, but now it was different.

Standing, I found this wasn't a barren area. There were mountains, trees, water, and there were also other living things—aliens, the evil ones.

A large group of them moved close to me. Standing there, not moving, I watched as the evil ones came closer. The power of their minds and weapons bounced off me, causing no harm. How could this be?

With a thought from my mind, they were gone. Searching again, I located where the leader was, and I knew he was hiding under ground. With a thought, I was there. It was becoming easier; my powers were expanding rapidly.

Landing in total darkness, my being brought light to it, chasing the darkness away, stopping me in my tracks, for standing in front of me was Nancy.

Aliens were standing around her; they held her in their evil grasp. My heart stopped me from moving. I knew that if I moved they would kill her. Doing nothing wouldn't stop them either. There was fear in her eyes that pleaded for me to help her. She struggled to free herself. It was a standoff for the moment. They were holding a weapon to her head. One of the aliens whispered something to her. With that she stopped struggling.

Someone came out from behind the aliens. They pulled Nancy aside. I could see who it was—Lori. She walked over to me. Standing there with a smirk on her face, she raised her arms in the air. Laughing, she asked, "Well, Mr. Big Shot, what are you going to do now?" as she continued laughing.

"Let her go. She hasn't done anything to anyone, except follow what her mother and I believe in—love. That love made us all choose to follow this path," I said.

She turned around and without saying another word, she walked back to Nancy raised her hand and struck her in the face so hard that Nancy fell to her knees, screaming out in pain. The aliens pulled her back up to her feet.

I yelled, "Stop," stepping toward her. I moved no closer, for there was no way of knowing what they would do. Again I pleaded, "Let her go, please."

Again Lori turned to me, laughing harder than before. "See, I said you wouldn't do anything. All humans are weak, even the ones they call the anointed."

Feeling helpless, I had to find a way to save my daughter. My mind and power had abandoned me. *Think*, I told myself, as I cleared everything from my mind. There had to be a way to stop this.

Lori signaled to them and started to walk around and leave. The alien holding the weapon moved it slightly away from Nancy. This was my chance. In less than a heartbeat, I mind-jumped toward them, hitting Nancy straight on. She fell backwards as the alien shot. It streaked past her, hitting one of the other aliens. The power of the weapon completely disintegrated him.

Putting the power of my protective shield over both of us, I now had the upper hand. I spun around the room; as light shot from my body, all the aliens that were around us were destroyed. But Lori had escaped. I had to find her. I couldn't leave Nancy. Holding Nancy,

I could feel the fear in her. Blood was running down her face from where Lori had struck her.

Looking down at the cut and laying my hand over it, I could feel warmth pulsating from my hand. Holding it there for a few seconds, I could feel the warmth fade. Taking my hand away, I saw that the cut was gone. There was no blood, and Nancy showed no signs of injury.

Nancy stood up.

"I was so scared that they were going to kill me, but I knew that you would come. Something came into my mind saying, *"Fear not, your father will come for you. Remember I am always with you."* Who was in my thoughts, Dad? And how did they know you would come?" she asked.

"There is a power greater than anything we can fully understand. I'm still learning about it. Maybe someday we all will know the answer," I said, hoping what I was saying was true.

"Dad, wasn't she the lady that we first met when we were taken by The Keeper to start this path? She asked.

"She was one of the people we trusted, but evil took over her soul. I'm not sure why," I answered, wondering how she could betray not only us, but The Keeper and most of all, The Creator.

"We need to go after her, Dad," she said, as she tried to go the same way that Lori had gone. Grabbing her arm, I stopped her.

If I let her go with me, what other dangers would come her way? I knew the time had come for Nancy to become part of our journey.

Taking her by the hand, I nodded. It was time we went after Lori.

Using my mind as we walked, I tried to locate any sign of her. There was nothing in any of the caves. Everything was empty. How could she disappear into thin air? I thought, *I guess evil can move like Sue, Skylar, and I can.*

Why were there only a few aliens with Lori? And what was so important about Nancy? Why was Nancy that important to risk their lives by going into the Valley of the Lilly? Did they know that she was protected by the Creator?

Something was going on. Was this planned before, and if so, by whom and why?

"Oops," I said. Something on the floor had caused me to trip. Looking down, it was partially covered with dirt. Bending down, I brushed the dirt off of it, carefully picking it up and turning it over slowly.

"What is it, Dad?" Nancy asked as she tried to see what I was holding.

"I'm not sure," I answered as I wiped it against my shirt; it was a small container. As I opened it, shock gripped my heart. It was one of the rings that Nancy had given to Skylar. Holding it in my hand, I felt fear trying to slip into me.

"That's Skylar's ring Dad. I gave that to her on her tenth birthday," Nancy said, her voice overcome with a sense of foreboding that something had happened to her.

How did Skylar's ring get here? I knew that she loved this ring, especially because Nancy had given it to her. They had a close bond.

Standing up, I took Nancy in my arms, holding her close trying to make everything all right, like I did when she was a child. Her body was shaking as sobs came from deep inside her.

"Nancy, it'll be okay," I said, trying to reassure both of us. The words didn't seem to help. Deep inside, something was telling me that now was the time to use my mind, not my heart.

Clear thinking was now the order. Evil was using everything possible to stop us. Some things were real, while others were not. How did the ring get here? Had Skylar been here, or was someone close to us helping the aliens?

Lori was the one who could answer that question, but I couldn't locate her. We had been looking through these tunnels for hours. We couldn't find anything. Even with the power of my mind searching beyond, it didn't help. What was I missing? Thinking, my mind hadn't sensed her leaving either by the help from the aliens or on her own. So she must still be here some place, but where?

I had to rethink everything, slowly thinking back over the last few hours. There was something wrong. They had risked a lot to take Nancy and John. Then why have only a few aliens guard Nancy and at the same time have the one person who was their biggest source of knowledge and information also here? It didn't make any sense.

"Dad, I have to go to the bathroom," Nancy said pulling away from me." I'll be right back."

Standing there, I watched as she turned and walked over to an opening beside some large rocks.

As she walked over to it, I was still trying to figure out why, and then I knew.

"Nancy!" I shouted, but she didn't stop. Shouting again, "Nancy, stop!" And now I knew.

Rushing at her, something burst in front of me, blinding me for a second. Trying to clear my eyes, I again started after her. The blast had blocked the opening.

"Use your mind!" I screamed at myself.

Closing my eyes again, I readied for the jump, but something stopped me. Opening my eyes, I surveyed everything around me. There were several large rocks lying next to what had once been the opening.

The answer came to me like a bolt of lightning. There were four rocks. Concentrating my mind on the first one, a light flashed from me to it. The rock disappeared. Taking aim on the fourth, I did the same to it. Only two more were left.

I spoke out loud. "Which one do I destroy now? Should I take the one on the left? Or maybe it should be the one on the right. Let's take the one on the right."

"Stop, Dad. It's me."

What I thought was a rock had now become Nancy.

"They forced me to deceive you. The ring was put there as part of their plan."

"What was the plan, Nancy?" I asked, as I could feel my body growing tense with rage.

"Lori took the ring from Skylar when everyone went to sleep the first night we arrived. Lori had access to some of your plans and knew you would come here to try and destroy the alien's cell. They moved the cell from here and set up this trap, using me as the bait," she said, her eyes trying to plead for me to believe that what she was saying was true.

"Nancy, how did you learn to change into a rock? That's a pretty neat trick," I asked, staring into her eyes. I had to wonder if she was telling me the truth or if this was another trick that evil was using to deceive me.

"Uh … uh, they made it look like that. But Dad, it was all a trick," she answered, trying to laugh.

"That's a very good trick, Nancy, or should I call you Lori? Because that's your real name, isn't it?" I said.

"What real name? My name is Nancy," she replied, looking around.

"I wouldn't try to run this time if you still want to exist," I stated, now moving close to her.

She started to back up and then stopped. What I said registered in her mind; there was no place to go. There were no more deceptions for her to use.

It was as they say, like watching a worm squirming. She slowly changed from Nancy to Lori. There was fear coming from her. If you could use the term *her*, for that is not what this thing was.

When I took my mind journey back to the beginning of good I saw the Abiatharians and how they brought divine judgment to all the worlds in the universe.

Along that journey I saw many worlds that used their power for evil; one of them was the world Arabia, known for what was mined from the ground—most of all precious stones.

The inhabitants of this world only thought the stones would make them wealthy. They forsook all for it. By some power they were able to become what they hoarded and over time learned to change into other life forms.

They could never become what they had started out as no more could they look upon their selves as beings of only rocks or imitations of others.

"Please don't destroy me," she begged, still looking around. "I had no choice but to do what they wanted, even if I'm not a true being. There is still life in me. The aliens took my family; yes, I have a family that I love. They would destroy them if I didn't help them to betray you and the rest."

At those words I was left not knowing what to do. Was she telling the truth or was it another ploy to trick me? Looking at it, there was nothing I could think to do.

My mind reached out for help far from here. Reaching into the stars farther and farther, my plea for help traveled.

My eyes slowly closed, no fear of the rock creature running away

What was it I needed to understand? When I opened my eyes, the creature was slowly moving. I blinked and when I looked I saw that it was still coming at me. My mind asked, *"Who are you?"*

Was I to fear it? *No*, the answer softly came to me.

My mind felt totally calm, my whole being opening to accept it. I felt my body and soul were being lifted into the air, as if a loving father was gently lifting his child and holding that child close to his breast, tenderly holding the child with an undying love, like the alpha and the omega of love, with no beginning and no end.

Words were spoken softly into my heart. *There can be good in all life forms. What is living has good and bad. Sometimes things beyond our control force us onto a certain path, some good and some bad. The strength inside you will not be made alone. Remember, I will always be there with you. We will walk side by side down this path. Times when you are too tired to go on, I will carry you.*

I knew that these words came from the Creator. In that moment I knew what I had to do and opened my eyes—eyes that now looked into the soul of the creature.

As I moved closer, the creature pulled back in fear. Reaching out my hand, touching it gently, my mind intertwined with its mind.

For a moment the creature stood there and then vanished.

How could Lori and Nancy be in the same place at the same time? There had to be an answer. I had to see them with my own eyes.

Turning away from it, I could hear a faint call for help deep in my mind. Who was calling me? Was it Sue? I asked myself. No, it was Skylar. Again I could feel something speaking.

Skylar! Skylar! my mind screamed.

I had to go to her. Closing my eyes I felt myself floating, then nothing.

Familiar words once again brought the answer into my mind.

Nancy was taken to the planet of the rock people. There she was brought into their fold, not as an enemy, but as a friend. Nancy was taken to a place of safety where the Gara couldn't find her. What you saw wasn't really there. I made you believe that it was Nancy, but it was another rock person who had taken her place, knowing that they would probably be destroyed, and this one did it for the larger good of all the others. Nancy is safe for now; when her time comes that will change.

CHAPTER SEVEN

When I opened my eyes, Sue and I almost collided. It was really weird—two people in entirely different locations using their minds to land in the identical same spot. I knew of only three people, including myself, who were capable of doing this, and if not for the circumstances, this would have been funny, but there wasn't anything to laugh about in this instance.

The world was facing destruction and yet, I found something to smile about. Grasping each other for a brief moment, we held on, wishing that this moment could last forever but knowing that evil wouldn't give us peace.

"Skylar," Sue and I said at the same time.

"I know that we both heard a cry for help and knew that it came from her and that she needed our help now," Sue said pulling away from me.

We needed to use all the power at our disposal to find her, for our time was running out. The evil that lurked in the darkness was trying to close its icy fingers around her.

"Sue, we need to use every ounce of energy that our minds contain to find her," I said, once again scanning the landscape. Neither of us was sure of where we were; everything was confusing and strange. Focusing my mind, this time I didn't close my eyes as I let my mind search around us, seeking anything that could help us. Sue tried the same thing. Both of our minds slowly crept over every inch of ground, in different directions.

Still exploring with our minds, we separated and walked away from each other. There was nothing.

Skylar, where are you? I kept saying to myself. Sue had to be doing the same thing. Would we find her in time?

We wouldn't let anything happen to her as long as one of us was still alive. Skylar trusted us with all her heart, and she knew that we would come.

"Sue, we have to be farther apart to cover more area," I said, looking at her. I felt this was our only hope of finding Skylar.

"I don't think we should split up to look for her. The evil power that the aliens have is growing stronger, even now you can feel it all around us," Sue said to me with a look on her face that I had seen before; one of fear and doubt.

Being married this long, there are certain things you know about each other. One of these feelings is you never have to say anything; you know what the other person is thinking.

We weren't having any luck by searching with our minds. It was going to have to be the old fashioned way, walking and looking.

It was like Sue said; I could also feel the evil hanging like a dark mist around us. Each step took us farther into the blackness. The hairs at the back of my neck bristled; I sensed that there was a hungry beast waiting to devour us.

Even the trees that surrounded us now had a strange appearance; as we moved through what had once been an ordinary forest, it was now like the place in your mind where all that scares you lies waiting for the moment to wake, leaving you with a feeling that there was something there, and then out of the corner of your eye, you could only catch a brief glimpse of a shadow.

Even our powers couldn't bring light into it. The shadows moved in the darkness, and I knew that evil lurked there. Taking each other's hand was the only way to know that we were side by side.

Noises around us grew louder—strange sounds, and then I felt something cold rush by us, brushing as close as possible without touching us. It made my skin crawl, as if someone was running icy fingers up my spine.

Sue gripped my hand harder, as her hand trembled; fear edged deeper into her soul. Small, panicky sounds escaped her, as she pulled me closer whispering, "I don't think we're alone. There is something that keeps touching me very, very lightly."

At that moment I pulled Sue closer to my side. Something lying on the ground caused both of us to fall.

Swoosh. Something rushed past us where we had been standing, missing us both by mere inches. I could hear it coming again. *Swoosh.* This time it moved lower. It was searching for us. Trying to track it with my mind was useless. I could feel and hear it moving over us at a fast rate. Whatever this was, it was moving closer with each pass that it made.

The darkness was now complete, making it impossible for us to see, so I had to feel around the ground with my hand, trying to find anything that could help us. Nothing was there. We crawled forward, not making any sounds; the only thing we could hear was the beating of our hearts.

There were dozens of them now. Each one darted around, stopping briefly, and then raced off again, like a vulture searching for the remains of its next meal.

My mind was able to put a shield over us. Maybe this would keep them from finding us. They knew we were here someplace, but couldn't locate where we were hiding.

The darkness had been a problem for us, and it was also a problem for them.

With my shield covering us and with the darkness, neither of us had an advantage. It became a game of hide and seek. We hid and they tried to find us.

This seemed to go on for hours, but I knew that it had only been a few minutes.

Crawling along the barren ground, it was if we had to almost become one with it, fearing that they had boxed us in. I didn't know what our next option was, and then my hand finally found something. A large hole, and if we had been running, both of us would have fallen into it. Moving my hand over the edge of the opening, I could feel air coming from it. We had to make a choice—try to keep crawling and hope they wouldn't eventually find us, or put our faith in the unknown and disappear into it, not knowing what lay at the bottom, but I knew that time was running out.

I could feel them starting to bounce off of the shield. They were close to finding us. I knew what we had to do. Pulling Sue tight against me, wrapping my arms around her I prayed, "Please be right."

Holding her close, I rolled over and down we fell.

The wind rushed past us. Falling faster, I didn't know what lay at the bottom; my mind was calm for some unknown reason.

Splash.

Our bodies landed in water—cold, very cold water. It took our breath away for a few seconds, and then we went deeper into the water. It was too deep to swim back to the surface.

Opening my eyes, I searched for anything. "*No, wait!*" my mind shouted. There—it was as if something was pointing in the direction that we were to go, when my eyes caught a sight of a faint light to our left. Pulling Sue, we started to swim to it, hoping that our lungs could last.

I knew that our power protected us from anyone trying to destroying us. What about this decision? We had chosen it. Again my body asked, *Will the air in our lungs last long enough to make it to the light?*

Pushing our bodies as hard as possible, I could feel the pain growing in my lungs. I knew that Sue was experiencing the same pain; I gripped her hand harder. Then slowly her hand began to go limp in mine

With the last bit of energy in me, I refused to let go of her. I used my other hand to pull us closer to the light, and as I did this somehow strength grew in it, not a lot, but my love for her gave me more strength; I hoped that it would be enough.

My lungs wanted to explode, the tightness was like a vice gripping them. As we moved closer, I saw that the light was getting brighter; as I pulled my wife, her body was limp; it was as if she had given up. This had become a race.

Only a few more yards, my mind screamed, *Fight. Fight. Don't give up!*" Sleep was trying to ease my pain—warm and peaceful sleep. *Close your eyes for a minute,* my mind said, as my arm began to slow.

As I looked at Sue's face, she was so beautiful; my love for her would be never ending. But for now my love and my life—I tried to let these words drift to her. I could now close my eyes and rest for a minute, knowing we would always be together. Our bodies moved together. Putting my arms around her, peace closed around us. It was a warm feeling. *Good night, my love.* One kiss, as my lips lightly touched her cheek.

I seemed to be drifting without reason through time. Everything that had happened in my life moved in front of my eyes, passing slowly. It was like a movie. But it was only playing for one—me.

As I watched it, there were laughter and tears. There was nothing spectacular, until almost the last part flashed on the screen. Like an old silent movie thriller between the hero and the outlaw, which one would lose?

"Joe, where are we?" Sue asked, tugging on my arm. I looked around with total confusion. Only a short time ago, we were surly going to die, yet here we were. Twisting around, we looked and there was the water bubbling up through an opening in the middle of the sand where we now lay.

"How?" was all I could say. There was no way we could have made it out of the water, let alone crawl this far from the opening.

This was to strange and caught me off guard. There was the opening, and here we were. The distance was at least twenty feet from us, but the biggest question was how we got over here. The sand showed no signs of travel between the opening and where we were. It was perfectly smooth. No marks of any kind.

I felt Sue touch me on the shoulder. As I looked over to where she was pointing, there was an opening on the far side of the cave. Tears were running down her cheeks, for there in the sand, I saw that there was only one set of footprints leading from where we lay to the opening. The prints were of someone not wearing any shoes of any kind. As I glanced down to our feet to reassure myself that we were wearing shoes, that confirmed that those prints weren't made by either of us.

There was nothing else to say except, "Believe and it will be so."

"Sue, we have to follow these footprints. Hopefully they will lead us to Skylar and safety," I said, standing up and pulling Sue to her feet.

There was no natural light in the cave, but somehow there was enough light for us to see. Following the footprints the light moved the darkness back enough for us to follow. At the opening the footprints mysteriously stopped; whoever made the prints led us to this point and we were on our own now.

As we left the area that lead from the cave, I noticed that the color of the sand was changing into a deeper shade, yet it wasn't as dark as when we first came together in the cave. Yet somehow without noticing we were now outside, it was silly how we had moved to this point without being aware of anything.

We both laughed. We were getting so old that things passed us by so easily. I knew that wasn't so. When we looked up into the sky it was like we were doing it for the first time. We wondered at the beauty of the heavens, and it was like you could almost reach out and touch it.

A bright light appeared ahead. It was moving toward us. Uncertain as to whether we should ready ourselves for another fight with the aliens, Sue and I stopped and prepared ourselves for whatever was to come and taking hold of each other's hand, we waited.

"Grandma and Grandpa," a voice called from the darkness. It was Skylar. The two of us ran to her taking her in our arms, asking nothing, only believing.

We stood there holding on to each other, never wanting to let go. Our hopes and prayers were now answered.

"How did you get here?" Sue asked, holding her tighter.

"Grandma, I really don't know. After the lady helped me," she answered.

"What lady?" I interrupted.

"The beautiful lady from, uh, uh, a place that is called Everlasting, I think," she squeaked. "I'm not really sure if that's the name. She said that I could stay there with her, but I wanted to come back to you, Grandma, no matter what, and then I fell back into the water."

"You were in the water?" I asked.

"Yes, Grandpa, before I met the lady and after I left her," she answered.

I was confused by what she was telling us, but we wanted to hear everything that had happened to her. Who was this lady and why did she want Skylar to stay with her?

"Go on, honey. What else happened to you and how in the world did you get here?" Sue asked.

"Grandma, after I got out of the water, it was funny. I wasn't even wet. Isn't that silly?" Skylar said.

"Yes, that's really weird," I answered. "Go on."

"But after I got out of the water, I didn't know where the two of you were, so I started walking. It was cloudy and dark. There was something evil and bad that was trying to hurt me. There were strange words, yet somehow I knew what they meant. Using them when I first got here, they stopped the evil beings from harming me. But more and more of them kept coming, too many for me to stop, and they were scaring me and they kept coming back. I tried using those words again. It helped for a while but like before, there were too many of them. You and Grandpa weren't here to help me. I couldn't find the lady either, so I started to cry. Everything was really scary, even when I tried to hide, they wouldn't stop. Then a man came to me."

"A man? What man?" I asked.

"Yes, Grandpa, I don't know who he was, but he was very nice to me. Taking my hand, he lifted me up into his arms. It was so nice. I wasn't scared anymore. All he did was raise his arm and I felt better. It wasn't dark anymore. Inside I knew the bad ones feared him and left. They were scared of him, but I wasn't," she answered with a laugh.

"But how did you find us?" I asked. Somehow, I already knew what she was going to tell me.

"We walked for a long time. He told me a lot of stories. Some were funny, but some almost made me cry," she said.

"What kind of stories did he tell you?" Sue asked, taking Skylar by the hand, as they walked over to some small rocks and sat down.

"He said that I could tell some of the stories, but others were a secret between him and me, that I couldn't tell anyone until the time was right," she said.

"Tell us some of the stories that he said you could share," Sue said.

"Well, he talked about all the different kinds of people that I would meet as I grow older," she answered.

"What kind of people and where do these people live?" Sue asked Skylar again.

"They don't live here, but far away in the stars," she said pointing to the sky.

"People that live in the stars?" I asked.

"Yes, Grandpa, but they aren't like us. They are all different looking, but all of them lived together in peace—all except one, and that one was evil. They made others evil, but there would be one place that three people would rise up and help everybody to cast off evil that bound them, and then other people would join with others to drive the bad ones away, but I like what he said last the best."

"What was that?" I asked.

"He said after the past, present, and future was mixed, this would come to pass. I asked how long. All he would say is that I would be a little older when that happens," she stopped for a moment, and then she went on with a sad look on her face.

"Skylar, tell me why you look sad." Sue said.

"He said that when the time came that you, Grandma and Grandpa, and my family wouldn't be with me anymore." Stopping for a time, she went on. "I asked him why, but all he would say was that it was in a book. I can't remember the name. It is also written that I would do great things for the people, some even before I leave. What does that mean, Grandpa?" She asked looking up at me, with a question.

I didn't know how to answer her. She was so young for all this to be laid on her shoulders. How do you tell a child that she could no longer be a child but would now have to be an adult?

There would be no more childhood games to play. Her life wasn't hers anymore. Everything that she did now would affect the lives she came in touch with.

"Skylar," I started to say, but she stopped me.

"Grandpa, I know what you are going to tell me. But you don't have to. The man already told me about the rest of my life," Skylar said.

"The rest of your life," I asked, wishing that she wouldn't have to go through it that way, but knowing inside that I couldn't change what was already predestined.

"Yes, remember the dreams I told you about? Well, other things were in them—things I didn't tell you about. How my life would turn out was one of them," she said. "That is one of the stories I can't tell you about," she said.

When Skylar stopped speaking, it felt as if time came to a stop. The Creator had accomplished his goal. We had now become one, as was written in The Book of Forever. Now everything around us was right. Relief was a welcome ally. There was something different. Bright lights filled us with warmth, and I knew it was time to go back. We had accomplished what had to be done here. The three of us stood together, holding hands, and closed our eyes. I could feel us move. In one beat of my heart, we were back at the cabin.

When I opened my eyes, I felt a warm breeze float over my skin. This helped me to relax for the first time in months, but in reality it was only a few days.

As I glanced over at Sue and Skylar, the expressions on their faces told me that we shared the same emotions. With our hands still joined, the three of us walked to the cabin. The Keeper appeared at the door, lowering his head slightly for a moment, and then he greeted us.

"It's good to have all of you back safely," he said raising his head.

"For a while there, I wondered if we would ever be able to get back," I said, firmly shaking his hand.

After shaking hands, he said, "You need time to rest." He turned and we went into the cabin, talking as we went.

"We need the quiet; it has been a long and tiring time, and I think we need to rest for a few days," I said laughing, and then I leaned over and whispered to Sue, "It's weird. I know that every time we return my body feels drained, and he always wants us to rest. I don't know why, but I think it has something to do with the waters of life that gave us the power to live for eternity."

"Unfortunately, you will only be able to rest for a short time. Things around the world are changing rapidly," he said.

"What do you mean?" Sue asked, as she turned to face him.

He shook his head. "Not now. I'll answer your questions later, but right now you need to rest. The journey will become harder," he said. I could see something in his face that told me that there something that he needed to say to us, but I couldn't figure out what it was; and I knew it wasn't going to be good.

"Saying that things are happening and leaving it at that doesn't help us to relax. Are they good or bad?" I asked.

"All I'll say for now is that there is good news about some, but others aren't. The three of you will need all your strength and power to help. No more questions. Please go rest," he said, motioning to our rooms.

Several of the helpers were readying our beds, but my stomach started to complain about the lack of food. We hadn't eaten for quite a long time. Looking at my watch, it was nine thirty—two days in fact. As we turned we saw a table set with food that had mysteriously appeared—a feast for us. For the last couple of days, food was the last thing we thought about. It's funny; under stress our bodies didn't require nourishment.

After eating we were led to where I thought we would find showers. The helpers signaled for us to stop. Once inside they left us alone. Looking at each other, we wondered what was going on.

The room became as bright as the sun but for some reason, it wasn't hurting our eyes. Something was starting to swirl around us. A blue mist filled the room. Each particle bounced the light into us; it was like bubbles bouncing off of us.

The feeling was fantastic. Every cell in our bodies felt like it had separated into millions of tiny, bright blue specks of light. They moved away from us to from a circle.

It was funny watching it for a few seconds. That was the last thing I remembered.

To my surprise, when I opened my eyes, I found that we were lying in our beds. As I stretched, my mind thought back to what had happened in the other room. I tried to think of a name for it, but all I could think of was the circle of renewal.

At the same time, Sue and Skylar stretched and slowly got out of bed. They came over and stood there for a moment smiling. I tried to push myself farther into the mattress, but it was no use as both of them reached down, grabbing my arms. Reluctantly I gave in and let them pull me from the comfort of my bed.

They looked at me; I shook my head, not knowing what to say. Each day something new took place. It was always different. I have no idea why this should surprise me; it was becoming second nature for things like this to happen.

How long had we slept? Glancing at my watch, this couldn't be true. Time hadn't moved. Somehow it was the same time as when we arrived at the cabin, yet I felt fantastic. I didn't know how this could be, but I accepted it.

Looking at Sue and Skylar, I could see from their expressions that they felt the same as me—fantastic.

I wondered how this was always possible? But in my mind I knew the answer; it had to be the Creator. Only he could cause this to happen—time within time.

The Keeper joined us. He pointed to a table beside our beds. We joined him at the table, and he began to speak. "Our forces are pushing the aliens out of more parts of the world, but we are facing strong opposition in several other areas. In those nations, evil is trying to push them into a confrontation with the rest of the world."

"What areas?" I asked.

In the center of the room, a map materialized. It appeared be suspended in the air. He pointed to several areas on the map.

"This is where the struggles are happening. There could be a world war. These nations have nuclear weapons. The aliens will use them to stop us. That way, they hope to remain secret. The time has come. You will need to go back to Washington and have the president address the United Nations. The world has to know. This can no longer remain hidden. We have people ready all over the world that, hopefully, will help us to stop them," he said.

"Where did they all come from?" Sue asked.

"Your husband knows. I will let him tell you later, but time is growing short," he answered.

I had to wonder again why it was always the same words, the same words all the time. Time is growing short... why?

"I know something stopped time here. Can't time be stopped around the world?" Sue asked again.

"No, we can only stop time in certain areas. People have to be able to have free will. By stopping time, we take away their choice. I know this is hard to understand, but in time you will," he said

Always in time, that seemed to be his reply to everything. Couldn't we have one direct answer? I said to myself.

Sue glanced at me and asked, "How do you know about these people?"

The Keeper glanced over to me and nodded that she should be told.

"Sue, when we were separated, I was taken on a journey. Not in body, but in mind, and I went back to the beginning of life in the universe. Two life forms were created. One turned to good, and the other turned to evil. For a very long time, distance kept them apart. The good people were from the planet Abiatharia. They are called Abiatharians. That name means *father of abundance whose house of divine judgment has been pronounce*," I said.

"What about the evil ones?" she asked.

"Their name is Gara. They are form the planet Haceldama, which means *field of blood*. Once their paths crossed, the Gara tried to destroy the Abiatharians, as they had destroyed others," I said, continuing.

The Gara forced the Abiatharians back to their home planet, and there they went for the final end. But something stopped the Gara. A protective shield was established.

Knowing that they couldn't win, the Gara retreated. For the next thousand years, the Gara slowly spread their evil from world to world. There was no conflict between them until earth became the prize. Several times, good tried to rise up and destroy the evil that was trying to enslave this world throughout history. But the battle between them was a tossup. Evil knew that they couldn't win completely so they changed tactics: work from within, by controlling the population, and the leaders of each country they hoped to win.

With our coming, they knew that victory was slipping from their grasp, and if the world destroyed itself, so what? And it's starting to happen.

It was time to go to Washington. The world's fate was in our hands, and I hoped that we were up to the task. I had to have faith.

CHAPTER EIGHT

We arrived in the Oval Office at the White House as the president came into the room. She had two of our agents with her. Ann was one of them, and they were to stay with her every place she went. The president was to be protected at all cost.

"Madam President, it's good to see you again," The Keeper said, shaking her hand.

Sue, Skylar, and I also greeted her warmly.

"Thank heavens you're here," she said, picking up several newspapers and handing them to us. "There are stories coming in from all over the world. Some of them contain good news, but others do not," she said.

Taking the papers, we started to read the headlines and stories together.

L.A. Observer headlined, "Everything West of the Mississippi." In the last few days, people all over the western states were sharing what they had with others, even complete strangers from housing to cars, furniture, and money whatever they had. Criminal activities stopped, no robberies, break-ins, assaults, thefts, murders; nothing bad was happening.

People were being healed by a group of strangers. No one was dying from disease; in fact, no one was becoming sick. According to the newspapers, it was strange, but a good kind of strange. The whole western part of the United States, from the Mississippi River to the Pacific Ocean was becoming the Garden of Eden.

My son, John, I thought. He's the one doing this, leading a group of healers; they were changing people's lives and giving new hope for a better life.

It was the same from south of New York to Florida. Good was working—no more despair, hatred, poverty, or disease. There were reports of people giving money, homes, cars, and anything you could think of to others that needed it. These reports matched those that were coming in from the west.

Even in South America where the three of us had destroyed the alien cell, peoples' lives were also getting better. It was becoming one world, not split up into smaller ones. Dictators were no longer in control. People united under one banner, developing hope and freedom.

Once evil was gone, the same thing was happening in Central America and parts of Africa. Good was fully developing in everyone's life. The future looked bright; dreams could now become a reality. No more would children grow up with a cloud of despair hanging over them.

Papers from other parts of North American cities like, Chicago, Cleveland, St. Louis, and New York City, painted a different picture and across the North, all the way into Canada, riots were breaking out. Evil still had a strangle hold on them.

People were destroying anything and everything that came into their reach. The police were unable to bring the riots under control. The National Guard and even the regular army that was brought in to help couldn't stop it. Some of the armed forces had fallen under evils control.

Evil was working in their ranks, pitting policeman against policeman, and one army unit against another. Even the people that lived in those areas fought against each other. Family members fought with each other.

We had to find the alien cell and destroy it, but we needed help to do this. If the three of us went alone, evil would use our own people against us.

The other newspapers from around the world told a story of a possible war between Russia and China.

China had amassed its military along its border with Russia and was also threatening to attack Taiwan.

North Korea was threatening Japan, South Korea, and others. Even the United States now acknowledged that North Korea had nuclear weapons and were going to use them if their demands were not met. But they wouldn't say what those demands were.

In the Middle East it was the same. Iran, Syria, Iraq, Egypt, and others now demanded that Israel be evacuated by all of the people that lived there, giving them only seventy-two hours in which to leave their country or they would be destroyed. Madness was sweeping through these areas.

The Gara were making their final stand. They wouldn't lose control over the earth, for they believed if that was going to happen, then the earth would destroy itself. Nothing would remain but a burned up cinder. Either way we would lose.

Putting the papers down, I looked at the president. Her face showed deep concern and questions.

Taking a deep breath, she started, "How do we stop this madness? Part of the world is like day. The rest acts as if the sun will never have light again." Standing up, she walked around her desk and stood in front, once again asking, "What can we do to end this madness that is trying to stop the good that is spreading across the world?"

Before we could answer, The Keeper put his hands out in front of us. We watched as something began to take shape in them. It was the earth. It moved up from his hands to float above him. He started to explain.

"See these tiny specks," he said, pointing to the spinning globe. "This is where our people are."

JOSEPH A. LUNINI, SR.

We could see thousands and thousands of tiny specks. They were in every part of the world. I knew that some of them lived here with us, but I couldn't imagine that there were so many of them and this plague of evil was still trying to spread.

"We have been living here from the time life started. The Gara also were here. We were able to keep ourselves hidden from them. They suspected that we were here, but they could never find us, until a few years ago. That's why they stepped up their plans to take control of the earth. Now everything about this world frightens them. There is something about these people that inhabit this world, people that they have never seen before."

"What about this world? How could it scare them? Their power is far greater than anything that we possess," I said.

He went on, "The Gara use evil. Their power comes mostly from inside the people they corrupt. In an all-out war against us, it would be about even, because their power is spread thinly over the universe. Time would also work against them as it does us, for they also know about *The Book of Forever*, which contains the knowledge that three beings will be brought forth to slay the evil ones. Those three come from this world. As you say, that would be the straw that broke the camel's back"

"Is that us?" Skylar asked with brightness shining from her eyes.

Touching her softly on the shoulder, he answered, "Yes, my child. You three are the anointed ones that the book says will come forward from the unknown but have always been known and written about in the book." He looked deeply into her eyes. "You are the Promise. The promise that was made and written in the book before time began and it will happen."

The president listened closely to what was said. As she listened to his words, they still didn't answer the question of how to stop the world from going over the edge. She knew that the three of us were the key to unlocking that knowledge. "You three control the future of this world. The answer lies in you and the helpers that live with us.

What can we do to stop the Gara from destroying the world?" she asked.

I think for the first time in her life, she truly didn't know what to do. Turning to The Keeper, she said, "The three of them have to stay together. When they are apart, evil can stop them.

There are too many troubled places. What can we do?" I asked, hoping that I knew the answer to that question—the helpers.

"Our people are coming together in those areas with people that have not come under the control of the Gara," he said and then turned to the door.

"What's wrong?" I asked, as we all turned.

"I want you to meet some of your old friends," he said, smiling for one of the few times since I had met him. This really surprised me.

The door to the Oval Office opened, and several people that I had never met before walked in the room. Then one figure followed them into the room, covered from head to toe in a long blue robe.

Stepping back, I was shocked to see who it was.

"What is she doing here?" I demanded to know, as hostility quickly raged through me.

The Keeper came over and put his hands on my shoulders, lightly pushing me back.

"Please calm down, Josaphat, and let me explain," he said.

"Explain a traitor. I left her back there in that desolate land. My mind told me to destroy her, but I let my heart win out and let her live. She took our daughter Nancy using some kind of magic, to make it appear that she was there standing in front of me. And now you have brought her here!" I shouted, and for the first time in a while, a feeling of hate rose up in me.

"Please," he said griping my shoulders harder. "Please, Josaphat. Calm down. I'll explain everything to you."

Sue came up, putting her hands on my shoulders. The warmth of her touch slowly eased my anger. I could feel a wave of calmness settle over me.

Closing my eyes for a minute, I could see Nancy's smiling face. A lump formed in my throat. I could feel tears trying to escape from my eyes as my body relaxed.

Sue spoke softly into my ear. "Joe, let him explain. I feel that there is something more about Lori that we don't know about. Please listen."

Opening my eyes, still fighting the tears, I reluctantly agreed to listen.

Lori walked over to us. The Keeper took hold of her arm. I listened closely and quietly as he spoke.

"Lori was never a traitor. What she did was to volunteer to act as if she betrayed you and us as well. We had to find out more about the people they controlled that were in high places of government."

"She was a traitor. What happened to Nancy, and why did so many others have to suffer?" I asked.

"In time you will understand. Please let me finish," he replied. "Her family was truly taken by the Gara, but she knew that without our help the Gara would kill them anyway."

"What about Lori's family?" Sue asked with concern in her voice.

"The Gara that was with her when you met were the only ones who could give the order to kill her family. If they knew she wasn't working for them, her family would have perished. By destroying them, they gave her family a chance to survive, because they would believe that Lori had also been killed," he answered.

"But what about my daughter Nancy? Where is she? If Lori wasn't a traitor, why did you let Nancy be taken?" I asked.

"It was a part of our plan to make the Gara truly believe that Lori was a traitor. We had to make sure that everything went right," he answered.

"If that is so, where is Nancy? Did she know that Lori wasn't a traitor?" I asked.

"No, Nancy didn't know Lori wasn't a traitor. It could have jeopardized our plan if she knew," he replied.

"You are still not answering me. Where is my daughter?" I demanded.

"Right here, Dad!" Nancy shrieked, running into the room, and joined us.

"Nancy!" the three of us yelled as we took her in our arms and twirling round and round like children. I hadn't been this happy in a long time. Sometimes you take things for granted until they are lost, leaving a hole in your heart. It's only healed when that certain thing is found and at this moment, it had indeed been found.

"I'm sorry, but it had to be done this way and Nancy, please forgive me for doing this to you," The Keeper said, with sorrow in his voice.

Nancy stopped jumping around and turned to The Keeper saying, "I know. It had to be done that way."

Going over to her, he surprised me again when he gently put his arms around her, but only for a moment. In her voice I could hear a woman speaking. In a short time, she had been tossed into a harsh world. She withstood the pain and was stronger for having come through it. *She was ready to join us on this journey, or maybe it was us who would join her*, I thought.

We turned our attention back to the president.

"This is some of the help that you will need, Madam President," The Keeper said, pointing to Lori and the others that had come with her. Even Nancy stepped forward.

"Nancy, what are you doing?" Sue asked, going over to her.

"Mother, you accepted the roll that was placed before you, so I must also accept. Each of us must do whatever we are called on to do," Nancy said, taking hold of her mother's hand and then she put her arms around her, whispering something in her ear and with that, Sue smiled.

I wondered, *Why?*

"What are our plans?" the president asked.

"Nancy has been taught the way of the rock people. She can become whatever image she wants to and will also have the ability to duplicate herself into two beings at the same time," The Keeper said, taking Nancy by the hand. "Nancy, Lori and the other two will go to four different countries. Once there they will assume the role as the leader of that nation, but Nancy's role will be different. Do not ask what it will be? Only have trust in her journey."

"What about the people that they replace? What will happen to them?" Sue asked.

"They will be taken to a place called Redemption," he answered, knowing that once there, they would remain forever, unless they changed from evil to good. Even though their bodies were dead, their souls still live.

"Once they have replaced the leaders, there is one problem: their power will last for only a few days. After that time they will change back to who they really are. And when that happens, chaos will break out in those countries unless we destroy the evil cell. New leaders will take control after that happens. We hope to have enough power ready to stop anything that they try until that happens," The Keeper said.

"While our people have control, we will take forces into the areas that are rioting and try to destroy the cells that control those areas," I said.

"Madam President, you need to address the nation as soon as possible about the force that will join your people in putting down the riots. They need to know that we are here to help," The Keeper said.

"Yes, I will. But first, my top people from the military and both political parties need to be told. We will need their help to convince the people not to be afraid and to help with our cause," she answered.

"I've already taken care of that, and they on their way here. By the time you get to the ready room, they will be there. We had better leave now," The Keeper said.

I took Sue's hand before we followed the president out. We had to say good-bye to Nancy. Not knowing when we would be together again tore at our hearts, for we knew she had to follow her own path.

For one brief moment, the four of us stood together, arms around each other. Not a last farewell, but see you later. One last look and then she left. We soon left the room and followed the president.

The meeting with the military and the politicians didn't go too bad. At first there was a lot of arguing, but after The Keeper showed them some of the powers we possess and what the Gara had done to other worlds and now was trying to do here on earth, finally they all agreed to stand with her.

The president was to address the nation at seven o'clock that evening. All those who attended this meeting would stand with her to show the nation's unity.

Time moved very quickly, and this drawn out process was in fact only a very short time. As the president stood before the cameras, our forces had gathered quietly out of sight. Nancy and her group had split up and left to start the switch. Everything was ready; the signal only had to be given for everything to begin. I hoped someone or something was watching over us. In my heart I knew that someone already was.

The president started, "My fellow—" She stopped for a minute. "I feel that instead of saying Americans that I should say my fellow people of the world. As you have seen on the television and read in the newspapers or have experienced in person, not only our nation, but nations of the world are facing a serious crisis. There is rioting that is happening in a numerous cities and towns around the world. Our freedom is in jeopardy. Some nations are threatening to use nuclear weapons against their neighbors. They are demanding terms of their neighbors that are totally unjustified.

"In America, as in other places, we cannot let this happen. So with the power of my office and with the backing of our military and the leaders of both political parties, I am declaring a national emergency. With all of this support behind me, I am also asking for help from foreign powers, one not of this world, but a group of worlds thousands of light years away from us. Some of these people have lived with us for a very long time. They are called Abiatharians, from the world Abiatharia.

All across America, people were startled to learn that aliens were living among us. "I know that this comes as quite a shock after years of your government denying the existence of such a people. We came forward to tell you that they, in fact, do exist, but you will have to put those arguments away until this threat is dealt with. I am truly sorry. I was aware that there were suspicions that they were here, even though the government denied their existence.

"People! People! We are doing this to ourselves, not from our own free will, but by the infiltration of a race of evil beings called the Gara.

"They have existed for thousands of years, destroying other planets and races of beings though out the universe. The Gara have battled the Abiatharians, pushing them back almost to the point of destroying them, till something greater than the Gara interceded to put a stop to this destruction.

"Now three people of our world have been called to help lead this fight against the Gara. The power of the United States and our allies will fight side by side until the evil scourge is wiped away from this world and if called to, we will take this fight to them. No matter where it takes us, so help me God," she said with a tone in her voice that reminded me of a football coach encouraging his team on to victory.

For a moment, the room she spoke in was deathly quiet, and then as if in a basketball game, at the last second, the ball was shot toward the basket.

Down by one point with only one second left, it found the bottom of the net, from defeat to victory. A deafening cheer went up from everyone; they stood chanting loudly, "*Yes, Yes!*"

I could feel inside of me that this was something that was happening all over the free world.

Next the president introduced us, "My fellow people of the world, I would like to introduce the three people that I told you about. This is Josaphat, his wife, Susanna, and their wonderful granddaughter, Joan."

A loud round of applause greeted us from those that were gathered there in the room. All three of us stood there for a couple of minutes. Not because of the greeting, but we were lost for words.

Finally as I regained my thoughts and composure, the president signaled for me to come forward, and I approached the podium, stepping up and taking hold of the microphone for support. You would think that with what we had been through the last few days this would be easy, but it wasn't. My knees were shaking and my stomach was tied in knots. I knew that the people had to believe and trust in us. My words had to ring true.

Clearing my throat and letting my heart speak instead of my mind, I began.

"Sometimes in everyone's life, things are put in front of you that you would rather give to someone else. I know when this first came to me and my family; there were large doubts in our minds. But deep in our hearts, we knew that we couldn't run away and hide from it. Not knowing would be far worse, because deep inside the truth is always there. This is our time to join the fight. Now it is the time for you, the people of the world, to join us. We will not disappear. The Gara will know the resolve of the human race to resist evil—to unite under one banner of freedom and justice for everyone. Today is the first day of our battle, and we will win that freedom. No darkness will stop us; we bring the light to the world and beyond. *Amen.*"

Again there was loud applause, but we couldn't simply stand here. Now was the time to act. Going back to the ready room, everyone was there. Satellite communication was set up between the White House and several other countries: England, France, Germany, Russia, Turkey, Greece, Spain, India, and other smaller countries.

They had watched our speech but before that, the government had sent by computer everything that we knew about the Gara to them.

Every country agreed to let America lead the fight. They put all their forces under our control. The people that we had in their countries would supply them with weapons and leadership, and they would show them how to fight the Gara.

Even with this help, the outcome would still be in doubt. We knew the strength of the Gara and the way they would turn people against each other.

The one factor that could give us the victory over them was how fast we could destroy their cells. Once the cells were destroyed, the rest of its control over the people would die and after that happened, we would drive them from this world and then, somehow, from all the other worlds.

The Keeper came up to us with some very bad news before we were able to launch our mission. "Our two transports that were hidden on the back side of the moon reported that they had picked up dozens of objects moving toward earth. We know they are space crafts controlled by the Gara; the only good news is that they wouldn't be here for several days. Once they arrive their power would turn the tide against us.

I felt my heart stop. No matter what we did before they arrived, it would make no difference; their power would be too much for us, and even united, we would be no match for them.

I looked at The Keeper. There was nothing I could think of to say. Emptiness filled me. That's the only way to describe it. What could we do?

Even with the two ships that the Abiatharians had given to us. Trying to stop them would be of little help. The Gara had the odds on their side. What could we do? Looking at Sue and Skylar, they didn't seem to have the same feeling of loss that I had.

They walked over to where I was standing. Both of them put their arms around me. "Joe, you need to have faith. Hasn't the Creator been with us every step of the way?" Sue asked.

"Yes," I answered. This wasn't the time to lose my faith, but there was something else. Would my faith be strong enough for what lay ahead, but there was no other course but to move forward.

Everything was ready. Our allies overseas were in place, and our people were standing side by side with them.

Nancy, Lori, and their people were moving into the assigned countries. Sue, Skylar and I were going to attack the cell in New York City.

Before we left we bid the president good-bye. She wished everyone good luck. The Keeper joined us, saying his good-byes and also wishing us luck, but there something in him that started to bother me.

Everyone left the three of us alone; they knew that we needed time to ourselves, even if only for a few moments. There wasn't a lot to say. Standing together, we felt the love that we shared wrap its' arms tighter around us. We had been through a lot already, but this was by far the biggest confrontation yet. I knew the time had come. We gave each other one last embrace, and I watched as Sue and Skylar closed their eyes. Now it was my turn. Slowly closing my eyes, my body rose into the air.

CHAPTER NINE

When I opened my eyes, I discovered that we had landed next to the site where the Twin Towers had once stood. There wasn't much light. When I glanced at my watch, I saw that it was almost nine o'clock at night.

Gunfire close by startled us. Turning, we could see police and military people locked in a fierce battle with other police and military personal. Which group was fighting for us? At that moment there was no way to tell.

Some of the civilians were trying to run and hide, but others were joining in the fight. As we watched in horror, there didn't seem to be any rhyme or reason to it. They were killing for the fun of it—well maybe not for the fun, but without any conscious thought as to what they were doing.

People caught in the crossfire were gunned down. Men, women, and children—it didn't make any difference. If you were there, then you became a target.

My attention was drawn to another group of people coming toward us. They wore a mix of uniforms. Civilians were also with them, but something else caught my eye. Some of them wore the blue uniforms of the Abiatharians; this was the one thing that made them stand out from the other groups.

This group moved quickly toward the two factions that were engaged in combat. Both had been under the control of the Gara. The power of this group overpowered the other two groups in a matter of moments, everything became quiet. Most of the two groups were dead; only a handful surrendered to our forces. Evil had tossed all the dead to the beast, and they let it devour each and every one of them.

Noise coming up behind us made me turn. There was a column of military trucks pulling up beside us. One of them stopped. The door opened and much to our surprise, The Keeper stepped out of the vehicle.

Skylar rushed over to him, throwing her arms around him.

There was a bond forming between them. He bent down and whispered something in her ear; she nodded in agreement with whatever he was saying.

Skylar turned and walked back over to us, followed by The Keeper.

Taking Sue's and my hands, she said, "He told me that Chicago is in flames. Most of the city is being destroyed. Someone has to go there to help, and I was asked to go."

"What about this city?" I asked The Keeper. "We will gain control of this city within a few days. We can't let her go there alone. The last time we almost lost her; someone has to go with her," I said to The Keeper.

"We can't let her go alone. Last time we nearly lost her forever. That can't happen again," I said to Sue.

A smile crossed Sue's face, "Joe, I'll keep her safe. Nothing will happen to harm Skylar," Sue said as she lovingly cupped my face in her hands.

"I know," I said, turning toward The Keeper. "Sue will go with Skylar. You knew this was going to happen, didn't you?"

"There are things that have to be. Some we can try to change; others we can't, no matter what. In both instances it isn't in our hands, but someone else's," he said, gripping my hands, hoping against hope that I would understand his meaning.

Sue and Skylar held hands, and in a flash, they were gone to a destiny that was written before they were born.

How many good-byes would we say to each other before we found the end of this path we were on? The answer was in me, but try as I might to bring the answer forward, I couldn't.

"Josaphat, you are to be joined by a group of fighters. You will need their help. The fight has only just begun. It will be long and difficult," he said, then turned and went back to the truck.

He always said words, but those words never came from his heart. They were just empty words that made me feel as if he thought I would know what he meant. I watched as the truck drove off. Then I turned to a large group of people standing there. It was a mixture of men and women made up of police, military, civilians, and our people. Everyone wore blue bands around their arms with the symbol of the world on it, surrounded by stars.

Fighting could still be heard all around us. Fire lit up the skyline. The buildings cast long shadows across everything, and I wondered if we really had the upper hand.

Our job was twofold. One to stop the destruction in the city, and the other was to destroy the evil behind it. We had to locate the cell that was controlling everything. But it would be hard. When we first arrived, I tried to use my mind to locate it, but there was something blocking me. Their power was incredible. The only way to find that cell was to search for it. The helpers did have power in their minds that they could use to search, but theirs wasn't as strong as mine.

Signaling to everyone to spread out, we moved forward. This way we could cover more area. Each building had to be checked. This would slow us down, but all rioters had to be stopped. They would cause more death and destruction if we left them alone, and we couldn't let that happen.

Our forces moved steadily toward the areas where the fires were the strongest. I hoped this would lead us to the main cell of the evil power.

We came under heavy fire from the rioters. They were more organized, and their resistance was strong. Each step was becoming harder to make. They were being pushed back slowly, but the cost to us in lives was becoming higher.

Our people were being cut down by heavy fire—not only from small arms, but by something much stronger. They were using strange weapons that cut large paths of destruction through our forces—the weapons that the Gara had probably given to them. The Gara were fighting alongside or behind, pushing the rioters to destroy the city and slow our movement.

Turning onto a different street, flashes of bright lights were followed by large explosions that ripped large holes in everything around us. Diving for cover, I looked up and saw several small crafts flying low toward us.

The lights and explosions were coming from them. More and more explosions erupted. The force of people that were with me was being torn apart. Something had to be done to stop the Gara.

As I concentrated all my thoughts into one direction, they formed a powerful energy that was released toward the craft, ripping it to pieces.

Moving that power from one to another, I watched as each one was smashed into millions of pieces. After a few moments there was nothing left above us.

Falling to my knees, my mind and body were drained of almost all energy. Two people came running over to me. Grabbing my arms, they lifted me back up to my feet. They pulled me behind a truck that had been wrecked as a large group of rioters led by several of the Gara came rushing toward us, firing their weapons at the spot where I had been.

Explosions tore large pieces of concrete from the street and side-walks. Our people fought bravely, but there were too many. One by one they fell. Not one backed up. They stood their ground. They were giving up their lives to save the world and me.

"We have to leave now," one of the men that had saved me shouted, pulling hard on my arm. I tried to resist, but my body was too weak to fight. They dragged me away from the truck and into a stairway leading down. Walking and half falling, I went down the stairs with what I now saw were police officers. At the bottom we moved across the room to a door. One of them tried to open the door, but it was locked. Taking aim with his leg, he kicked at it as hard as he could. The door splintered apart and fell away.

Stepping over the pieces, they pulled harder on me. "Come on," one of them shouted to me. "If we stop we're done for so keep moving."

"Where are we going?" I asked weakly moving back.

"I work this beat," one of the officers said, pushing while the other one pulled on me again. "This building has an old bank safe down here, just ahead; it's hidden behind a fake wall. It's only a little farther."

In the distance behind us, I could hear shouting. The Gara were trying to find us, and they were getting closer. If we found the stairs, it would be only a matter of seconds before they also found them.

"James, take him. I'll stay here and try to delay them," the one officer said who was pushing me from behind.

James looked back at him, his face showing fear, not for himself but for his friend.

"Take care, Bob. And when this is over, I'll buy you a cold one," he said. Taking both my arms, he let me lean against the wall. He walked a few feet away. Putting his hand on a small picture and twist-ing it, part of the wall moved, exposing an opening.

Struggling to my feet, I tried to see what was there. It was a large, old safe. The door was partially open.

Coming back to me and taking hold of my arms, he dragged me to the opening and shoved me through. Falling to the floor, I could hear screams coming from where Bob had stopped to try and hold the Gara off. James quickly slid the wall back in place, and then he closed the door to the safe.

Holding our breath, all we could do was hope that if the Gara tried to used their mind to try and find us, they would not be able to penetrate the safe; its walls were made of lead and steel.

I used the last of my energy to form a protective shield over us, in case they did. I hoped it would work. This was our only chance.

Time stood still. Waiting was the worst of it. We listened but there were no sounds at all. My eyelids became heavy. Sleep tried to take control of me. I had to fight it. My body began to shut down. *No*, my mind tried to shout. Slowly, I entered the quiet world of sleep; there was no fighting it now.

"Hello," I heard someone behind me say. Turning, I found a woman standing there. "My name is Diana." But she stopped me before I could ask a question. "I know who you are," she said, smiling. "Don't look so confused. You are known to many people, and good is always with you."

"How do you know who I am, and where am I?" I asked.

"Your granddaughter told me," she answered, still smiling.

"Joan told you?" Stopping for a second, I said, "You're Diana, aren't you?"

"Yes," she answered with laughter in her voice, for she had already told me her name.

"Why are you here?" I asked, thinking she had come to me.

"I'm not here with you. You are here with me," she answered.

Looking around, I found that I wasn't in the safe any longer, and James wasn't with me either. "What's going on?" I asked, still confused.

"Did Skylar tell you about her chance to stay with me and be safe or that she could return to you?" she asked.

"Yes, but I wasn't sure if it had truly happened or if it was a dream," I said.

"You knew it really happened to her, didn't you?" She asked.

"I knew that it had, but sometimes everything doesn't seem quite real," I said, walking over to a pond. Sitting down, I looked into the water. It wasn't my face looking back at me, but something different. It was a place and time in the future that contained great beauty and peace.

"How can this picture be in the water?" I asked, looking up at Diana.

"The future is not a picture in the water, but it is what you make of it. The control is in your hands. I am here to offer you what I offered Skylar. The choice is yours," Diana said, pointing to my heart.

Everything started to drift away. Diana's words reached into my soul. Her words would be left there forever.

I knew Diana could offer me the chance to stay, but I still felt that she wouldn't, and then something was shaking me. As I opened my eyes, I saw that it was James and he was saying, "Come on wake up, we have to go. I think they gave up and left."

My body and mind felt stronger. "How long have we been here? James, how long did I sleep? Are we still in a safe?" I asked as I rose to my feet.

Looking at his watch, "About thirty minutes, and yes, we are still in the safe," he said, walking over to the door. Taking hold of a lever on the back of the safe, he turned it and pushed the door open. Sliding a section of the wall aside, we stepped out carefully. Finding nothing, we slowly walked back toward the stairs.

"James you said thirty minutes. I know it had to be longer than that, and where is Diana?" I asked, wondering why he said it had only been thirty minutes.

James looked at me strangely. "Yeah, it's only been thirty minutes, and who is this Diana?" he asked.

"You saw her. She met us at the lake," I answered him as I wondered why he was questioning me.

"All I know is that for the past thirty minutes we have been hiding in the safe, and there was no one else with us. You blacked out for a while and maybe you dreamed about whoever this Diana is," James said.

Maybe I did black out, or maybe it was Skylar's story about Diana. No, I know I went there, and she was waiting for me. But if he didn't see her, then I guess it was all dream, I thought. "Come on. Help me find Bob," James said, looking around with a panicked look on his face. Seeing nothing, he frantically started pulling debris up, pushing aside anything that was there. But Bob was nowhere to be found. Finally he stopped and stood there with anguish on his face.

Taking him by the arm, this time I was the one who led us up the stairs. Reaching the top, we carefully looked around. Gunfire could still be heard in the distance. But nothing was close to us. We could still see fires raging around us and then, it all suddenly came to a stop.

There was an eerie quiet that lay like a sleeping animal, waiting to awaken. Where had everyone gone? For another thing there were no bodies lying around that we could see. There was no one close to us, alive or dead. What had happened to everyone?

My mind was now strong again. Using it, I started to search around us, not going out too far. If the Gara sensed me searching, I didn't think the two of us could stop them. We had to find help. Had all our people been killed?

Moving and searching again very carefully, we still couldn't find any sign of the Gara or anything. Night was slowly turning into morning. Time was our enemy.

"Wait," I said, feeling that there was something ahead and to the right. Touching James on the shoulder, I motioned to him that there was something right ahead of us?

Moving slowly, I felt it again. Could it be some of our people or what was it? No, I could feel good coming from it, not evil.

Look, "there it is," I said pointing. Moving forward James followed me as we moved closer. It was a fairly high building, eight maybe ten floors. What I was feeling was coming from the basement.

Taking no chances I formed a protective shield around us. Entering an open door I sensed and felt nothing and we continued our search.

"Do you know where the stairs are?" I asked, looking at James.

He nudged me; I turned and followed with my eyes as he pointed to a door near the back of the hallway. Moving as quietly as possible we went to the door. Reaching for the handle I started to turn it, but stopped, I could sense fear coming from somewhere in the basement.

I twisted back to James and putting my hands on his shoulder and whispering, "Close your eyes, ready," and with that I mind jumped us to the basement. This was only the second time that I tried this with another person other than Sue or Skylar.

To my surprise it worked. We were standing behind a group of people—our people. A sigh of relief escaped my lips.

James opened his eyes wide, shaking his head. I could feel him trembling. A smile crossed my face, such a brave person, afraid of a little mind jump.

There was no time to calm him now. Someone in the group had heard movement behind them. Before they could do anything my thoughts moved over them, reassuring them it was all right.

Everyone turned back to us. Because I had calmed their fears first, this had stopped them from firing their weapons, before they knew who was behind them.

Some of them recognized me and ran over to us cheering.

"Quiet everyone," James said, having calmed down. "We don't know where the rioters are, so we must be quiet."

"Thank God you are still alive," one of them said taking my hand in hers, "we thought you had been killed, after the alien crafts had been destroyed. They sent hundreds of people against us. We were lucky a gas line exploded blocking them from us. If that hadn't happened they would have killed us all for sure. The explosion and fire gave us enough time to escape. We were lucky to find this place to hide from them.

"What happened to all the other people?" James asked.

"Most of them were killed, the others, I'm not sure what happened to them," someone in the crowd answered.

"We can't stay here. Our only chance is to go on the offensive. Here we can't do anything; their strength will grow if not stopped. I don't think they know we are here, that gives us a chance, a small one, but a chance none the less," I said.

James walked over to the stairs, "let's get the heck out of here!" he shouted with a laugh, "Our team is not beaten, and the game has just begun."

Going up the stairs, we could see that the sun was shining brightly. Once outside we still couldn't find anything. Everything was quiet; there was no gunfire, no noise of any kind. It felt like the quiet before the storm, this scenario kept repeating itself. Destruction then nothing, over and over again like a vicious cycle.

I signaled for our group to spread out, I tried something new. Bringing my mind into focus the protective shield formed over everyone.

Moving ahead I could see that people were now moving our way. I could sense that they were not friendly. Lifting my hand I signaled for everyone to get ready.

The other group moved toward us, without counting I knew that we were outnumbered by at least twenty to one. We stopped and took cover and then we waited readying our weapons. They rushed at us firing their weapons but the fire bounced harmlessly off my protective shield covering us.

We held our fire until they were close, "Now!" I shouted. Flashes of light erupted from our weapons and formed into one powerful energizing force sweeping from one side to the other. It looked like leaves falling from trees in an autumn storm; in a few seconds it was all over.

Then more and more came, but each time the results were the same. You would think that would have learned by now that our power was equal to or more powerful than theirs. As we started moving forward, wave after wave still kept coming. Eventually they stopped, I could feel the sun bathing us in the warmth of its rays as the smoke slowly cleared and I wiped sweat from my face.

Two scenes lay in front of us, one of beauty, the suns warm rays, the other of horrible carnage. Hundreds of bodies lay around us. Some bodies were stacked on top of each other. There was no room to walk between them. It was a terrible sight; most of the bodies were in pieces.

Amazingly we hadn't lost anyone, the shield had protected us. Starting forward again there was little resistance and after a few hours there was no one to challenge us.

I still hadn't located the main cell. Looking around I saw several groups of people coming our way, once again I signaled for everyone to prepare for another attack.

"Stop, stop!" I shouted, for on their arms they wore the bands of World Freedom Fighters. At last reinforcements had arrived.

Hundreds of them poured over us like waves thundering ashore.

Something else caught my attention. I had an uneasy feeling in my mind. I could sense the darkness of evil moving closer to us again.

James saw movement ahead of us. He took his gun from his holster, firing several shots into the air. Everyone started to run for cover. "Stop, stop," I shouted. "The Gara are coming, we have to get ready to fight."

Everyone stopped and moved into position preparing for what we thought would come.

But they didn't come any closer. We watched as they formed a barrier in front of what looked like the entrance to the subway.

James signaled our group to fan out before we started moving forward. The rubble from the partially destroyed buildings forced our groups out into the streets. Some of them used the alley ways to move forward, but they faced more of an obstacle than we did because the allies were narrower and some places were almost totally blocked. Once we were in the streets we reformed and moved toward the enemy cautiously. I went to the front of our group; there was only about one block between us and the people standing in front of the subway entrance.

I saw someone was moving toward us. Raising my hand I signaled for our group to stop. The figure kept moving closer. Who was this person? I could feel the fear in our group as it was starting to move through them. I couldn't let it control them.

What! my mind screamed. Shock moved swiftly through me. Marsha was the person who was moving toward us.

"Hold your fire!" I shouted.

James could hear the urgency in my voice, he began running back and forth in front of our group, telling them to hold their fire.

Marsha still kept moving towards us. What did she want and above all, what was she doing with them? Sue hadn't told me about Marsha being with the Gara. I knew Sue was aware of the fact that Marsha had gone over to their side. I knew in my heart why Sue hadn't said anything to me. She wouldn't have wanted to see the hurt in my eyes when I found out that my youngest daughter had gone over to the other side. I didn't know that Marsha had betrayed us.

Standing there I watched as she came closer to me. My mind was in a state of confusion. How could my daughter be with the Gara? I was happy to see her. But why was she with them?

She was standing in front of me now. My heart wanted to take her in my arms, but my mind held me back. We stood there for a few seconds eyeing each other.

Finally I spoke asking, "What is going on? Why are you with them? Don't you know that they want to destroy this world and kill all of us?"

She stood there, a strange expression on her face.

"What's wrong with you anyway? I asked a question, please answer me." I was almost pleading, trying to look into her soul, my mind pulled back in horror. What I saw and felt was pure evil. How could this be my own daughter? Why was she helping the Gara to destroy our world?

Finally she answered with contempt in her voice, "Father it's so nice to see you again. How have you been?" A smile formed on her face, a smile that showed nothing but disdain for me.

Walking around me, she moved closer to our group. Then, putting her hands on her waist, she shook her head back and forth in contempt as she laughed with pure evil delight.

"This is what is going to defeat the great Gara? You have to be joking." Still laughing, she turned and walked back to me. She stood close in front of me and looked directly into my eyes.

I could see hate in those eyes, eyes that once showed love. What had caused the change in her? She had always been a problem child, but nothing that love couldn't overcome.

"Marsha," I said, trying to reach out to her.

"Don't 'Marsha' me!" she screamed, moving back. "Dear old Dad, always trying to protect me. What do you think about me now? I'm not the one who needs protecting. You're the one who needs protection now."

"Since you are my father, I have been given the honor to accept your surrender. If you don't feel like giving up, well, I guess we will have to kill you and all your group of so-called heroes, too."

I didn't know what to say to her. This was not the loving little girl I knew. She was always kind, no matter what her problems. There was something that had changed inside of her after giving birth to Skylar.

She shoved her finger into my chest, bringing me back from my thoughts.

"Did you hear what I said?" she asked. "As the old saying goes; surrender or die, which will it be, Father? We will give you five minutes to decide."

She turned and walked away. It was if she was walking out of my life. Her life now belonged to evil.

James walked over to me, asking, "Who was that and what did she want?"

"That was my daughter," I answered as I followed her with my eyes.

"Was?" James asked not fully sure of what I meant by was?

"Yes, *was*. She is one of them now. They have given us five minutes to surrender or they say we will be destroyed."

I turned to him. "James, move everyone back behind the crumbled buildings," I said, pointing. "Once they are there, wait for my signal, and then rush from all directions. We won't give up without a fight."

Everybody moved back behind the crumbled buildings like I instructed. When I looked back, I watched as Marsha disappeared through the barrier of people in front of whatever they were trying to protect.

We waited and waited, and I could hear the seconds ticking by on my watch. The ticking of my watch got louder with each stroke. Sweat started to drip off my face; my heart was pounding. My eyes didn't move as we watched and waited for them to make their move.

Then they started to move, slowly at first, then faster, firing their weapons at us. Out of the corner of my eye I caught something coming from above. Six of their crafts dove at us.

This was the moment I had been waiting for. I lifted my arm toward our group and gave the signal. Everyone rushed forward, weapons raised, hollering and firing as they ran.

One group ran past me as I stood still. Both groups moved closer to each other, one good, one evil, firing their weapons with complete hatred for one another.

"Time," I signaled. James raised his arms above his head and shouted, "Stop and drop, stop and drop!" everyone stopped moving and dropped to the ground as planned.

This was the time to make our move, gathering every ounce of energy in my mind I released it. Light shot upwards and at the same time moved across the Gara's forces. The whole area in front of me lit up like ten suns exploding all at once. The ground shook like an earthquake had started. Fire erupted from the sky, so intense that anything close started to melt from the heat.

In an instant it was over. I waited for the smoke to clear. Finally my eyes could see the spot where our enemy had once been. Nothing remained, only rubble of the collapsed building and ashes.

I could feel that my powers were growing stronger each day.

Once again my body was drained, I noticed that every time I used the powers that were given to me my body paid a price, and I didn't know what that price was. I tried to stop myself from falling. James ran back to me and taking hold of my arms he held me up.

Shock from what everyone had gone through floated over all of us. As everyone began to struggle to their feet and slowly moved forward, looking carefully they could see that the only thing that remained of the evil was ashes.

I slowly began to regain my strength. James helped me to move closer to where the subway entrance had been.

Several people that had fought with us came running over to help us. They began moving the debris away from the entrance. Looking down into the subway I wondered about Marsha. Had she been killed? I had to find out, I put my hand on the wall and then I started down the stairs, with James and several others following.

My heart was being torn apart, but I had to let my mind take control over everything now. Nothing mattered, only the destruction of evil, even though I knew that part of it was Marsha.

At the bottom of the stairs I could feel something dark and evil trying to overpower us; that's what I had hoped for.

Using my mind, I let the evil lead me. Standing on the platform, James once again helped me to climb down onto the train tracks Cautiously I stood on the ground between the rails, not knowing whether electricity still flowed through them, then turning to the right I could feel evils power as it grew stronger. This was the most powerful effect that I had ever felt from it.

James and the others had followed me, turning to him and the others, I said. "Please stay here, I have to go on alone."

This was my war now. Moving deeper into the subway, the darkness closed tightly around me. I had to see with my mind.

There was a wall blocking my way, movement behind and to the left caused me to turn, but I stopped. I had to let the energy in me do the work. There was a flash of light, striking where they were standing and then all was quiet, again my mind sent a second and third flash of energy, and then there was nothing.

The wall had to go, concentrating on it, there was a flash followed by a large explosion, causing pieces of metal and concrete to bounce off me.

In front of me the room went from darkness to light. Walking forward, there the evil being lay, quivering, in my mind I could feel it begging for its life. It could do nothing against my power. Watching it I felt no compassion, in fact I felt nothing inside to help me make the decision of whether to let it live or die. Turning and walking away, there was a flash behind me.

Returning to James and the others all I said was, "It's over." Yet I still wondered about Marsha, had she also been destroyed or was she able to escape.

Going back the same way we had come, we stepped outside. For the first time, this city and everyone in it could no longer feel the evil that had once darkened their path. It had been replaced with peace and harmony. Goodness rapidly moved over the city. Looking up into the sky I could feel the sun healing our hearts and souls.

Evil was gone from here. We had won again. I should feel happy, but I couldn't. "Marsha where are you?"

CHAPTER TEN

Sue and Skylar opened their eyes and looked around and thought, "So, this is the Windy City." they had appeared by the old Sears Towers. This was not what they had expected; nothing was out of place, no destruction of any kind.

Cars and trucks moved up and down the street cutting each other off every so often with horns blaring, people walking and running to homes, work or wherever. Some were smiling, others talking, everything looked like it was supposed to, there was no right or wrong.

This was totally wrong. If evil was controlling this city what kind of evil was it? They were completely confused.

Walking through more streets, it was all the same. Could they be wrong? Had The Keeper made a mistake? What was going on?

"Grandma," Skylar said, "this isn't right. I have this weird feeling, it feels like we are playing hide and seek. We are the seekers and evil is hiding.

"I know Skylar," Sue said, "Even the hairs on my arms are standing on end. There is an icy feeling here. I can't put my finger on it, but there is something definitely wrong."

After walking some more they still couldn't find anything that could help them discover what was going on. Finding a bench they both sat down. Looking up into the night sky, Sue watched the stars, their lights twinkling as clouds passed between the stars. One second they were there, another second they were gone. Back and forth, back and forth, every time it was the same. The pattern kept repeating itself, never changing.

Wait, how could that be? Watching closer, the clouds were all the same, never different. The stars also stayed still, it was all the same. Wait, that can't be right. How can the stars, and clouds not change, they have to change. Nothing in nature stays the same.

Skylar looked up at the sky, then at Sue. "Grandma there's something wrong with the sky. My wishing star isn't in the right place," she said pointing up.

"You're right, something is wrong, nothing is changing. Everything is staying the same," Sue answered. Turning she watched the cars that were moving around them. It started to become a game between her and Skylar.

Counting out loud, "One, two, three, four, five, six, seven, eight, nine, ten, eleven, now start again," she said as a blue Ford Taurus went by.

Skylar started to count, when she reached eleven, the blue Ford drove by again. Over and over it happened. The same blue Ford drove by them at exactly the same time.

As they watched, all the cars and trucks kept repeating never changing their pattern. It was like a carrousel at the fair. Round and round.

Sue's attention was now drawn to the people. It was the same with each person, never changing. Everything was the same. This wasn't real; something or someone was putting on this charade, for them.

Was this to put them off guard, to delay them? *Why? Why go to all this trouble? It would be easier to attack and drive us away or to even try and kill us?* Sue thought.

Maybe they knew that our power were too strong for them. They wanted to fool us into thinking everything is all right and then maybe we would leave. Did they really believe we would come here, take a look and then leave? They might have conquered vast parts of the universe but Sue doubted it was through brain power, only through strength.

She began to have strange thoughts that rapidly moved through her mind. Grabbing Skylar by the arm she whispered so that evil wouldn't be able to sense her thoughts, she didn't want to put them in more danger than was necessary, "Skylar are you ready to run for it?," they stood up, looked around, and then ran between two buildings, down a long alley, across a street and into another alley, across another street into another alley. Sue hoped that by running like this, they would lose whoever was observing them.

Stopping in their tracks, this too was repeating itself. Moving down the street, another alley, but it was the same on every street.

Back and forth, up and down, but every building, every street, cars, trucks, and people were the same. No matter what they tried it was always the same.

Breathing hard Sue leaned against a door that was in one of the buildings. She and Skylar had to catch their breath, and rethink of a way to stop this madness. The alley closed in around them. The pain in Sue's side was unbearable, her lungs felt like they would burst. She pressed herself harder against the door as she waited for the pain to ease.

Skylar was on her knees holding her side; she had to fight hard to catch her breath. She started to cry; looking up at Sue with tears streaming down her cheeks she said, "Grandma what's going on? Why won't they let us go? I can't run anymore." Sobs were coming from her.

Sue was trying to figure out what they should do, but she was too tired to think. Looking down at Skylar, Sue felt herself starting to lose control. Somehow she had to regain her composure.

Suddenly Skylar stood up, her breathing was back to normal and her strength had also returned. Looking around she grabbed Sue's

JOSEPH A. LUNINI, SR.

hand, "Come on Grandma," she said pulling hard. Sue had to struggle to keep up with her; whatever had entered her granddaughter entered her as well.

They walked to the center of the street, which surprised her; she could feel the urgency in Skylar's grip. Sue thought that Skylar would want to run, but no, Skylar stood firm, taking her time.

What was going on, she thought to herself. Sue knew that she must put her trust in this child.

Once in the center of the street Skylar gently pushed Sue to the side. Skylar slowly started to rise into the air, light started to glow around her, then she started to spin around faster and faster until she was only a blur.

The light around her body was growing more intense. Sue shielded her eyes for a moment; she could see small streaks of light coming from the glow that surrounded Skylar. More and more streaks flashed into the darkness.

Then Skylar's body suddenly came to a stop, but the light continued to swirl around her like she was in the eye of a hurricane.

Suddenly a scream came from Skylar, then a strange voice came from deep inside her, everything around them began to shake. "*CARO-GE-FI-IEK-VIRS-RIG-OWE-O-MI-SU.*" (Creator God of the universe, bring power to my soul.)

Streams of bright blue light came from her, sounds of thunder crashed across the sky almost knocking Sue to the ground.

Sue heard more strange words coming from Skylar, "LL-TE-ORD-S-NE-MI-RET-DA-IA. AMI-E-GN. LATI-E-ROD." (All the world is in my heart and mind. Darkness be gone. Evil be destroyed.)

More light flashed, not only in the sky, but across the heavens. The ground began to crack as fishers began to appear. Everything around Skylar turned a bright blue with yellow highlights around the edges.

Winds started blowing, soft at first. Then they intensified. Sue grabbed onto the pole of a street light, locking her fingers to keep from being driven into what was left of one of the buildings close to Skylar that hadn't been destroyed. Sue didn't know how long she could hang on.

It was like a scene from a biblical movie in which God was trying to destroy evil in the world. All that was needed was the sea to part in two and wash over everything. She could feel her hands slipping and didn't know much longer she could hold on. Trying to use her powers didn't help either. Everything inside her was being pulled toward Skylar, she didn't know what her fate would be if she let go of the pole?

A voice spoke to her, "*Sue be not afraid, I am with you, what you see is my wrath against evil. I have given the power to Joan so that she can direct it anywhere and at any time that she chooses.*" Sue released her hands, her fate now rested with Skylar. She felt herself being propelled toward her; she watched as the blue light around Skylar reached out and surrounded her. She freely and gently joined Skylar, almost becoming one with her.

Sue's body was now filled with the power that radiated from Skylar. It almost felt like she was being torn apart, and the feeling was unbelievable. She watched in amazement as her body became part of the light, higher and higher she went, feeling like she could reach out and touch the stars. Her hands moved toward them. She was almost there. Just a little more. Straining, they were almost hers, and then in an instant it stopped, the light was gone. The thunder faded away and Sue's feet touched the ground.

She looked around, and then found Skylar was standing behind her. "Grandma," she softly said. When Sue turned around it was like she was facing a different girl, Skylar was no longer a child. Sue saw something else in her; she saw a future leader, one who would travel far from this world conquering evil, bringing goodness to those worlds that were scattered though out the universe.

But that was in a future time and place for now there was evil here that had yet to be dealt with. The future would come soon enough.

Skylar and Sue looked around, it was now daylight, and Sue could feel that evil had faded into the darkness; it feared the daylight and them. It was afraid of her … No … maybe not her … but Skylar.

The city had taken on a normal appearance, but she still had a bad feeling inside that kept gnawing at her. Evil had put on a fantastic show in the night. But in the light there was nothing, where had it slithered off to?

"Excuse me," a young man said as he bumped into her, dropping his brief case.

Sue bent down and started to help him pick up the papers that had fallen from the case scattering over the ground. She said, "Here let me help."

Handing him the papers she turned and started to walk away but he said, "Excuse me, Sue."

Startled Sue spun back to face him once again with a surprised look on her face she asked, "How do you know my name?"

"My name is Jesse. I've been sent by The Keeper to help you. Please come with me, we have to hurry," he said. "Evil is still with us hiding in anything that casts a shadow, it could be in your shadow, we have to be careful, evil is watching and waiting to strike.

They quickly followed him to a car. Once inside, he sped off at a fast rate of speed. He looked in the rearview mirror several times to make sure that they weren't being followed.

"I have been waiting several hours for you. I was starting to worry that something had happened to you," he said.

"It's a very long story, but I can wait till later to tell you," Sue answered, looking around, watching people as they sped by trying very hard to forget the last few hours. Everything looked normal, but it did last night too. She was cautious about her surroundings.

They drove along Lake Shore Drive for several minutes. At the same time, Sue felt they were being followed. Finally the car pulled into the ship yards, moving past several buildings, then slowing. The car pulled into a large building.

The door to the building closed behind them. Then she saw that there were several people standing at the other end of the building. The car pulled up to them and stopped.

Sue counted six people standing there; one of them reached over and opened the car door saying, "Thank heavens you made it. We were so worried about you. We thought that you would be here last night."

Before Sue could answer, a young woman interrupted.

"Sue, my name is Juanita; I am the leader of this group. The Keeper told me about your problems last night. Glad to see you're all right."

Getting out of the car, she shook Juanita's hand saying, "For a while, I had some doubts too. But it's good to find that we have friends."

"Thank you," Juanita answered. "I would like you to meet the other members of our team. This is Glen, Mark, Kevin, Matt, and Dawn," she said as she pointed to each one.

"It's good to meet all of you," Sue answered, shaking each of their hands. "But why have we been brought here?" Sue asked.

"I'll let Mark explain everything," Juanita said as she turned. "Will you please follow me?"

As they walked, Mark started to tell Sue and Skylar what they had found. "The Gara have taken control of only a few people, but they are high up in city government. The Gara have been moving large amounts of materials to this area and once here, then it's taken at night by barges to the middle of Lake Michigan and in the morning, the barges come back empty."

"What happened to the materials?" Sue asked.

"We're not sure. Two of our groups tried to find out, but they went out and didn't come back. We think that the Gara killed them. When they didn't come back, several other groups of people searched the area around these buildings and all the way to the docks, but they didn't find anything either," Juanita answered.

"We're lucky that there's a room hidden behind that wall," Dawn said, pointing to the end of the building. When both groups didn't return, the Gara started searching for us, and we were able to prevent them from finding us by hiding in there."

Then Matt came running over to us. "They are coming. Quick! We must hide."

Following Matt, we ran to the other side of the building. We stopped as he grabbed what looked like a large fish hook and turned it. The wall moved back...

"Quick, inside," Matt said, pushing us in.

The wall quickly and quietly closed behind us. We listened as steps and small chatter could be heard now. They were speaking in low voices, and Sue couldn't make out very much of what they were saying. Straining, Sue could only understand a few muffled words. Something about time and arrival was about all she could understand.

After several minutes it grew quiet. They had given up looking for us and left. Checking carefully, Mark looked through a small hole in the wall. No one was there. He slid the section of wall back, and we all stepped out.

"What do you think they meant by saying time and arrival?" Juanita asked, looking at Sue.

"We know that before we left for New York, the Gara had a large group of ships heading toward earth and that they would arrive in seventy-two hours. I think that is what they were talking about," she said. "This place may be one of the control areas for their attacks. Chicago has a large population of people, and it's a good location to direct their attacks."

"Where's the place that they take the materials to?" Sue asked.

"Come on," Mark said. We followed him as he headed over to a side door that led to outside the building. Looking carefully, he continued on. Passing several buildings, we moved behind several large containers of freight.

"There." He pointed past the docks toward the water.

He pointed to a place that was several hundred feet from the shore. Scanning the area, Sue noticed that there were two small boats that were tied to the dock. There were three men standing by them. Sue noticed something else: weapons strapped to their waists— ones like the Gara carried, only smaller.

She sensed evil coming from them and also to the place that Mark had pointed to in the water. This had to be it. This is what they had been sent to Chicago to find …

The hair on the back of her neck was standing on end. *I've found you,* she said to herself, letting her mind search the water. Deeper and deeper she searched with her mind. The feeling of evil grew stronger.

Turning to Juanita, she said, "They are here. We have to go into the water. It's the only way to destroy them."

"How are we going to destroy them when they are at the bottom of the lake?" Matt asked. We don't have any scuba equipment."

Skylar thought for a moment. "We don't need any."

"What do you mean?" Dawn asked. "We can't breathe in the water. We need oxygen."

"I know," Skylar answered, walking up to Dawn, and taking hold of her hand, she said, "Close your eyes." In that moment Dawn and Skylar were standing at the bottom of the lake.

There was shock on Dawn's face. She grabbed at her throat, but then stopped. She was breathing, and there was no need for oxygen tanks. Somehow the water gave her what she needed.

"*Stay here,*" Skylar said to her, not with words, but with her mind.

Skylar went back to the others, taking them one at a time to join Dawn. Now it was Sue's turn. Skylar took hold of her hand and they instantly joined the others.

Using her mind to communicate, she led them through the murky waters, searching for the source of the evil. They moved slowly and carefully forward.

For several long moments she couldn't find where the evil was hiding.

Where are they? Her mind asked. Why couldn't she find them? What was wrong?

Then she heard a voice deep inside of her saying, *Let your mind be free. Stop looking. They will come to you.*

Skylar stopped moving and, letting go of her thoughts, she could feel her mind expand. It moved through the water, faster and faster.

Suddenly her mind stopped searching. There was something there, and she could feel herself being pulled toward it. Letting her body go free, she floated over to it.

The others followed close behind, not knowing what was about to happen. Had they found the source of the evil? Their hearts were pounding.

They tried to see through the water, but it was too cloudy from the pollutants that had been dumped in the lake. All they could do was to follow close behind Skylar. Each of them hoped that Joan knew what she was doing. She stopped moving and, raising her hands, she could feel the hard surface of something as she ran her hands over the skin of whatever it was. Then she tried using her mind, but she couldn't penetrate into it.

Skylar felt something moving toward them. Pulling back from the object, she signaled to the group to move back. She had forgotten for a moment that they couldn't see her clearly, so she tried to use her mind to signal them. But it came too late. Something flashed through the water, striking Matt and where he had been the water turned red, Matt was gone.

Everyone else started to swim, trying to find a place to hide. Another flash tore into Glen with the same results.

In Skylar's mind, words started to form, and she shouted, "*REC-KI-MR-TE-LATI*." (Protect them from the evil.) Even in the water, Skylar's words were clear. Light shot out from her. Moving through the water, the light covered everyone in a blue glow. Sue swam up beside Skylar; they joined hands as they moved along the object. Their minds formed together into one.

They stopped and placed their hands on the wall. As they did this, the water around them began to churn as the light from their joined minds struck the object. For a second nothing happened. Then a crack started to form in it.

The crack slowly began to grow longer and wider. Flashes of light bounced off of them, having no effect. Their joined power was too great.

Turning her thoughts toward the lights, Skylar said, "*RO-KI*." (Destroy them.) A powerful light flashed from Skylar. The water almost began to boil around them, then nothing.

Turning her attention back to the object, Skylar concentrated harder. With a loud bang, the object burst open like a balloon filled with too much air.

Sue and Skylar let go as they were pulled inside the object. The water filled the chamber. Once inside, Skylar turned to the opening. In a few moments, she saw that the other four had joined them.

Facing the opening, everyone watched in amazement as the break began to close. In a few seconds, the opening was once again a solid mass and, surprisingly, the water was gone…

They turned toward Skylar. What kind of person was she? Her powers were beyond belief, and they kept growing in strength.

Sue turned and looked around the chamber.

"There," she said, pointing to a door. "Stay here. I'll be right back."

Closing her eyes, Sue felt herself being pulled toward the wall. Slowly her body became part of the wall. Moving through it, she stopped before reaching the other side of it.

Her eyes could see into the next room. It was empty. Sue moved along the inside of the wall. Several more rooms were empty; again she searched as she moved.

Sue suddenly stopped. There it was again—that feeling of evil—and slowly, she moved. The feeling was growing stronger; evil was close.

In the next room, she found some Gara guarding something. She looked closer. There was an object behind them in a clear glass case. Moving forward, something stopped her.

She moved back and went down another wall. She could feel something blocking her again. She tried several other ways, but it was still the same. What was stopping her? Trying one more time, her mind slammed into something that sent a shock through her. She could hear an alarm go off.

The Gara started firing at the walls, tearing large holes in them.

Sue moved swiftly, trying to get to safety. She knew that she was vulnerable now. The strength of the object was also her only protection.

They were getting closer to her. In a matter of seconds, they would find her.

Something flashed before her eyes. She felt nothing.

W*ait*, she thought. There was no pain. Looking around, she saw someone standing in the room with the Gara. Trying to clear her eyes, it was Skylar standing there alone.

Skylar pointed toward the Gara. Fear rose up in them. Dropping their weapons, they tried to flee, but there was no place to go. They were pushing and shoving each other, fighting to escape, but escape was impossible.

"*MI-SU-S-OWE-KY-FOU-SA-TE-FOU-DA-KI!*" (My soul is power. Bring forth the light and destroy them!) Skylar shouted.

Light swirled around her, lifting her into the air. Faster and faster the light moved. The chamber began to move. Her power was truly given by the Creator. In that moment the Gara were gone. Nothing remained but ashes.

The light faded. Nothing was moving. Skylar slowly floated back to the floor.

Sue emerged from the wall and came up beside her. Skylar looked into Sue's eyes for a second, and then she turned and looked into the glass case.

There lay the creature, squirming with fear. Its long, thin arms flaying into the air, and its bulging eyes held only fear. It was trying to crawl away, but there was no place for it to go. Skylar stood there watching it. Then she turned to Sue and taking her arm, they mind-jumped to where the other four people waited, and then they mind-jumped again and now all of them stood on the dock. Looking over at the water, it started to bubble faster and faster. Then it simply erupted like a volcano, but instead of red hot lava, a blue light poured out.

"What happened to the evil? Was it destroyed?" Mark asked, as he continued to stare at the water.

Skylar and Sue stood there for a long time; neither one of them spoke or moved.

"Sue, what's wrong?" Juanita finally asked, touching her on the arm. Why wouldn't either one of them say anything?

After what felt like an eternity, Sue took Skylar's hand. Both turned and started walking away but stopped abruptly, saying, "Something in the universe created all life. Or do you believe we came from nothing and were formed through evolution?" Sue asked.

Juanita answered, "I believe there is a supreme power, a being that made all things. Without it, nothing would exist."

Sue looked at Juanita, then at Skylar. She knelt down and looked into Skylar's eyes and placing her hands on her shoulders, she asked, "If there is this supreme being that gave life to us, making good and evil at the same time, and we are given the choice to choose between the two, some choosing good, while others chose evil, then there had to be something or someone that was given the power to keep the two in balance. For if one overcame the other what would our reward be for choosing that one over the other?"

Skylar reached up and placed her hands on Sue's cheeks and answered, "Power has been given. Look not unto others, but in you. The answer lies deep in your soul. Use the answer wisely, for that answer only comes to us once. Choose carefully and look to the water. The one who walks among us was there," Skylar said, as Sue got to her feet, and then she stood by her side.

"Evil has been destroyed here with this victory, and the other areas have also thrown off the shackles of evil. People are now free to help each other, from Chicago to Cleveland, New York south to St. Louis. New Orleans over to Miami, up into Canada, as far north as the Arctic Circle, and completely down to the tip of South America."

CHAPTER ELEVEN

Nancy and several of our agents quietly and quickly moved into the capital of China. By the power that had been given to them they were able to disappear from one place and then appear in another place, they were able to locate where the Chinese leader was staying. It was night, and due to what was going on in the world, he was being guarded by a large contingent of guards.

The country was almost on the verge of civil war. Government leaders were leaning toward an attack on Russia. Not all were under the control of the Gara. Those that weren't wanted to pull their troops back from the border.

To keep those that disagreed in line, some disappeared without a trace. It was a way of saying, if you want to keep on living, agree with the government's policy or shut up.

Thousands of people were rounded up and simply disappeared. There were no civil rights. Some people thought there was even less freedom now than before. It was simply, "keep in line or else."

To the southwest, the military were even preparing to attack India, Turkey, and Greece. Mass amounts of troops, armor, vehicles, and even nuclear weapons stood ready.

This region of the world was about to exterminate itself. The only chance to diffuse the situation was Nancy and her small group; she hoped that more help would soon arrive, if it was coming at all.

But Nancy couldn't wait. She had to work her way into his home or office, and there wasn't a lot of time to accomplish this. There was no one outside of her small group that could be trusted. It looked as if they would have to do this alone.

Her group planned on ambushing a diplomat's car that they had learned was going to a meeting with the Chinese leader. Nancy could touch the ones she loved and those that had been given supreme power by the Creator. By simply touching others, they could move into their bodies. The security guards were the first people they used their powers on, thus changing who they were. Then they would set up a checkpoint. Standing in the road, they waited for the car to approach.

When they saw that the car was coming, they waved their arms to stop it. Once the vehicle had stopped, they moved from behind the barricade and walked over to the driver's side.

"Rolling down the window, the driver asked, "What's wrong?"

"We're checking for enemies of the country," one of Nancy's group said. "Would you please step out of the vehicle?" Only after a heated argument did the driver do as he was asked.

The three people in Nancy's group, Peter, Carol and Roy, went around to the other doors and asked the others in the car to do the same.

Slowly, the other occupants stepped out of the car. As they were wondering what was going on, Nancy and her group simply reached out and touched them. In an instant their bodies switched with the occupants of the car. Looking through different eyes, Nancy looked down at the four bodies lying on the ground, and one of them was her lifeless form. There would probably be a small article in the paper about four Americans being found dead on a lone road in China.

They were dissidents that were trying to overthrow the Chinese government.

Before they could get in the car, something caught Nancy's attention. Someone was coming over to them—a small boy about twelve years old.

Speaking in perfect English, he said, "My name is Lee, and I know that you are good people. I want to help you. I know that you want to stop this madness before the world is destroyed. What can I do to help?"

For some unknown reason, Nancy trusted him. "We need to get to the government building where the leader of your country is staying without getting caught," Nancy said, wondering who this boy was.

"My father works there," he said. "I will show you the way. There is a secret entrance into the building that he showed me."

Nancy's plan was that once they got there, she would go in alone. Peter, Carol, and Roy would go with the boy to join her later.

After getting in the car, they drove for several miles. They didn't go into the main part of the city but stopped about a quarter of a mile away, Carol, Roy, and the boy got out of the car and headed into the woods.

The car continued toward the compound. Guards at the gate stopped them. One of the guards came to the driver's side asking to see their papers; Peter showed him what he wanted to see.

After looking at them for a minute, he signaled them forward, and they drove the car up to the building which was guarded by dozens of soldiers. As they pulled up to the entrance, several of the soldiers came up to the car. One reached over and opened the door.

Nancy got out of the car and from here on she would be on her own until the others could join her. She felt tightness in her chest. She followed two of the soldiers into the building, as four more followed behind her.

They led her through several long halls and down a set of stairs. She found herself in a large room. Without saying anything, the soldiers left her alone. She walked around the room looking at the art work on the walls, pretending to admire them. Nancy could feel eyes on her. They were watching her. Holding herself straight, she walked over and sat in the only chair in the room.

Waiting for what she thought was hours, sweat started to appear on her forehead, her nerves were starting to fray, but she knew that she had to keep herself under control.

Finally a door opened and two men walked in. They weren't soldiers, but they were armed. Each one carried a machine gun. Coming over to her, they told her to get up and come with them. Standing up, she followed them through the door. Again they went into several rooms and down several more flights of stairs. Standing to the side, they motioned for her to go into the room. She did as directed. A woman led her to a large table in the center of the room. Nancy accidentally brushed the woman's arm, and she wondered, *How was this woman saved?* When she looked into the woman's eyes, she knew that the answer would come later. The woman pointed to a chair and Nancy sat down. On the table there was a container. The lady told her it was tea and asked if she would like some.

Nancy nodded her head yes. After pouring a cup, the woman left without saying a word. As the woman was leaving, a group of men entered and they were followed by a half-dozen heavily-armed men.

The first group sat down at the table with her. Another door opened and people came in carrying food. Three of those people were Peter, Carol, and Roy. How did they get from the car and in here to serve the food? That was another question that would have to be answered later.

They sat eating quietly; when one of them finished, he pressed a button under the table. The door opened and again her people came in gathering the dishes, wiping the table off and then left.

"You have the weapons code," one of the men sitting with her asked, reaching his hand toward her. "The code, please." This time his voice didn't have any patience in it.

Nancy's mind tried to figure out what to say.

"What about our deal?" she asked, hoping to bluff her way out.

The man sat back in his chair, pressing another button. Another woman entered the room, carrying a brief case. She sat it on the table in front of Nancy and left the room.

Nancy reached over and opened it. Inside were stacks of money. It had to be over ten million dollars.

"That's our part. Now the code," he said, putting out his hand again. "You have ten seconds to give me the code to arm the missiles, or you will be shot."

She could have been wrong about whom the evil controlled? Maybe it wasn't the Premier, but a group of rogue politicians. Where could the Premier be? Nancy had a feeling that he was being held captive here by these people. They were running everything.

His counting unnerved her, bringing her back from her thoughts. "Eight, nine," The count, "ten," she heard. "I want it now," he said louder, standing up.

The door suddenly opened. She heard Peter saying, "Excuse me, sir. We forgot to give you your desserts. He walked in carrying a tray.

"Get out of here!" the man standing across from Nancy shouted at him.

As he turned to look at Peter, it was the chance Nancy was looking for. Standing up, she reached over the table, grabbing his hand. A look of fear flooded his face for a second then was replaced with a brief smile.

Nancy looked across at the body she had occupied. It lay across the table, not moving. The other people stood up.

She was in charge, but no one else in the room knew what had happened. Turning to the soldiers, "Get this worthless body out of here, and bring me the other one that came with him," she said.

Several of the soldiers rushed in and lifted up the body and carried it out of the room. She sat down. She began to drink her—uh, his—tea. That was easy. She had destroyed one member of the group, but there were still the others, and the Premier had to be found and freed. Maybe there was still a chance that this madness could be stopped before this part of the world destroyed itself. She could only hope.

In a few minutes other soldiers came rushing back into the room. "Sir, we have found more bodies a couple of miles from here, and they are Americans."

"What do you mean you found dead Americans? How did they get there? Do you know who killed them? Nancy asked, standing up from the table shouting at him. "I wanted all foreigners captured alive!" Laughing in her mind, she thought, "*If they only knew.*"

"But sir, we found one boy in the car. There was no sign of a struggle. It appears that someone left him in the car with all the dead bodies lying around," he answered. "We also found two more bodies in the kitchen."

"Bring me some more tea, and have somebody clean up this mess!" she shouted, sitting back down.

"Sir, what mess?" he asked with a puzzled look on his face. He would do and say whatever it took to save his life, so he turned and shouted for someone to come and clean up the mess that wasn't even there.

"Just do what I said, or you could end up like those that were found in the kitchen," Nancy said, trying to sound hostile. "Bring me the person I asked for earlier."

One of the soldiers answered, "But there is no other person, sir."

"What idiots. If I say that someone's there, then all you have to do is go find them. Now I suggest you do just that," Nancy said.

The soldier didn't know what to do, so he said, "Yes." He turned and left the room.

The three others at the table looked at each other with confusion running through them. *What mess? Someone had cleaned the table right after everyone had eaten. What about all these bodies that kept turning up?* they wondered.

Nancy wanted to leave them all in confusion as to what was going on, and so she acted like everything that was happening was normal, knowing that the others had seen how evil acted and would simply believe in what she had told them.

Turning toward the door, Nancy watched as Peter, Carol, and Roy came in, carrying a large pail.

They started wiping the table then handed a small towel to each of the three people sitting at the table with Nancy. As each of them took the towels, they also touched the hands of the group.

Everyone in Nancy's group all looked down at the three new bodies that now lay on the floor.

The soldiers in the room didn't know what to do. Nancy stood up.

"What's going on!" she shouted at them. "People seem to be dropping like flies."

"Get these bodies out of here. After that I want none of you to come back in here until I call you." she said.

The soldiers were confused, but they knew better to than to question what they had been told.

Waiting till they had taken the bodies out and left the room, Nancy turned to Peter and the others saying, "This is almost too easy."

"I know," Peter answered back, shaking his head.

"There is a group of people, not the Premier, who is orchestrating this war. They have him hidden somewhere in this building. We have to find out where. Hopefully he can stop this madness, but time is running against us," Nancy said.

"We need help in finding him. We can't ask people where he is. We're the ones who brought him here," Carol said, looking at Nancy.

Nancy thought for a moment. "Roy, get one of those soldiers back in here. I have an idea," she said

Roy got up from the table and walked over to the door. Opening it, he spoke to one of them. Turning, he came back over to the table followed by the soldier.

"Sit down," Nancy said, motioning to the chair at the same time. "Do you know that you are one of my most trusted guards?" she asked, looking at him and acting like they were friends.

"Thank you, sir. I am your most humble servant. I will do whatever you ask of me," he said, bowing.

"Good. That is what I needed to hear from you," she said, continuing. "We have traitors among us that want to stop us from our glorious job of spreading our ideas and beliefs throughout the world.

"We must find and kill them!" he stood and shouted.

"Good. I knew you were the right person to help us," Nancy said.

"You are to be the one who will head the group that is guarding the Premier. Do you think you can do that?" Nancy asked.

"Yes," he answered, trying to salute and bow at the same time. Nancy, Peter, Carol, and Roy all stood up and saluted him in return.

"Now, you will lead us to the Premier," Roy said, still saluting.

"I am to take you?" he asked with confusion on his face.

"Yes, if we go first, it will look like you are nobody, but with you in front, everyone will know you are in charge of guarding the Premier," Roy said.

For a few seconds he stood there.

"You're right," he said. "Everyone must give me respect, and watching me leading you, they will know and give it to me."

"Oh, you are so right; someone's going to give it to you." *But it's not going to be what you think,* Nancy said to herself.

"Lead on," Nancy said, as all four stood at attention before him.

Turning, he walked over to the door, and Roy ran past him to open it. Once in the hall, Nancy made it clear that this fine soldier was to be in charge.

You could see the confusion on the other soldier's faces. He was only a lowly and not very bright guard, and now he was their leader. Some of them must have thought that we were fools.

Walking behind him, everyone could see the ignorance in his face. He walked with an air about himself—one of complete stupidity.

Following behind him, they went down a long hallway, stopping by a double door guarded by two soldiers. Nancy signaled for them to let us pass. The guards opened the door and Nancy's group was led down another hall that was lined with dozens of soldiers.

Stopping again, they stood in front of a steel door. Nancy signaled and then it slid to one side. Entering, they went down a flight of stairs. At the bottom they were met by more soldiers and another steel door, the same as the one before. With a signal, it was opened. Moving inside, they were standing in a small room. At the other end of the room, a door opened and a man walked in, coming over to us. He looked at the lowly guard who had brought us here and he demanded, "What are you doing here?"

Nancy walked up beside the soldier. "He is in charge. Now whatever he wants, you will get it for him. Understand?" Nancy said with a threatening tone in her voice.

There was a startled look in the other man's face. He tried to argue briefly.

"This man can't be—"

Nancy cut him off in mid-sentence.

"I said he is in charge. You are to follow his orders, or do we have to replace you?" she said, pointing her finger at him.

"Yes … yes, I understand," he stuttered. "What do you need?" he asked.

The lowly guard turned to Nancy. Leaning over, he whispered, "What do I want?"

Nancy whispered back, "You want to see the Premier."

"Oh, yes. That's right." Turning back, he said, "I want you to bring the Premier to me right away!" he demanded.

"The Premier," the other man asked, looking past him toward Nancy.

She nodded her head.

He turned and left the room. *So far so good*, Nancy thought. In matter of minutes the door opened. The soldier returned and three people were with him. Nancy recognized one of them as the Chinese leader from the pictures that she had seen in the newspaper.

"You may leave him here with us," Nancy said to them.

"We are not to leave him alone. That's the order you gave to us," one of them stated.

"I gave those orders to you, so I can change them. Now leave!" Nancy demanded, pointing to the door.

There was hesitation for a moment, and then they turned and left.

Nancy could see fear on the Premier's face. Moving closer and leaning over to him, she whispered, "Don't be afraid. We are here to help you."

There was a startled look on his face, but quickly it changed to hope.

"How are you going to help me escape from here? There are too many soldiers."

The soldier that had brought them here turned to Nancy.

"What do you mean you are going to free him?" the soldier that had brought them there raised his weapon.

Roy had moved behind him. He reached over and took hold of his shoulder. Roy looked down at the body that had once been his and then dropped his weapon.

The Premier couldn't understand what had happened.

"Don't be afraid, sir," Nancy said to him as she continued. "We have certain, uh, things that we do, that others can't do. Our bodies are capable of moving from one person to the next. But when we do, the body we were in dies."

Roy finished, "That's why we can't touch any living form, for if we do, we become the new one, destroying the other. The only way to return to our original bodies is by going through a process that we have on our home world. You are wondering how this person that we call Nancy is able to do this. She was taken through a time warp back to our planet and her form was changed. This is something that she chose to do, fully knowing that she had to refrain from touching any living form until the time she went back to her our world and at that time, and if desires she could remain there forever.

"We have to leave right away," Nancy said to the others. Roy, who was now the soldier, walked to the door that they had first come through. Opening it, they found the hallway empty. Something was wrong, but she knew that they couldn't turn back.

Going slowly into the hall, Peter gave a small object to each one. Nancy looked; it was a small handheld weapon.

"You hold it this way," Carol said to Nancy. "Press here and it will give off a burst of energy, destroying everything it comes in contact with."

They could hear people coming toward them from two different directions. Using their weapons, they were firing at them. Bullets struck all around.

Raising their weapons, they fired in both directions—Nancy and Roy one way, and Peter and Carol the other way, keeping the Premier between them.

After a few seconds, it grew quiet again. They started back toward the entrance. More bullets rang out around them, but they kept moving forward.

Reaching the top of the last set of stairs, they slowly moved toward the door.

Suddenly a large blast hit, knocking them back, then another and another tore at the front of the building. Once again, bullets started to come from behind them.

Nancy knew that they were trapped between two forces that were determined to destroy them. Her mind was trying to figure out what to do.

The explosions were getting closer to them, and it was only a matter of time until the explosions would be right on top of them. There was nothing they could do to escape.

Taking something from their belts, Peter and Carol started toward what was left of the door.

Turning to Nancy, Peter said, "If you ever make it back to our home world, give this to my family," he said, tossing her a small packet. Carol did the same. "Tell them to always keep us in their thoughts, for when they look they will see us looking back."

Turning back, they rushed out the door. Looking through a large hole in the wall, Nancy could see bright flames explode outwards from what they carried in their hands.

Everything in front of them was engulfed in flames so bright that it looked like it was day for a few moments.

Nancy didn't have a lot of time to watch them. The people that were coming up from behind were getting closer.

She and Roy stopped firing their weapons and for a moment, everything was quiet. Then once again she could see a barrage of bullets that were being fired at them bouncing off the walls, all the while getting closer and closer to them. In front of her, she could see explosions drawing nearer.

The Chinese Premier tried to stand up, but Nancy shouted, "Get back down! What are you trying to do, get yourself killed? We didn't come here to let that happen."

He looked at Nancy and even though he spoke in Chinese, she could understand his words. "I cannot let all of you die to save me."

"If you die," she said, "the evil that is taking control of your country will win; do you want that to happen?"

He knew that what she was saying was right. This was for them to do; his job would come later.

Nancy turned back to the battle that was going on around her and for a moment, her mind tried to escape to a place that was full of love: her home.

She felt something rip into her arm. Looking down, there was a liquid dripping from the wound. It wasn't blood, but part of her life. She was drawn back by a voice.

"Nancy," Roy shouted. "It's time," he said, also tossing her a small package. The same as what Peter and Carol had said to her.

Standing up, he pulled something from his belt, waving to Nancy, a last good-bye. He charged down the stairs. Flames shot out from him.

The light from it was so strong; Nancy had to look away again. She could feel tears running down her cheeks.

It was quiet again, not only in her mind, but everywhere. Holding her arm, Nancy stood up.

"We have to get out of here before more of them come," she said to the Premier.

"I have to get to the nearest television station; the people of China have to know that I am still alive. This madness has to stop," the Premier said, moving toward the door.

Once outside, all that could be seen was destruction. Nancy knew that if the Premier couldn't let the people know he was alive, this part of the world would surrender to the Gara and their evil ways. But where could they find it? Nancy turned around looking in all directions, there was nothing but darkness. From the rubble of the compound came a small figure. Straining her eyes she tried to make out who it was.

"Lee!" she shouted. "How did you survive in there? What about your father? Is he all right?" She asked.

"My father is all right. He protected me from them," he answered.

"Lee, I have to get the Premier to a television station so that the people know that he is still alive," Nancy said.

"Mr. Premier, I need you and Nancy to come with me, please. My father told me how to get there," Lee said.

"Where is your father, Lee? He needs to come with us." Nancy asked.

"He has gone ahead of us to wait for your arrival," Lee answered.

Why would he leave his son alone? Nancy thought.

Lee turned to Nancy. "He didn't leave me alone. He is always with me," Lee said.

Now how did he know what I was thinking? Nancy asked herself.

They followed Lee through a wooded area. Behind them, Nancy could hear the arrival of more troops, knowing that the troops would find nothing.

Walking for several miles, a tower came into view. Funny, everything was dark except for the tower.

Lee didn't slow down; in fact, at the sight of the tower, he began to run, dragging her behind. "Wait, Lee," Nancy hollered. "The Premier can't move that fast. Please slow down!"

Lee turned and came back to us; he reached over and took the Premier into his arms, lifting him up as if he was as light as a feather. How could someone so small lift the Premier so easily? Then Nancy heard, *Nancy, do not question. Believe.*

Turning, he started to run faster. Nancy could hardly keep up with him. As they reached the tower, Nancy leaned against a wall that was part of the base; she was completely out of breath.

Lee stood the Premier back on his feet.

"Go in, sir," he said. "There is no one here but us. Once you begin to talk to the nation, the people will come to your side to help stop this madness."

The Premier went in. Nancy went over and started to follow him inside, but Lee reached out. He placed his hand over her heart.

Nancy moved back in fear of what her power would do to him, but she couldn't move. Something was holding her.

"Nancy," Lee said. "Our job is finished, by those that gave their lives without question and also what you have chosen to sacrifice. Evil has been destroyed; there will be no more madness. Only peace and harmony will now move across this land."

"How do you know?" Nancy asked. Who was this person that was telling her about the past and the future at the same time? He was only a boy.

"How were you able to touch me without being harmed?" Nancy asked.

"The answer lies in you," he said, looking into her eyes. "The choice you made to change and become one of the stone people would seal your fate. You knew this and still accepted it without fear. This was done for the good of all."

Lee changed before Nancy eyes. Falling to her knees, she started to weep; tears of joy fell from her eyes, forming a pool around her.

Lee walked closer to her. Nancy raised her head looking lovingly into his eyes.

"It's time to go home, my child," he spoke. She could feel warm wind from his breath flow through her lifting her high, and then there was nothing.

CHAPTER TWELVE

We had managed to clear evil from the Americas. Nancy's group had stopped it in the Far East. Our attention was still focused on this world, making sure our enemy couldn't retake the areas that they had lost; the other threat came from space, which was a larger concern. There were less than thirty-six hours before the Gara's fleet of ships were close enough to attack the earth, and we still had two major areas on earth that evil was still controlling. The Middle East was one and the other, surprisingly, was the North Pole.

The ice in the North was melting at a rate way above what it should be. Our feeling was that the Gara were turning their attention from control to destruction of the earth.

We had people in the Middle East, but they weren't making a lot of headway against them. Our forces were becoming too thin, and we knew if the Gara managed to melt the ice cap, it would flood the coastal region. That would cost thousands of deaths and massive destruction.

Standing there, I looked at Sue and Skylar, asking them both, "Well, are you two ready to go and freeze?" trying to make light of the situation, knowing in my mind that this could be our biggest test yet. We were given heavy clothing and supplies to protect us from the cold.

JOSEPH A. LUNINI, SR.

Taking a deep breath and holding hands, we slowly closed our eyes. In less than a heartbeat, we were someplace in the Arctic Circle, as a cold wind bit into us.

Opening our eyes, all that could be seen was white. It was bitter cold. My mind tried to search around us. But the cold shut it down.

"Do either of you sense anything?" I asked, as I continued to search.

"Nothing," Sue answered. "I've never felt so cold in my life." She was trying to let her mind search, but her mind was also being affected by the cold.

"Me neither. Wait," Skylar shouted, pointing to a small speck that was moving toward us.

Sue and I looked to where Skylar was pointing; we strained our eyes, trying to figure out what it was.

It was coming closer toward us at a high rate of speed. Skylar touched my arm, saying, "Grandpa, they are here to help us."

Turning back to whatever was coming toward us, I wondered how she knew this, and then I could see several more objects following behind it. Within moments they were close enough for us to make out that they were snowmobiles. Very quickly, they moved up beside us. One of the riders got off the first snowmobile and came over to us. Reaching out his hand, he said, "Good to have you here. My name is Gary."

He shook my hand then Sue's and then Skylar's, bowing to each of us in civility.

"Come on. Climb aboard. We need to get you out of this frigid weather before the Gara come," he said, motioning for us to get on the machines, and there was fear in his voice.

We struggled through the snow, over to the vehicles. Once we were seated, they began to move across the snow and ice. I marveled at such a beautiful setting. How could this be a threat to the world?

It felt like we traveled for miles. My mind tried to drift off to sleep; it was like I had taken a sleeping pill.

Finally I could feel the vehicles slowing down. When I opened my eyes, I saw that we were in front of some low buildings that were almost buried by the snow.

Once we stopped we were rushed inside one of the buildings. Inside, it looked as if no one had lived there for years. *Why are we here? Could this be right?* I thought as I looked around.

"Come this way," Gary said as he pulled up a piece of carpet from the floor and pushed it aside. He reached down and pulled up a section of floor that was made of wood, exposing a flight of stairs.

We followed Gary down the stairs. Once at the bottom, I heard something behind us. Looking up, I could see someone was closing off the entrance to the stairs.

When I looked back at him, he motioned for us to follow him to a door; it looked like it was made of steel, but instead of opening it, he bent down and pushed a small panel aside that revealed a button. Gary pushed it, and a section of the floor behind us slid to one side. This door was there to fool anyone into thinking we had gone through it.

Standing back up, he went over to the opening, and I could see that there was a ladder going down. Standing at the opening, we looked down into the darkness.

Following him, we slowly climbed down into the darkness; my mind searched but found nothing. Standing in the darkness, I looked up as the floor above us closed.

In that brief moment, my heart had stopped beating. I couldn't feel or hear anything. After what seemed to be an eternity, everything returned to normal. What had happened to me?

Then suddenly dim lights around us started to slowly get brighter, pushing the darkness aside. My eyes slowly adjusted to it. We found that we were standing in a tunnel. Looking around, it had no beginning or end. The light started to move away from us in both directions, as if we were the power that gave life to the lights.

Gary moved forward, or it could be backward, depending on your choice. The three of us followed close behind, in total confusion as to who he was and where we were going.

Staring at the walls and ceiling, I tried to figure out what they were made of and then I took off one of my gloves reached out my hand touching the surface; to my amazement I discovered that they were made of ice, yet there was no coldness to it.

Where my hand had touched the surface, it began to melt—water running down and refroze within a few seconds, blending back into the surface like it had never been disturbed. I had touched this surface, and I knew that it was made of ice, and because there wasn't any chill to it, I couldn't figure out how this was possible.

Because I had been totally absorbed by the wall, I hadn't noticed that the surface on which we were walking had changed and this new feeling brought me back to where we were and looking down I felt my heart jump. No, not a jump; a thud. I could feel my blood rushing through my body. What had caused the change in my heart was the sight below me. We were standing on a bridge that was suspended in the air—nothing supporting it, amazingly it simply floated in the air.

Light cascaded into the abyss of darkness. There was nothing, only an empty chasm with no end.

The bridge jerked, causing us to grab onto the rail that was stretched on either side of us. The bridge slowly started moving down; everything grew brighter as we went lower. Everything was so quiet and this floating bridge—well there was no magic trick that could top this. After descending for what I thought was several miles, we stopped. The bridge had settled onto something that I couldn't see.

The light began to change and for the first time our eyes could really see what was around us; there was only one word to describe what we were seeing: *awesome.*

"At one time untold thousands of years ago, someone came here and started a new life," Gary said to us, with a kind of sadness in his voice. "I think you called it the Lost City of Atlantis. I have heard of a book that told of this place, a place of beauty and wonder where everyone lived in harmony, until darkness moved across the city, turning it into something that angered the one who had first walked upon the streets. It had been built where the sun would always keep it warm, but upon seeing that evil now possessed its soul, anger was released, striking at the heart of the city, burying it forever under the snow and ice, and there it would remain until the three anointed ones would once again raise it from the depths of blackness and bring it back into the sun."

"This is the City of Atlantis?" Sue asked, looking at the ruins of what must have at one time been beauty beyond words.

"When it was destroyed, where did the people go?" I asked, bending over and picking up a piece of broken pottery. Moving it around in my hands, I could feel someone else's hands holding it a long time ago.

Walking over, Gary also picked up a broken piece. He held it firmly in his hand. "You can feel a life force in each and every broken object that is here. For as many broken pieces, they are matched by the same number of hearts that was destroyed through …,"

"The story of this," he said moving his arms in a sweeping motion, indicating all of the ruins around us, "is about betrayal brought here by evil. Once you let it become your friend, it consumes your soul. It becomes a need that you can't control, forsaking all things good, destroying everything for its power. It gives you whatever your heart desires, until the time comes that you have nothing to give back to it. Then it destroys you, leaving what you see here."

"Gary, is the evil still here?" I asked, turning to him.

"Yes, that is why the ice is melting. It started to melt very slowly at first several hundred years ago; so small that no one noticed it until ten or twenty years ago. Now it has increased so much that if it isn't reversed, most of the ice masses will disappear in a few months.

How do we reverse it?" Sue asked.

"You have to destroy the evil that hides amongst it. By doing that, you will heal the hearts that lay broken here," Gary answered.

"On the surface I tried to use my mind to find the evil, but I couldn't," I said to him.

"It's not your mind that can destroy the evil here; it's your heart that you must give. You felt it on the way down," he said to me, taking his hand and laying it on my chest over my heart.

I could feel warmth pulsating as it entered my body and took hold of me. I felt joy, but there was also sadness. I couldn't figure out why. Did this mean that I would lose someone close—a family member, maybe?

"It's time to start," Gary said, walking away from us, through the broken pieces of what once was a land that had given us life.

The three of us followed behind him not saying a word, wondering how the three of us could bring life and wholeness back to the city and raise it once again into the sunlight. We traveled for a couple of hours. The landscape around us started to slowly change from broken beauty to a land of barren snow and ice. The winds whipped fiercely through us, snow swirling into our eyes blinding us. Cold reached its icy fingers deep into our souls, almost to the point of freezing our hearts.

The visibility was down to zero. I felt Sue and Skylar reach out for my hand. Reaching back, I was able to take hold of their hands. Even though they wore gloves, I could feel the coldness in them.

There had to be shelter somewhere. I knew that we weren't supposed to be destroyed. But I wondered if we could be frozen out here, lost forever in this God forsaken wilderness?

At that moment of doubt the winds stopped blowing, a feeling of warmth descended around us from the sun that was now shining. Its rays pierced deep into us.

Rubbing my eyes, I couldn't see Gary. Only Sue and Skylar existed. The sun around us went on forever. All we could see was snow, nothing but snow.

What is happening to us? my mind asked. Suddenly the snow under our feet gave way. We tried grabbing the edges, but I couldn't find anything to hold on to. We were falling. I tried to find Sue and Skylar's hands and then somehow, I felt the warmth of their hands take hold of mine. Our bodies landed softly on a cushion of snow. I lay there shaking my head as I tried to get to my feet, but my legs were to weak hold me up.

Skylar pulled on one of my hands, and Sue pulled on the other one as we all stood. Something flashed across my mind: The Promise. *Three will overcome one.*

Standing there together hand in hand, strength moved through us, as a voice softly spoke in my mind, *"Nothing is ever forsaken. Remember, I am always with you. Use your heart and it will help lead you to the evil ones."*

"*I* don't know how," I said out loud.

"Grandfather," I heard Skylar say. I looked down at her.

"Close your eyes," she said. "It will lead you."

"What have I got to lose?" I heard myself say. Was my faith losing the battle that was now raging in me?

I slowly closed my eyes. My mind relaxed. I saw a light through my eyelids, and it was glowing and moving away from us. My legs began to move like someone else was controlling them. Step by step, faster and faster, I moved farther into the light.

Sue and Skylar moved with me. The light propelled us faster. Everything became a blur.

In an instant it stopped. I felt like I had run into a wall. Opening my eyes, it was there ... Was this the answer?

"What is this?" Skylar and Sue asked almost at the same time. Removing her glove, Skylar reached out and touched the wall of ice in front of us. She noticed that it wasn't cold, it was like when I had touched the ice, water ran from the spot she had placed her hand and froze below.

Ice, I thought, *How do you melt ice from something warm when it's so cold?*

"That's simple. With the love in our hearts that we share with each other," Skylar said, reading my thoughts.

"Come on," I said to them. "Let's put our hands one on top of the other."

Laying our hands together on the wall of ice, water began to cascade down as the ice rapidly melted. We could see something on the other side. In a few minutes, the ice was melted enough for us to see into it.

What we saw was strange; it had all kinds of lights that were blinking on and off, levers and handles of all kinds and shapes.

Holding each other's hands, we went into it. What was this? Is this the answer to why we came here? I couldn't figure it out.

"Grandpa," Skylar said, walking over to a row of lights on the wall that weren't blinking. "Look at the color of them."

Taking a closer look, they were all blue—the same color of blue that was at the cabin.

Skylar raised her arm and began to touch them, not in any order, but in a pattern that she only knew. The room began to buzz like a nest of bees were there; lights took on a blinking pattern of repetition. They kept repeating the same pattern, and then they stopped.

We looked at each other, wondering what would happen next. The wait wasn't long. Suddenly the wall in front of us parted. There was another room.

We slowly went in and once inside, the wall closed behind us. Bright lights started flashing around us; I could feel our bodies being lifted into the air. What about the roof? But as I looked up, I saw that there wasn't any.

We moved at a high rate speed. I couldn't tell where it was taking us. Everything started to rush by us faster, at an incredible speed. It was hard to breath.

Then it was over. Standing in a different room, we looked at each other with puzzlement in our minds and eyes.

"Welcome," a voice said from behind us. Turning, there was a man older than time. Somehow, in my mind, I could tell that he had seen many years, more than the grains of sand in an hour glass. He walked over to us; taking my hand, he said, "I have waited for a very long time to meet you."

I was taken aback by his words. What did he mean that he had waited a long time?

"Who are you?" I asked, still shaking his hand.

"My name is Helicus. I am the one that holds the book," he answered, letting go of my hand and turning, he walked over to a shelf at the back of the room.

"What book?" Sue asked following him over to the shelf.

"I have had this since the beginning of life on this world," he said, picking up a book, turning he walked back to me.

The book looked very old; dust covered it, and it looked like it hadn't been opened for a very long time.

"As evil in this world grew, my power started to weaken. You have seen what it can do. You fought and won bravely in the outer world. The strength that is in you will be needed here," he said

"We were told to use our hearts instead of our minds, but the power we possess comes from our minds not our hearts. How can we use it to destroy evil?" I asked.

"Here evil can only be destroyed by the power your heart carries," he answered.

I was confused by his words. *Our hearts only carry the power of love,* I thought to myself.

"You are using your mind. Let go of it; let your heart lead you," he said, looking at the book that he held in his hands.

Closing my eyes, I let my mind shut out everything. I slowly put my hands out, and he laid the book in them. Energy flowed from the book into me, not into my mind, but into my heart.

There was a sadness that also crept into me. Opening my eyes, I watched as the book started to glow and then began to vibrate. Slowly the book opened, as the pages lifted, and fell over, finally stopping.

Looking down, I began to read. "Sometimes to strengthen our hearts, it must endure the pain of sacrifice."

Helicus came over to me, saying, "My time is over; the book has been passed to you. Evil waits here for you to destroy it."

With those words he faded from sight. I turned to Sue and Skylar. Before I could speak, the ground started to shake. The walls around us started to move. Snow started to pour in over us and as it touched us, it melted in an instant.

Flashes of light exploded around us. Our battle was back in full swing. The Gara, for some reason, had waited until now to attack. Maybe we were unknown to them or maybe the power Helicus contained kept them from seeing into this place. But once he was gone, the power in him existed no more.

Sue shouted, "Joe, you must use your heart to reverse the melting that is happening. Skylar and I will stop the Gara!" she said, as she and Skylar floated up to the surface. The snow which was coming through the opening covered both of them, letting them become a part of it.

I knew that I probably had a surprised look on my face. Thinking wives don't tell their husbands everything that they can do, and I turned back to the book that I still had in my hands. What was I supposed to do? Nothing was making any sense. In the background I could hear the battle between Sue, Skylar, and the Gara.

Something was pulling me back to the way we had come. I had to let something unknown lead the way, not resist. I followed. As I moved there was a hum. The further I went, the louder it became. Suddenly I stopped. Looking around, I saw a small door to my right. Carefully I walked over to it.

What now?

My body stiffened. Evil was close to me. My senses were screaming for me to run. *No!* I would not leave; I tried to use the power of my mind. But again nothing happened when I tried.

"Okay," I said out loud. Reaching over with my hand, I pushed the door open, and something hit me hard in the chest, knocking me flat on my back. Scrambling to my feet I jumped to one side, looking for anything to use as a weapon.

And there lying on the floor was a large metal rod. Lunging forward, I picked it up. There was another flash, but this time I swung the rod and deflected it back toward to whoever was firing at me. Again and again it happened, but I was able to hit it, like playing baseball. So far I was batting one-hundred percent.

As I moved forward, I could see someone firing at me. As I walked closer, their shots bounced off me.

I could feel the power in my heart rise up. Without my knowledge the power of my heart put up a shield to protect me.

I watched as lights now flashed toward them. Screams were the last sound, then quiet. Walking past to where they had stood, there lay my enemy. This was too easy. Standing there, I ended its evil life with a thought, but the thought came from my heart, not my mind. Now there was a warm feeling coming from me—compassion. But why? How could I feel this way? It was evil; maybe the answer would come to me some day.

There was something behind it that looked like some kind of a control panel. Moving over to it, I turned one lever, and the hum that I had heard earlier jumped into a thundering roar. I could feel cold start to increase. We had reversed the melting with a turn of a switch. I guess the Gara used strength not knowledge whenever possible. Now I had to find Sue and Skylar.

Running as fast as possible, I let my heart lead me. The wind was blowing in and around me. Except for it, there was nothing else moving. A deathly quiet had closed in around.

Finally I found the opening that the Sue and Skylar had gone up through. Climbing I was soon outside. They had flown, but I had to climb. It didn't really matter. What really mattered was finding them.

Once I was outside, my body started to shiver from the quickly dropping temperature. Light was giving way to darkness, not complete darkness; an eerie light cast shadows over everything.

Where were they? My mind reached out, trying to find them; it came back empty. Worry started to creep into my thoughts.

I searched for hours, still nothing. My body ached, and every muscle had lost its strength. *Sit down for a few minutes*, my mind said.

"Just for a couple," I answered talking to myself. Was I losing control of my mind?

Nothing mattered now; I didn't seem to care if I was going nuts.

Dropping to my knees, I rolling onto my back and let peace move over me I relaxed the last of my resistance. My eyes now surrendered to sleep.

I rested for a long time; snow covered me like a blanket. Waking I tried to push it off. Finally it gave way. Standing, I looked around. Checking the time, I saw that I had been asleep for only one minute, but my mind and body were refreshed. I knew the Garian ships were now less than twenty-four hours from earth.

Standing there, I truly felt alone and lost without Sue and Skylar. It didn't matter what happened to me without them. I was lost.

Then I felt a hand on my shoulder. Turning, I was met by a small boy of about eleven or twelve years of age. He was wearing a robe, nothing else to keep him warm.

"My name is Lee," he said, extending his hand toward me.

Taking his hand in mine, I could feel warmth coming from him. A kind of peace came over me. Tears started to fall from my eyes. I could feel something wrapping its arms around me.

"Do not lose faith, my son. It is true that to strengthen your heart, you have to lose something close to you, but you have already suffered that," he said.

"Suffered what?" I asked.

"In time you will know, but for now it's a time to rejoice," he said, pointing, as he faded from sight.

Turning, I saw Sue and Skylar running to me.

As they came closer to me, I could feel something in me that happened almost two thousand years ago. Another person doubted but was shown and believed. I must believe without seeing.

Wrapping our arms around each other, those thoughts disappeared from my mind.

We had fought and won again. This time with the help of others, it was different. We had learned enough to finish driving evil from our world; the last of our struggle was moving closer.

In the back of my mind, there were still two questions. Who or what had I lost? Removing the book from my backpack that Helicus had given to me, as I opened it, to my amazement, I saw that the pages were all blank. I knew that my faith wasn't as strong as it needed to be, because if it was, the pages of the book would be filled with words.

The snow was falling heavier now, but it had a warm feel to it. Reaching out my hands, I could see that each snowflake was different but yet the same. But we were like the snowflakes—different—but we each had our own inner beauty.

The world was taking on a new look. Something was slowly evolving. Like seed to a flower, the wonder of each part that together formed something elegant.

"Let's play in the snow," Skylar shouted, pulling away from us, running and falling into the fresh beauty of snow that was given to us.

Laughing, she made a snow angel, and then she was standing, saying, "Look, Grandma and Grandpa. It looks like the angel in my dreams. Come on, both of you make one."

Sue and I laughed. Running toward her, we grabbed hold of her arms and spun around and around. All three of us becoming dizzy, we fell into the warm arms of the snow.

This might be the last time that our souls felt the warmth of the love that was flowing between us.

Our laughter faded; as we looked up, we saw the snow swirling faster. Something moved over us, lifting us up, and we were held in a warm embrace of never-ending love.

Everything around us started to fade; we were drifting into the conclusion of our long journey.

CHAPTER THIRTEEN

The snow was replaced by the warmth surrounding the cabin. We were home—well, our adopted one. This was where we started and always ended.

Warm sun bathed us as we drifted back. As usual, when I opened my eyes, Daniel was there to meet us.

"As always, it's good to have you back. The three of you accomplished great things. The Gara have been pushed back. Their power only exists in one remaining place: the Middle East."

As he spoke I noticed several cars were coming up the road toward the cabin.

"Who are they?" I asked, watching the cars as they pulled in behind the cabin.

Skylar turned to look. "Wow, Grandpa. Look at all those big cars!" she said, trying to pull her hand out of mine. There was still a small part of her that was a child.

"Skylar, you have to stay here. We don't know who they are," Sue said, with concern in her voice.

I looked over my shoulder at The Keeper. "Who are they?" I asked again.

Before he could answer, one of the car doors opened and the president stepped out. I continued watching as more car doors opened. I recognized some of the other people that were there.

The French President was one, also the leaders of England, Canada, Spain, Germany, and many others that I didn't recognize.

I asked The Keeper, "What are all these people doing here?"

"The fleet of alien ships is now within our solar system. Their ships have slowed down. There are twelve of them, and they are spreading out. It looks like they are moving into attack formation. We believe they are going to stop before striking us," he answered.

"Why do you think that they won't attack?" Sue asked.

"They think that the earth can still be of some use to them," The Keeper answered.

"You think they will stop and simply ask us to surrender?" I asked. Hoping they would, it could give us some much needed time.

"Yes, they don't want to destroy us yet, not so long as we have something to offer. We only have two of our own ships stationed between us and their ships," he answered.

"Why don't they blow something up and scare us into surrendering?" Sue asked.

"I think they aren't sure of your powers. Combine that with the two ships, it makes them leery of attacking us," The Keeper said. "That's why we have called some of the world leaders here. There needs to be a plan laid out before they arrive."

"How much time do we have?" Sue asked.

"Less than four hours, I believe," he answered.

The president came over to us, followed by all the rest, saying, "Our satellites have picked up their massive fleet moving closer to the earth. We have been tracking them for several days. I know the people aboard our battle cruisers are willing to give everything, even their lives to defend our world."

Several of the other leaders voiced their concern about what we were planning to do. A couple of them wanted to surrender, but most wanted to fight.

"Let's go into the cabin. I have laid out some plans for us to go over. There isn't much time left," The Keeper said, pointing toward it.

We followed him over, and once all of us were inside, The Keeper laid out a couple of plans.

After a short time, it was agreed by everyone that we would fight. Surrender wasn't as option. There had to be a plan of attack. We were facing an enemy on two fronts—one from above us in outer space, the other was from the Middle East.

Our only defense would be the help from our two ships that were stationed on the back side of the moon, and the odds were stacked against them six to one.

Something that The Keeper had said bothered me. I turned to face him.

I asked, "You said that they knew about our two ships that are stationed on the dark side of the moon." To my knowledge only a handful of us knew about those two ships.

The Keeper was taken aback by my question. Regaining his composer, he answered, "With as many spies that they have hiding amongst us, the Gara are bound to know about our ships."

His answer bothered me; it was like he wanted our enemy to have knowledge of our ships. Not wanting to have discourse among us, I let it go.

He continued, "In the Middle East, the Gara have pulled in all of their people from around the world to reinforce rogue government leaders and mercenaries that would fight against us for the promise of riches and power that the Gara said they would give them."

While discussing our plans, one of President Mary's secret service agents rushed into the room, saying, "Madam President, we have received word that two small ships were launched from the Gara invasion fleet, and they have been tracked by radar and are heading to North America. We believe they are heading toward this base."

Turning to the president, I asked, "Does anyone other than those here with you know about this place?"

For a moment sadness moved over her face. She lowered her head, choking back tears, and then she raised her head, as she took a second to compose herself.

"Yes, I told one person about this place," she answered.

"Who did you tell?" I asked.

"Jim," she responded, looking down again.

"When did you tell him? You weren't supposed to see or talk to Jim until we were ready for it to happen," The Keeper said, trying to keep his voice under control.

This was the first time I had seen any anger in him. It only lasted for a moment, and then it was gone. Continuing, he asked, "Who helped you?"

"Ann," the president answered.

"We're in a lot of danger. If it's true that the Gara know about this place, there's not a lot of time to prepare before they get here,' Sue said.

"I didn't know that Jim was still under their control since we had driven evil out. I thought he had changed back to being a good person. I still love him," Mary said, her voice breaking   .

"Ann should have known that he was still under their control," I said.

"She is a kind and caring person. Her biggest fault is that she is young. Evil can disguise itself to fool even the strongest," The Keeper said, coming over to me. Putting his hand on my shoulder, he continued, "Remember what you were told."

Standing there, the words came to me, silent words. *For your heart to grow, you must lose something close to you.*

Then I turned around and walked over to Mary and reached out and took hold of her hand, saying, "We all make mistakes and I mean all, and as time goes by, there will be more and more. Every time it happens we learn."

Sue joined us, saying, "He's right. No one that walks this world does it without making mistakes."

At that moment another man rushed into the room, shouting, "We have spotted the alien ships. They have landed at the edge of the clearing close to the cabin!"

"How many people do we have to fight them?" I asked.

For a few seconds everyone looked at each other, waiting for someone to answer.

"I'm not sure," the president said, as she turned to The Keeper.

"I'm not sure how many people we have, and right now there's no time to count. I need all of you to get out of here right now," one of the president's personnel said, motioning us all to the door.

The Keeper turned, saying, "Everyone, follow me. There is an underground shelter behind the cabin."

Once everyone was outside, all except the security people followed him to the shelter. I knew that at this moment I was the only one who could lead our defense. I looked around and took a quick head count, I had to know what our strength was.

There were thirty security people and twenty-one of the Abiatharians, counting myself. That gave us a total of fifty-two. There was no way of knowing how many of the Gara had landed. We had to play it by instinct. The Abiatharians and the security people were told to spread out around the cabin and at all cost, they were to hold their ground.

We could only wait and see what would happen; I could sense a lot of different feelings coming from everyone. Fear was the one I could feel was the strongest.

There was no movement. Everything was quiet. I used my mind to search the area, but I couldn't sense anyone or anything.

"Where are they?"

I caught movement out of the corner of my eye, but it was one of our people. He had stood up and started to move behind some low bushes that ran along a creek bed. There was a flash of light, followed by an explosion. The force of it tossed him into the creek bed; I knew without a doubt that he was dead.

Then everything broke loose; dozens of explosions erupted around us. We couldn't tell where the firing was from. What was blocking me from locating them?

Several more of our people were hit and then suddenly, it stopped. Someone started to walk toward us carrying a white flag.

"We want to talk to you about surrendering before we have to destroy all of you," the person said. As the person walked closer, the voice sounded familiar to me. I wondered who this could be.

"Wait. That was Marsha's voice," I could hear myself say out loud. "Hold your fire!" I shouted to everyone, not believing that she was really here.

They were trying to break my will to fight by using Marsha, knowing that she was my daughter. They knew that I would hesitate to harm her.

She walked over to me and stopped several yards away.

"Marsha, what are you doing here? I see that you have truly been corrupted by evil, so much so that you would help them kill all these people, as you have done before?" I said, trying to figure out why she contained so much hatred for me and everyone that stood with me.

"It doesn't matter if they live or not. They're worthless people to me," she said with a smile.

"You want to kill and destroy without any remorse? We didn't bring you up that way," I said, trying to figure out why she had become so evil.

"What's in the past is long gone. Tomorrow is all that counts. What you can gain, that's what it's all about," she answered.

There was no use in talking to her; she had shown before what she had become.

"Are you ready to surrender to us, or do we have to destroy all of you? Our power is too strong even for you, the one who is supposed to save the world?" she asked. Evil was radiating from her.

"And if we do surrender, what happens then?" I asked.

"Once that happens, we will merely kill all of you," she said, with more of an evil laugh.

She was a monster, pure and evil. Somehow I would have to … the words wouldn't form in my mind. Even if she had become someone I didn't know, I didn't know what I would do if push came to shove.

"There is no way I will let you harm these people," I said, as my mind formed a protective shield over me, and then I turned in disgust and walked away from her.

I had taken no more than a few steps when I felt the force of something hitting me in the back, knocking me forward. As I hit the ground hard, I rolled over seconds before another blast hit, covering me with debris. Several more tore into the ground around me.

Several bright lights flashed past me toward Marsha, but she had already disappeared into the thick brush. Scrambling to my feet, I stood my ground. This all had to change. There was no way that we were going to let her and the Gara win.

My eyes moved along the edge of the wood. I used my mind as I hunted for the evil.

We had fought hard and long to get this far. We were close to driving evil from our world, and now it was time for good to rise up with all the power and might that it contained.

"Shoot anything that doesn't look right!" I shouted. Our people started firing, ripping large sections of forest apart. Screams started to rise up as our fire began to find the Gara.

My mind also became a weapon of destruction. Walking forward, all of our forces joined me. It was like we were a sharp knife that was slicing through the fiber of the woods.

To our left, one of the Gara ships rose into the air, firing at the cabin. Explosion after explosion tore through it and all around it. As the ship turned, it moved toward us. Something had to stop it. The fire from our weapons was useless and bounced harmlessly off of it.

The ship aimed its fire back toward the bunker. In a few more seconds, they would destroy it. That would throw the world into turmoil.

Something had be done fast. Drawing all the power in my mind, I concentrated on the ship. There was a bright flash that traveled from me to the ship; it exploded with a deafening sound. Pieces of the ship scattered over a large area. My mind had destroyed their ship.

My body was now drained of all energy; I had used my mind on two fronts—one on the ground and the other in the air.

Standing there, terror suddenly gripped me; a scream tore from me, shaking my soul. I knew that something terrible was wrong. Sue was in trouble.

Turning, I started to run as fast as possible to the bunker. Once I reached the bunker, I saw that it was empty. How could I have been so stupid? Marsha and the Gara had sacrificed one ship to us and while our attention was drawn to it, they had used their other ship to flank us gaining entrance to the bunker. We hadn't left anyone behind to protect everyone that was in there.

I stood there lost. Not only was everything we had done over the past few weeks in jeopardy, but Sue and Skylar had been taken, along with all the world leaders that were here. The way Marsha was acting, it was very possible that she would harm them. I had to keep my wits about me and stay calm; I knew that this was probably my only way to save them. Where was The Keeper? Rage boiled in me, as I shouted for everyone to hear—especially him.

"You were supposed to stay and protect them."

So why did he leave them alone?

My mind couldn't make sense of any of this. The Keeper had helped us from the start. He had shown us everything. What was going on now, and who should I trust?

Sue and Skylar weren't the only ones who needed my help; I needed to save all the others too.

Walking out of the bunker, everything was quiet—too quiet. What was going on? I carefully surveyed the area surrounding our camp. Everyone had disappeared. I walked to the edge of the clearing—still nothing.

Next I used my mind. In my mind's eye, I searched, but I found nothing. Not even our enemy, the Gara. They had also disappeared. No life at all, except for me and the animals that lived here in the woods. It felt as if everyone who had been here to fight alongside me were now only ghosts.

Once again I searched the woods with my mind. I felt that something was there, and it gave me an uneasy feeling. An alarm went off in my mind. *What is wrong*, I asked myself, as a cold chill ran up my spine. The feeling was growing stronger with each step that I took. It was so intense that even the movement of the wind rustling through the leaves made me more edgy. It was like when a storm is brewing; all the birds and insects seem to vanish in the gloom of the approaching storm.

Pinching myself, I needed to know that I was still here and not in a dream.

"Ouch," I said. "It's not a dream."

Slight movement on my right forced me to stop. My instinct immediately knew the danger was close.

"Now is the moment," I thought.

In self-defense, my protective shield formed around at the same moment that a large section of a tree came hurtling toward me.

It struck my body, and the force of the blow tossed me hard against another tree, sliding down landing face first in the dirt.

For a brief moment, I lay there, all my senses stunned, but I knew that I couldn't delay. Now was the time. I put mind over matter. I rolled away as another tree slammed into the exact spot where I had been lying.

Scrambling to my feet, I ran behind a large tree as two more missiles came hurtling toward me. Both hit the tree with such force that it was snapped in two.

Something was out there trying to smash me into nothingness. So far I couldn't detect what or where it was. I forced my mind to concentrate; I searched in all directions, trying to figure out where the objects were coming from.

Then my mind stopped. Looking closer my eyes caught the movement of something as it tossed another missile in my direction. It came crashing down right behind me.

This was my chance. Seconds moved by as if they were hours. It happened again.

Yes! my mind shouted. There was something there. Each time that it threw another object, I moved closer. Whatever it was wasn't very smart, because when it threw an object, it looked up, and it hadn't noticed that I was closing in. Now I was lying right next to it. I prayed that I was right.

Only perfect timing would give me my one and only chance. Finally as it threw another missile, it became visible. That was what I had seen earlier; each time it threw an object, it had to become visible.

When it rose up to throw the tree, I slid under its protective shield, which was giving it its power of partial invisibility.

Once I was under its protective shield, I looked up and what I saw completely surprised me. It was a Gara, but not like the others. This thing was at least three times the size of the others.

When I saw him, he noticed me. Reaching down, he tried to smash me like a fly. Ducking to one side, my mind let loose with a burst of power that was followed by some kind of mess that covered me. What I saw made me sick to my stomach. It covered me and everything around the area with a greenish yellow slimy odorous matter. It reminded me of one of my foolish days in school when I went out all night and partied, drinking way too much, and then awakening the next morning to find myself covered with my own vomit.

Trying to control the urge to throw up, I bent over, taking several deep breaths of air to settle my stomach.

Once I had myself under control, I looked around. Why send this monstrous creature here? There had to be something of great importance that it was protecting.

Wiping the slime from my eyes, I said, "Wait."

I could see what looked like an entrance to a cave, about a hundred feet away.

There was something that drew me to it; I had to find out if there was anyone inside. Moving closer to it, my mind tried to search deeper.

As I neared the tunnel, I tried to search for any life forms.

Suddenly my mind stopped. There was something inside the entrance that was very cold, and it blocked my way. I was beginning to realize that cold limited my powers.

I knew that I couldn't use my mind, but I had to find out what it was, so I had to, carefully and silently, move close to the entrance. A movement deep in the shadows forced me to quickly hide behind some trees.

I watched as two figures came out of the cave. They were Gara, not as large as the one that I had fought—it was like standing between a motorcycle and an eighteen wheeler. That is the difference between what I had fought then and what I was about to fight. They had their weapons raised. They must have heard the explosions.

They stopped a few feet from the entrance of the cave. Something was bothering them. Not knowing what had caused the explosion, they were being very careful.

I had to get between them and the entrance. I picked up a rock and tossed it as far to the left as I could. This brought an immediate response from them, and they fired in the direction of the noise and then ran over to find out what it was.

I knew that with the cold affecting my powers, I couldn't use my mind-jumping. I had to run between them and the entrance to the cave. They heard my movement, but before they could turn, they were gone. This surprised me. I looked down at my hands, and I felt heat radiating from them. I knew that this was the answer to how the Gara had disappeared, but how? I didn't think my powers would work in the cold that surrounded the entrance to the cave. I knew that I would have to accept whatever happened.

Once again it felt as if I were being drawn to the entrance of the cave. Again I tried using my mind to search, but my powers were still being affected by the cold. Knowing that evil lurked in the darkness, waiting to pounce on unsuspecting victims, I was afraid to enter the cave unprotected and unarmed. But something was telling me that Sue, Skylar, and the others were in there.

Slowly, as I entered the cave, darkness closed around me. I looked ahead; I could see a light reflecting off of something large and white. What was it?

My mind couldn't penetrate it because of the cold. Moving closer, I felt the cold intensify around me. When I finally reached it, once again my body was drained of all energy.

As I stood in front of the object, my eyes could barely make out something inside of it. Taking my hand, I tried to brush away some of the ice covering it.

I could feel heat pulsating from my hand as it touched the icy surface. Water started to run down from where I had touched it—not slow, but cascading in waves. When I moved my hand in a sweeping motion over its surface, it was like a water pipe had burst, gushing to the floor.

As the ice melted, two figures started to appear in the melting ice. Straining my eyes, I tried to make out who they were. "*Oh my God!*" I shouted as my heart started to pound in my chest. It was Sue and Skylar.

I moved like a machine. All the energy that was left in me was concentrated to melt the ice. The heat from my hands was tremendous. In matter of minutes, they both were free from the ice.

Falling to my knees, I cradled Sue in my arms. Her body was still warm, but she wasn't moving. Lifting her up, I carried her to a dry section of the cave. Laying her down, I went back to pick up Skylar, and I laid her next to Sue. Both were warm but not moving.

My mind was lost.

"What am I supposed to do?" I screamed out loud.

A voice penetrated my thoughts, saying, "*Remember your heart; it is your most important ally.*"

Putting one of my hands on each of them over their hearts, I felt Sue move first with a jerk, and then Skylar took a deep breath; moans came from both of them as they opened their eyes.

"Joe," Sue said, putting her arms around me. "Where are we?" she asked.

Before I could answer, Skylar took hold of my hand. "Wow! Grandpa, that was really strange," she said laughing. She was still a child in age, even though that didn't correspond to the maturity of her mind.

Taking hold of their hands, I help each of them to their feet, and we stood in a group hug.

"Excuse us." A voice came from behind of what remained of the block of ice.

I was in a state of total confusion. Everyone who had been at the cabin stood there. I had to ask myself, "*How can this be possible? What was going on, and whom or what had made this happen? Was it the Gara?*"

"How did all of you get here?" I asked, walking over to them. Looking at each other, Mary answered, "I don't think any of us are really sure."

"Have any of you seen The Keeper?" I asked, trying to see if he was there.

"He was with us in the bunker before everything went blank," one of them answered.

"Before everything went blank?" I asked again. Sue and Skylar walked over to me.

"We were in the bunker when coldness crept into it, but it only affected Joan and me. The cold moved so fast that we didn't have time to try and escape. In a matter of seconds, we were frozen solid. That's all I can remember before we blacked out," she said.

"What about you, Madam President? Were you and the others frozen? If you weren't, then you must know how you got here." I asked.

They were at a total loss as to what had happened. But I needed to know all the facts.

"When Susanna and Joan started to freeze, none of us could move to help them," she answered. "It was as if we had been given a sleeping pill that acted so fast that there was nothing that we could do. The next thing any of us remembers was finding ourselves in this cave behind this frozen block of ice."

I knew who had brought them here. But the bigger question was: Why? I asked myself.

"I don't know what's going on, but we need to get everyone out of here before more of the Gara come. There were three of them guarding this cave; I was able to destroy them. I don't know if there are more of them close by," I said, moving toward the entrance. Everyone followed behind me. I stopped and turned.

"Please wait here."

I slowly scanned the terrain. Sensing nothing, I signaled to them that it was safe to leave the cave.

Once out of the cave, we were able to take deep breaths of the fresh air, letting it fill our lungs with the sweet scent of nature. It all was different, but that all changed in a flash. Everything was rocked by a large explosion that landed in the distance behind some trees.

Looking in the direction to where the explosion had come from, we saw a large cloud of smoke filling the sky where the cabin and bunker had once stood.

This was sign that the Gara were near us, but where?

Taking cover as we ran, we moved up to the site of the smoke, but the only thing there was a large hole in the ground.

Standing by the large gaping hole in the ground, the president turned to me, saying, "My God, if we had still been there, all of us would have been killed. There must have been someone watching out for us."

Who had that person been? I wondered. Then something caught my attention. Turning, I saw a young boy coming toward us. As I looked closer, I saw that it was Lee.

He came up to us, saying, "It's good to see that all of you are safe, I was worried that you had been injured."

"How did you know we were here? And how did you find us?" I asked.

He stood there for a few seconds before answering.

"My father told me that you were at the cabin, and he knew something bad was going to happen to you. So he moved you to the cave," he said, pointing to it.

"Your father?" I asked. "Was he here? I don't remember anyone of Chinese descent being here."

"My father is made up of several different types," he answered, and then he walked past me, stopped and bent down and picked up a small brown sack.

Where did that come from? I hadn't noticed that there before.

He turned and walked over to the group of people that had followed me. He opened the sack saying, "It is time to turn the final pages in this chapter."

I couldn't remember what book he was talking about. *"Maybe The Book of Forever,"* I thought. *"Was that the book I had been given at the North Pole?"*

He continued. "You people have to go back to your homes. Your people need to see you at the head of the table. You are entering the final and the greatest struggle of mankind."

Reaching into the sack, he took out a small sphere, holding it out and again speaking, "Each one of you will reach into the sack and take one. Hold it close to your heart; it will guide you to your homes."

Each person walked forward and, without hesitation, reached into the sack, taking one out. When Sue, Skylar, and I went forward, he closed the sack. All he said was: "It is not yet your time."

Something fantastic began to happen. The spheres started to turn blue; a glow shone around them. We watched the spheres; they started to expand, moving to completely cover each person as they held it. Once that happened, the spheres started glowing brighter. Slowly they lifted into the air, scattering to the far corners of the earth. In a moment they had disappeared.

He now turned to us, reaching once again into the sack, saying, "These are yours." Looking at me, he continued, "Remember three will always overcome one. You will once again move into the Valley of Death alone. In time you will once again be together. Your flight will be thousands of miles apart for now."

"Lee, if everyone was taken there for safety, I don't understand why the Gara seem to be protecting the entrance of the cave. I want to know why everything happened the way it did," I said.

Lee looked at me for a moment, and then he spoke.

"Today, you were tested to see if your faith in the Creator was strong enough to give up yourself for others."

Lee's words left me wondering what their meanings were. But before I could ask, he raised his hand, as if to stop my words. Then he said, "You may never fully understand … you only have to believe."

Sue, Skylar, and I stood together, our arms wrapped around each other. Our hearts blended together for a final embrace before we had to move apart.

"It's time," he said, handing Sue and Skylar each a sphere.

As before, the sphere covered them. In a blink they were gone.

It was my turn. Holding out my hand, he started to place the sphere in it, but stopped, saying, "Are there any other question you want to ask? Who am I? Where is The Keeper, but most of all, who came into this valley and raised their staff to save all? You have only to look into your heart, for the one that you think is lost is not, but with you forever. Believe in that and they will be with you. Your hearts are one, never to be separated."

I tried to ask, but my mind was blank. All I could do was put out my hand.

Looking down, I watched as he placed the sphere in my hand. Slowly, it began to expand, moving over me. I wanted to close my eyes, but they wouldn't. My sphere started to lift into the air and then with a jerk, it moved rapidly through the clouds. I looked up as the stars moved toward me. Looking, I could see the earth. It was a beautiful sight. I wondered if this would be the last time that I saw it.

What about Sue and Skylar? Would I ever see them again? Deep inside I knew we would be together. Our spirits would be linked by the love we have for each other.

CHAPTER FOURTEEN

Our two ships, the *Temperance* and the *Hornet,* sat at the dark side of the moon, hidden in the darkness of space, waiting for the evil that was coming our way.

Commanders Stephens and Titus were in constant communication with each other as they watched the viewing screen on their own ships. They were using satellites that the Unites States and Russia had installed to circle the moon, giving them uninterrupted view of space.

What they saw on their viewing screens sent shivers up their spines. Even these hardened warriors still had the same feelings that you and I have. Fear was the one thing that they didn't want the others to know that they also dreaded. Fear was like a plague; once it started, this disease could run rampant through the ranks. They couldn't allow this to start.

"Commander Titus, this is Commander Stephens." Even though these two had been friends since the academy, the two of them were always professional when others were around.

"Yes, Commander Stephens, I am at my ready," he answered back, knowing what Stephens was calling about. He was watching the same movement of the Gara fleet.

"Switch to a secured frequency," Stephens said.

At that, Titus gave the control of the bridge to his second in command.

"Take over, Captain," he said. He walked over to the elevator. As he approached it, the doors opened automatically as entered he removed a key from his pocket. He placed his hand on a numbered panel. Once his hand print had been identified by the ships security, a small plate slid to the side that was concealed and known only to him.

As it slid away, he took the key, inserted into a slot, and turned it to the right. Then he heard the soft whisper of sound behind him and without hesitation, he turned around as he removed the key, and the panel slid back into place.

Taking his communication device from his belt, he pushed the bottom button. At first, there was only a static noise and then the clear voice of Commander Stephens came through.

"Anthony, what do you think our chances are?" he asked.

"Adam, I don't know, but I would say Custer had a better chance than I think we have." He said this with a false laugh, for he knew that the odds of any of them surviving were very unlikely.

"That's not what I wanted to hear you say, but at least you didn't say zero," Adam answered, and both of them were laughing, even though the two of them were not joking about their odds in this war against the Gara.

"What about our crews, Anthony? How do you think they will hold up once this thing starts?" Adam asked, knowing that his people had been handpicked to serve on his ship, even though they had all volunteered for this tour of duty. They were aware that there was little hope of returning home.

Many of them had families that they had left behind; still others were related somehow. Whether it is a husband, wives, brothers, sisters, sons, or daughters, this was making the ultimate sacrifice. These people had left their homes in secret. No one could know where they were going or what they were chosen to do.

Anthony also thought about their two ships. Both had been made in secret on earth by the Abiatharians and all the others who had volunteered. Although they knew that they hadn't been picked to serve on the ships, they still had something to be proud of. They knew that they couldn't go back home until the two ships were launched into space. They could still carry the knowledge that they had been part of helping to save mankind against the Gara. It had been decided to proceed in this manner for fear that one of them could be swayed over to the Gara side and give them information about our first lines of defense—taking away our only chance we had of surprising them.

"Adam," he heard on his voice communicator, bringing his attention back to the present, which cleared his mind immediately.

"Adam, are you all right?" Anthony asked with concern.

"I'm sorry, Anthony, but sometimes I can't help thinking about the sacrifices our people have had to make," he answered.

"Me too," Anthony replied. "But they knew that it had to be done this way, and they are proud to be the ones to serve with us."

"It grieves me to know that so many of them will lose their families. It's so sad," Adam said, as he thought about his son and daughter who were serving on these ships. They were both fighter pilots, but there was one other person that he missed very much. His wife, after her death, left a large void in his heart, and he would do anything he could to have her back. His eyes started to fill with tears.

"I know, my friend, but if what we give saves lives, it's a small price to pay. Everyone here would agree with what I am saying." Anthony answered, as his mind thought about his family.

When Anthony was first offered the command of his own ship, he turned it down, but his wife wouldn't let him. He didn't want to take the position because she was suffering with a form of muscular dystrophy.

Her words would always remain in his heart.

"Anthony, we are but two grains of sand in a vast desert, and if those two never move, maybe all the others would be destined to be imprisoned in that spot for eternity. Still, if the winds swirl through them, they could be lost forever in that wind. But if you move them, there is a chance to preserve them. Even if it is only in your mind, you know that you tried," she had said to him.

Most of all, he could still feel her frail hand as she touched his face that one last time.

Thoughts of the past had to be put away for another day and another time and place. His only prayer was that they would be together once more, to live forever in the peace of eternity

"The president wants to meet with us today," Adam said.

"How? We can't forsake our duties and leave our commands to give the president a tour of our ships. What is she thinking?" Anthony answered, with disbelief in his voice.

"No, let me explain. The president and I were worried that you wouldn't understand, and the president felt that if she came to our ships, it would boost the morale of both our crews. She requested that a fighter transport her from earth to where our ships are hiding in space." Adam replied.

"Okay, but what about the Garas detection system? It hasn't picked up our location. But if we send someone out to transport her here and then return her to earth, surely they will notice. One flight might be able to go undetected, but four? I think that would really be pressing our luck and putting our commands in danger at the same time," Anthony said, questioning him.

"Wait, I don't remember receiving any communications about the president coming here," Anthony said again.

"I know, I know, but somehow I guess using our satellite communications, I was able to receive word regarding her request to meet with us today." That was the only way he would have been able to know what she had wanted.

Then he thought, *No wait. There weren't any messages from earth for me. So how did I know what the president wanted?*

"Anthony, I know that this is going to sound really weird, but did she contact you and then me?" Adam asked.

"No way," he answered, with strong confusion in his voice. He wondered if his friend was starting to think that things were happening when they weren't.

A voice speaking softly crept into Adam's mind. *It was I who let you know that Mary wanted to meet with the two of you. You do not have to fear me, for I have been with you since you were formed, as I have been with all the others throughout time. When you despaired, I stood with you; when you grieved at the loss of your wife, I lifted up your heart and as you now face this fork in the road, I am ready to lead you through the darkness to the light, if only you will reach out and take my hand, if not that is your choice to make."*

"Adam," Anthony's voice came through the communicator and brought him out of the dark and back into the light.

"Where did you go? I have been trying to get your attention for the last ten minutes. I was about ready to contact Jonathan to see what had happened," Anthony said; his voice was filled with worry and concern.

He shook his head, trying to remove the thoughts that were still swirling through his mind.

"Yeah, yeah, ah ... I was going over some figures about how to get her here. I don't think the Gara will be concerned with a small ship moving back and forth; they will probably think that it's one of our satellites

"You're joking, right? Come on, Adam, the Gara can't possibly be that stupid to think it's a satellite moving straight, not orbiting around the earth? Come on, old friend. Level with me. What's going on?" Anthony asked; there was a true sense of concern in his voice.

"Don't question what I am telling you. Have I ever let you down before? There is no way that I would do that now," Adam answered, not really knowing what to say or if he should even wonder about what had happened in his mind.

Looking at his watch, he was surprised to see that no time had gone by. It was, according to his watch, the same time now as when he started to talk to Anthony, which surprised him. With all the confusion that was going, he thought maybe he had looked at his watch wrong.

"Anthony, have one of your fighters leave immediately to pick up the president!" he shouted. He realized the tone of his voice was harsh, but in this instance it didn't seem to matter.

His tone surprised Anthony, but he didn't argue, but simply agreed with him to send a fighter to earth and bring back the president. He still wondered why his friend was acting this way. What Adam had ordered him to do could put everyone and everything in danger. But an order was an order; he had been trained to follow it. Maybe it was wrong. He wondered if he should go personally to Abel's ship and talk with him. Only he figured that, that would only cause a wider disagreement between the two of them.

Closing the secret compartment, he left the elevator and went back to the bridge.

"Captain, send one of our fighters to Washington to pick up the president and bring her back here," he ordered.

Upon hearing this strange order, the captain stood up and asked, "But, sir, won't that give our location away to the Gara and lead them straight to us?"

Anthony thought carefully about the order he had given to his captain. Even though it was wrong, for some reason inside, he had to do what was ordered of him. Why?

At that moment he heard a voice in his mind speaking, *Do not question what you are about to do, for it had been foretold before time itself began. The path has been chosen. As it was written, today you shall be with your wife, and it will be like she had never become ill; now both of you will be together throughout time, in peace and love.*

What had he heard in his mind? Did someone speak to him, or was it the stress of what he was about to do?

A warm, gentle feeling entered his heart, and it leapt with joy, lifting the feeling of doom that was there. Still he had concerns about the future; he had to wonder, were the words only talking about him and not the others.

He moved closer to the captain and placed his hand on his arm, saying, "Roger," not addressing him as he would normally, which would be to use his last name.

Anthony said, "I understand your concerns about what I am ordering you to do. I asked the same questions when I heard this plan and why we are to follow it. The only thing I can say is do what is commanded of you for it is written."

Roger didn't understand what Anthony was saying to him. They had fought side by side through many struggles, and knowing that Anthony had felt the same way when he was given orders, he also would follow suit and obey.

"Yes, sir," he said. He turned and pressed a button on the control council and gave the order for a fighter to be sent to Washington.

"Bay one, Fighter Bay One, prepare one fighter for a special mission."

The speakers squeaked, and then a clear voice said, "Yes sir, where is it going?" It was a normal question to ask where the mission was headed, and the person had the right to ask.

There was nothing he could say that would make any sense of this mission, for what he was ordering would be like opening a page for defeat.

By bringing the president to the ship, not only would it be endangering the mission, but it would also endanger the life of the president. He had to wonder why it was being done then.

The conversation he had with Anthony didn't make much sense. Why give away the location of not only yourself but the one person who may become the world's leader?

It didn't have any normalcy to it. Still he would obey the order that had been given—no questions, only actions.

The fighter was readied for its mission to earth where the president was waiting to be picked up. Our fighters were capable of flying at speeds up to two hundred and forty thousand miles an hour. This flight would take roughly three hours.

Our top fighter pilot was chosen to handle this; so much was riding on a successful mission. The pilot knew that the president was to be his one and only concern and was prepared to sacrifice himself before letting anything happen to her.

Both commanders watched as the fighter headed for earth, hoping that the color—black—would blend in with the darkness of space. Where all the others were silver, this one had been specifically painted black to conceal it in the darkness of space so that it couldn't easily be spotted. It was a one in a million chance that it was this color. The reason for that was that it had never been top coated with silver. Why? It could happen to you. They ran out of paint and therefore, they had to leave it black. The ugly duckling of the fleet could well be the savior of this particular mission.

The next several hours would creep by at a snail's pace. The only thing they could do now was wait and hope.

Meanwhile the president was preparing herself for the trip. Everyone around her was nervous; most of her inner group kept looking at their watches, wishing that this mission was already over.

Mary gave some final orders to her staff, one for the possibility of her not making it back and the other for her successful return. The latter of the two was what everyone hoped would be the outcome.

The fighter finally landed at the secret landing zone, very close to the White House; in fact, it landed right on the grounds of it.

The president was waiting, dressed as a fighter pilot. She watched as it landed and then she was quickly taken to it. The hatch was open and ready for her; they helped her into a seat, and then strapped her in. She waved to her staff as the door closed.

There was no communication between her and the pilot; speed was at the forefront. The enemy may have already found out what she was doing.

Mary felt the ship lift from the ground. It slowly rose, and she wondered to herself, "*How are we ever going to get to the ship in less than three hours at this rate?*"

In a sudden burst of power, the fighter soared like a streak of lightning through the clouds, catching her off guard as she was pushed back hard into her seat. As she tried to move parts of her body, she soon found that this was useless. The pressure was too great; it felt like there was someone standing on her chest. Breathing was becoming next to an impossible task.

Mary struggled to breathe. Using the muscles in her chest, she was finally able to take small breaths of air, and even with the mask over her face pushing oxygen in, it was still difficult to get enough air to fill her lungs.

Slowly her system started to adapt to the pressure. She wondered if all the fighter pilots went through what she was experiencing.

"*Well I know one job that I never want,*" she thought. "*This one. No way, no how and from this point on will I ever think my job is becoming too difficult. I will remember this experience, and that will quickly change my mind.*"

As the ship left earth's atmosphere, the blue was replaced by the velvet blackness of space as the beauty of the stars shimmering on this sight of heart-stopping beauty made Mary almost forget why she was here.

She thought, "*Now I know why they go through all the unpleasant-ness of the takeoff, plus the terrible knowledge that at their fingertips, they could unleash a powerful destructive force and whatever hit it, it would no longer exist.*"

Her eyes never left the stars until the pilot said, "We are nearing the moon, Madam President."

She turned her eyes toward this bright object that lay on this velvety blackness. The stars sparkled, but in comparison to this, it wasn't even close.

"Wow," she said out loud.

This caused the pilot to chuckle.

"It's something all right. Seeing it from earth is one thing, but when you're this close, what you said is the best description of the moon that I've ever heard."

What she had said embarrassed her, and knowing that the pilot had heard her exclamation of "wow" made her cheeks blush. She decided she wouldn't say anything else until they landed; all she did was watch as the fighter swung to the dark side of the moon.

It went from day to night. As they now moved from the brightness to the darkness, her eyes tried to adjust, but with the fighter completely dark and no light on this side of the moon, it was utterly impossible to see anything now.

The only way she knew where she was, was to turn and look back at the stars. They were the only lights around her; even the landing bay was completely dark. How would they be able to find it, let alone land? Still Mary knew that the pilot had everything under control.

Then from the darkness, a small light appeared. She could see that he had turned the fighter toward it. Mary could hear the engine begin to throttle down, yet she felt nothing. But she knew the fighter was slowing. The light grew brighter as they neared it.

They slowly moved toward it until she could see what looked like a landing pad. She had never seen a real one, but this looked like the ones that she had seen in the movies. There was a yellow line straight down the middle of it, with numbers on either side of it that read from two hundred yards to zero in increments of twenty-five feet.

She watched as they approached it. This was the only sign that the fighter was moving in this darkness.

As the floor of the landing bay door grew closer and closer, she could hear the landing gears drop into place. Then she felt the wheels touchdown, and she watched as the fighter glided past the numbers on either side of the runway. This was the only thing that told the pilot how close he was to the end of the bay.

Once the fighter had stopped, she glanced back and watched as the door to the hanger close, and then there was a hissing noise as the area was pressurized and filled with oxygen. Once this was completed, people started coming from all directions and made the necessary preparations to open the doors for her to disembark the fighter.

The pressure of the fighter's doors was released and slowly swung out and up. As this was happening, a small set of steps moved out and down from the hatch, allowing her to step out.

The two people dressed in white protection suits with markings and numbers moved at the same time stepping up into the door of the fighter. One went to the pilot and unstrapped him from his chair. The other did the same to her. Once her straps were released, there was an immediate relief of the pressure, allowing her to fill her lungs with oxygen and breathe normally once again; this sudden intake of oxygen gave her a strange feeling, like her lungs might burst, and also gave her a feeling of light headedness. Thank goodness neither sensation lasted for very long. It was actually more of a relief than anything else.

The person who was helping Mary had the name Elis printed on the front of his suit. As she read his name tag, she spoke to him.

"Thank you, Mr. Elis, for your help. I would have fought these straps all day," she said, as his hands brushed them away. A small smile crossed her face, causing him to laugh.

"Everyone says the same thing the first time they fly in one of these. Even pilots who have been trained by the book do it too. All they want to do is learn how to fly and fire the weapons, but they forget once the fighter lands how to release these straps so that they can hop out of the fighter. We stand around waiting, and then you can hear them all say, 'How in the heck do you get out of these straps?' So we have to show them. It's like putting a child in a car seat and then taking them out," he said as he laughed even harder; this also made Mary break into laughter.

As her laughter subsided, a thought crossed her mind. This was the first that she had laughed this hard in a long time. It felt really good to laugh and to be able to forget about everything else.

Saying those words brought everything to a loud crash in her mind. It felt like a scene from an old movie where they throw water in a person's face and whatever had caused their laughter in the first place stopped immediately.

Elis noticed that she had stopped laughing, and he saw a sudden sadness on her face, the look of someone who had just remembered something terrible.

"I'm sorry, Madam President," he said, looking down. He became quiet.

She noticed his actions and at once tried to ease how he was feeling.

"No, it's okay. It's good for us to laugh once in a while. I think this shows we are still human and alive," Mary said, as she put her hand on his arm, knowing that he felt bad. Maybe this small gesture would somehow ease his discomfort.

As he looked at her, a small smile formed on his face. He placed his hand over hers saying, "Thank you. I know the burden you carry, Madam President, but a day will come when it will be all right to laugh. All others will laugh with you, for brightness will cover the universe again."

Mary felt déjà vu as she looked into his eyes, but she couldn't remember why. All she knew was that they gave her an inner peace for a small moment, like one small grain of sand that fell in an hour glass.

"You!" she heard the pilot bark at him. "Come on and hurry up. We haven't got a lot of time, and this isn't the time to stand around talking."

"Yes, sir. Sorry, sir," Elis said, as he helped Mary from her seat and then helped her step down the ladder to the floor. Once that was done, he looked at her again, smiled once and said only one word to her: "Until," and then he turned and walked over to the hanger doors and was gone.

She didn't take her eyes off him until he was through the doors and had disappeared from her sight. It was only when she felt someone touch her arm and say her title that she realized she had been staring at the door although no one was there.

Shaking her head slightly, Mary turned around.

"Good to have you on board, Madam President."

She recognized Commander Stephens at once. He held out his hand and she grasped it, shaking it firmly.

"It's good to see you too, Commander," they had only met once before, but she never forgot a face or name.

"I'm glad to see that you remember me after all this time. I thought maybe you wouldn't remember me. One of my largest faults is meeting someone, then running into them later, and then not knowing who they are. I'm not even old enough to use that as an excuse," he said. There was no smile or laugh, only honest words.

Mary thought that this was kind of strange, but she knew the job he had to do, and maybe he felt it would be out of place to do either one. She respected him for that.

"I may not know everything, but people are one thing I do know best and when we met before, I sensed something strong in you, and that feeling is still there."

Mary didn't know what she should or could say; even if she had the words, she wasn't sure how to say them. She could sense a deep sadness in him, like when a person seems to be trying to keep their distance from you.

"Madam President, I don't want this to sound negative, but with the Gara about to attack, I would have thought you would want to be in D.C.," he said, with what appeared to be a look of annoyance on his face.

"I'm sorry, Commander, but for some reason, I'm not really sure why, I only know I had to come here, but I don't think that I can truly say that either. Maybe it was to…"

She had to stop these thoughts of Elis, and then she continued, "…see you again, and I have no idea why. Well, maybe it was to come and meet some of the people who would play such a large role in our struggle against the Gara and maybe to say thanks for what you do. Even if a person thinks what they are doing isn't all that important, it is, no matter how little. You think it counts; everything counts, even when one of your crew… Oh, I didn't get his first name, but his last name is Elis," she said, looking around to see if he might have returned, but he was nowhere in sight.

As she turned back to look at the Commander, she could see a strange look on his face.

"Did I say something wrong?" she asked, puzzled by his expression.

He learned over to the person to his right who had helped the pilot out of the fighter and whispered something to him.

The man shook his head and turned back to her saying, "Um, Madam President, there isn't a crew member by that name on this ship. You might have the name wrong."

He looked at the man beside him and asked, "You don't have anyone working with you named Elis, right?"

"Are you sure someone helped you?" he asked with a kind of confused look.

"Commander, two people came aboard the fighter. One helped the pilot and the other, named Elis, helped me. We talked and even laughed for several minutes," she answered, as her voice rose in anger.

"Please, Madam President. Sometimes space travel causes confusion, and it takes a while to stabilize your senses. It's possible you could have seen someone who you thought was named Elis, but there is no one here by that name," he said as he patted him on the back.

Mary stood there for a few seconds, as her anger rose like a volcano getting ready to erupt, its lava burning everything it touched, and she was about to erupt the same way. Then she felt a hand touch her shoulder. When she turned around, she was ready to torch whoever was there. Only, to her surprise, it was Elis who was standing there with a smile that filled her with calmness.

She was thinking to herself that she was right and she was ready to tell that to whoever was touching her.

"See I am right he—"

In mid-sentence Mary stopped as she looked in amazement, and then she realized that everyone was frozen in time, except for Elis. No one moved. Everyone was like statues.

She slowly turned back to Elis, saying, "What is happening? Maybe I'm going crazy or maybe this is a dream?"

"Mary, do you really think it's a dream?" he asked

For a moment she couldn't think straight. What in the world was happening here?

"No, Mary, this isn't a dream. And yes, it's really happening. Here, reach out and touch me, or even one of them," he said, pointing to Commander Stephens.

She turned her head to look at the others but didn't walk over to touch any of them. Slowly, she looked back at him and taking a deep breath, she asked, "Why are you doing this to me? Can't you see what's going on around us? The world could be destroyed in the next few days, and you're playing games with me."

This time when she spoke, there was no anger in her voice; it almost sounded like she was a child who was being bullied and begging for it to stop.

"Oh, Mary, I need to explain why I brought you here so that you will understand. I'm letting you see the future—your future—for it will come to pass that your spirit will float among the stars—the ones that you marveled at as you made your journey here, for what seems to be the end to others, you will be the one to know that it's not.

When some despair that the end is upon them they have nowhere to turn and become lost in a void of their own making. The future will become the past, and the present will become both the future and the past. You will enter a land of beauty to wait for the moment when the Creator calls you back to right the wrong and to serve together as one. It will be then that you are called to be a part of this greatness and when it happens, the three will join as one. Evil will be vanquished, and then you will be brought forth to lead all nations to peace," he said.

His words confused her.

"I don't understand. What you are telling me?" she asked.

"Child, do not worry. For when the time comes, you will know without remembering any of this, for what you see did not happen. You were brought here so that you would understand the flaws that exist in all of us. For you have met the weakness in the one, who, with friendship, will betray all for love," he spoke, with warmth and love to her.

"I will know when it is time?" she asked.

"When all seems right and you belong to another, you will be asked to give it away for others and only remember it in your dreams. It will be over fast and then, all will be right. Both of you will walk together, as the two who were first here, only you will be faithful to the one who gave you life," he said, as he turned and walked away, and then he was gone again.

"Madam President," Commander Stephens said. "I would like to thank you for coming here and putting yourself in harm's way to let us all know you will be by our sides no matter what happens."

"No, Commander. I want to thank you. It has been an honor and a privilege to speak to all of you, and now I must return and prepare for what is to come our way."

Turning, she walked back over to the fighter for her return trip to earth and to face whatever came.

"Madam President," she heard Larry's voice. "You have a phone call on red line one."

"Wh…what?" she mumbled, as she tried to focus her eyes, and when she had herself composed, she asked, "Where am I?"

"You're in your office. You fell asleep; I had to let you sleep for a little while. I know that you haven't slept for over twenty-four hours straight, but I heard talking coming from in here, so I came in to check and see if everything was all right." he said.

"What about my trip to the moon?" she asked as she tried to figure out what was going on. She wondered if it was all a dream.

"I was sleeping. Wait a minute," she said as she looked at her watch.

"Madam President, there wasn't any trip scheduled for you to go to the moon. I think that sometimes when our minds become overstressed, we try to find a place to escape to, and maybe yours was going to the moon. Whatever, maybe it was only a dream. You didn't leave your office since the last time I checked on you, and that was over an hour ago."

According to her watch, he was right; it had been an hour since she had seen him. She had only slept for an hour. Walking over to the window, she pushed aside the drapes and looked up at the heavens. Night had come and the moon was full, shining in all its glory.

Mary stood there wondering, *"Was it a dream or did it really happen?"*

Did what she was told foretell her future? But the words were so confusing. Her mind couldn't grasp the full meaning of what they were trying to tell her. There was a message there for her, but right now she couldn't figure out what that might be.

Without even realizing it, Larry had quietly stepped out of the room, leaving her alone with her thoughts. Turning, she looked back at her desk. She watched the light as it still blinked, telling her that she hadn't answered the call yet.

CHAPTER FIFTEEN

Once all the world leaders who had been with the president arrived back in their own countries, it was obvious that convincing the people in those countries wouldn't be as easy as they had once hoped.

Even with most of the evil gone, with exception to the Middle East, it was becoming someone else's problem now. They were enjoying something new, a complete well-being, a life full of happiness with no wants. That was what each and every one had always hoped for and now, they held it in their own hands.

Meeting after meeting was held. There was no real anger amongst them, but each had lives. It was what they all had hoped for.

The only problem was that evil still had not been completely destroyed, and as most would say, if you cannot see or feel it, it won't hurt you.

Leader after leader frantically called the White House, asking, "What can we do to convince them that there is still evil among us? Even if it's not with us now, if it is not completely destroyed, it can spread like a cancer waiting silently to strike before you even feel it, and when that happens, it is too late."

Mary tried and tried to change people's attitudes about what was still with us—evil—but each time it was the same.

Had we not really changed, still only thinking of ourselves? Mary prayed that was not the case. Yet what could she do to hopefully draw everyone together for this, for what she prayed would be the last battle?

She hadn't had contact with Josaphat, Susana, Joan, or John; even The Keeper couldn't be found. Mary felt alone.

Sitting in her chair, she wished that whatever the experience had been, whether it was a dream or reality, she wished that she was there now and not here. The weight on her shoulders was as strong as the feelings were about the trip she took to visit the two ships on the back side of the moon. But that had ended in a strange way. Now this she was not so sure about.

As she sat at her desk, she laid her head down on her arms, wishing that it would be different. She jumped when her intercom next to her head buzzed in her ear.

She tried to regain her composure before she answered the call. Rubbing her eyes, she was surprised to feel the small amount of moisture. She sniffed, wiped her eyes and nose, then she cleared her throat. She reached over and pushed the intercom button, saying, "Yes, what is it?"

"I'm sorry to bother you, Madam President. This may sound really weird, but there is a child standing in front of me, and I don't know how he even got in here. I . . . I turned around, and he was standing there looking at me. None of our systems alerted me, and none of the security people came. He was just here. I didn't want to leave him alone, not knowing who he was or where he had come from. The only thing he said was that he needed to see Mary. I said, 'Do you mean the president?' He nodded and then stood there looking at me, so the only thing that I could think to do was to buzz you."

For some reason Mary wasn't surprised by this. Stranger things had happened before, so why not this? All she said was, "Well, then send him in."

"Are you sure, Madam President? I can call security and have them to escort him out."

"No," she answered. "Send him right in." Walking over to the window, she took one last look and then sat down in her chair. She turned and faced the door, waiting for this surprise visitor. After a few seconds, the door opened, and a young boy entered, greeting her with respect.

"Thank you for seeing me," was all he said.

Mary watched as he took one of the chairs and brought it over, placing it next to her. Even this action didn't startle her; it was completely normal.

She waited for him to say something, but he only sat there, a small smile crossed his face.

She waited for several long moments for him to say something. Still, he said nothing and as she grew impatient, Mary spoke first, not really knowing what else to do or what to say.

"Well here goes," she thought.

"I don't know how to start, but I have to start somewhere. First, how did you get past security? Second, who are you and third, what do you want?"

He didn't answer her questions right away. He sat there and continued to smile. Finally he started.

"The answer to your first question is: they didn't see me and second, my name is Lee, and lastly, I am here to help you."

Mary thought about his answers.

"I can believe that no one saw you, and okay, your name is Lee, and no, there hasn't been anyone that could help me so far, except for Josaphat, Susanna, Joan, and The Keeper. But as of right now, I don't have any ideas of where they might be. So why not you? ... Okay ... tell me how."

"Well, I know you feel abandoned and you have to make all the decisions without any help, right?" he said.

Taking a deep breath and looking around the room, she spoke, "Well not to sound facetious, but do you see anyone here besides us?"

The smile did not leave his face. He turned his head first to the right and then to the left. Then he looked up and then down and finally, he looked under his chair.

"Nope," he said.

For a minute Mary didn't know what to say. Finally she broke into laughter and for a few seconds, she couldn't get herself under control.

"Well, you managed to make me laugh, but that's not the kind of help I need right now."

"I know, Mary; my first step was to show you that all was not as dark as you thought."

"Okay then. How do I bring everyone together? Because time is running out, and this has to be done soon," she said.

"How was your trip to the moon?" he asked.

Looking at him, she answered, "It really did happen, didn't it?"

"Only you know that. They say dreams can foretell what is going to happen," Lee said, as he raised his hand to his head.

Well, his answer didn't help her.

"Did it happen or didn't it," she thought.

Rising from his chair, he walked over to the window, and lifting his head, he asked, "Can you see the moon?"

Mary turned and lifted her gaze toward the sky.

"Yes, I can see it, but that doesn't tell me if I was there or not."

"Whatever happened, you were told all would become known at some time. Believing in something will bring you that answer," Lee said.

"This is getting me nowhere fast," she thought to herself.

Then she started to ask, "Well how do I get it done? It's seems like you are making a movie or writing a book, trying to create knew scenes so you can make it longer. So tell me how to do this or leave."

As she spoke, Lee turned to her.

"Everything takes time. But if you wait, the answer will come to you. Remember, all good things come if you have the faith."

"Words … words … Help me. So far the only thing that you have given me is a headache," she said, rubbing her forehead, as anger filled her voice.

"There," he said pointing at her. "Peace and calm is okay, but you have to lead, not wait. Use what you feel inside, and make all the others aware."

In anger she thought, "*That's what is needed. It's time to show that we have backbone.*"

Reaching over her desk, she pushed the intercom button.

"I need to set up a news conference, and I want it televised right away," she said.

What would she say to stir them into joining the forces before it was too late to stop the Gara from swallowing them one at a time?

Mary waited impatiently, pacing back and forth. Finally she heard a voice over the intercom.

"The television news conference has been set, and you will go on the air in one hour. But we have a problem. For some unknown reason, the satellite at the White House is not working. You will have to leave the White House and go to the nearest television station."

She hoped that by appearing on television and over the internet, this would bring their heads from the clouds, force them to fight instead of ignoring the inevitable.

"Lee, this is the only way that I can …"

Looking around, she saw that she was talking to herself; he was gone. But he had left her with the answer.

When it was time for her to leave, several of our agents went with her. As she left the building, there were several black SUVs outside the entrance. Guards were everywhere; helicopters flew overhead. Guns were exposed and ready to protect her from any attack that the Gara might launch.

Once inside the safety of the vehicle, she felt a little more at ease. The vehicles, with their darkened windows, completely hid her from view. This way, there was no way for them to know which vehicle she was in. The Gara would have to attack all of vehicles. That was the only way to make sure that she was eliminated from their plans and thus weaken all resolve throughout the world.

The motorcade slowly moved out flanked on all sides, security forces giving her protection as best as could be expected, hoping that they would make it to the station without incident.

The station was several blocks away, and the drive was estimated to take about fifteen minutes. Mary could hear every beat of her heart. Sweat appeared over her brow, and taking a hankie from her purse, she tried to dab it away.

"Would you please turn up the air? It's so hot in here," she said to the driver.

"Madam President, it's on high now, and it won't go any higher," he answered.

"Just keep calm," she told herself. *"Everything is going to be all right."*

As her thoughts ended, the vehicles stopped in front of a very large building. It had several floors, but she couldn't see which station it was.

Before they had come to a complete stop, one of the guards opened her door, saying, "Madam President, please," as he motioned for her to get out of the van.

Moving swiftly, she was out of the van and across the sidewalk and into the building in a matter of seconds. They hurried her up the stairs, not in an elevator, for security reasons. They didn't want to give the Gara any opportunities to try anything. They could cut the electricity, trapping her in the station.

Even though the building had been cleared of all non-essential personnel, they still couldn't be completely sure that all those left were to be trusted. Even though they had been cleared to stay, it was no guarantee that one of them hadn't crossed over to evil.

Mary stood off to the side, waiting to go on the air. She was try-ing to figure out what she had to say to bring all countries together; words alone wouldn't do it. She had to show an image of what this world could look like if evil was successful in defeating us as they had done hundreds of times in other worlds.

Doubts started to creep into Mary's thoughts. There had only been a couple of times in her life when uncertainty had been her com-panion, and most of them had occurred in the last few weeks.

Mary closed her eyes; she saw images of what lay in our path. Loud noises around her brought her out of her thoughts. When she opened her eyes, she was no longer in the station; she was standing in the desert, and explosions shook the ground as she saw the destruc-tion around her.

Red was covering the sand. She could hear screams, and the cry-ing of children also penetrated her, and wherever she looked, destruc-tion lay before her.

There were two groups that were engaged in conflict; she knew one was evil and the others were our people. The people of our world—yes—there were even beings from places other than earth.

A lot of them wore blue; some were dressed in military clothes, but a vast majority looked to be regular civilians made up of men, women, and even children. Some carried weapons; others had what-ever they could find that they could use as weapons to fight with.

Still, the power of their foe was far more powerful than what they carried. That power had taken its toll on them; vast amounts of those fighting the evil were being destroyed. Sections of their defen-sive lines had large, gaping holes where the enemy's power had struck.

Mary's eyes moved over this field of destruction, and then she saw that those fighting the enemy were not made up of all nations of the world and then in the next moment, quiet moved over everything.

"Why?" she thought. She had an urge to turn around, and what she saw brought sadness to her heart, for standing in the center was

a pole in which a white flag waved in the air for a moment. Then suddenly it went limp, falling against the pole wrapping around it.

White flags were usually a sign of peace, but this one was a flag of surrender. Evil had become the victor, and all was lost.

Beings that made up our forces stood like statues. Whatever weapon they had held was dropped on the ground at their feet. Then as if the scene had been choreographed, they all raised their hands into the air at the same time and fell to their knees.

She could still hear crying, but now it wasn't in pain; it was in despair at what the future held. They would be held in bondage, not freedom, only servitude to the will of whatever evil desired.

Death would be swift if you didn't follow their commands. It would be painful. You would be used as an example to force all the others to obey. Families would be torn apart. The only thing that you would be needed for would be to serve their needs.

Mary could see in her mind the darkness of evil. It was like a plague moving over the earth, blocking out light. The stench of it would fill your soul with despair. Life would be worthless. Your desire to live would vanish; it would become a copy of the history of long ago wars, evil that controlled all your actions. They had no concern for the person, only what they could trick the people into giving made each one of them think that by doing evil's will that they would be able to survive.

Camps were set up around the world; everyone had a computer chip implanted in them that recorded their every movement. It also kept track of the amount of sleep that each person was allowed, which was very little. Most of their time was spent working. They were allowed time to eat their one meal of the day. No time was spent with their families.

If the chip that was implanted in them didn't match with their activity, a small amount of bacteria was automatically injected into them, causing terrible pain. After a few days spent in delirium, they could no longer function. At that time, they were removed, and what happened next was anybody's guess.

After years of this abuse, the population of our world was only a tenth of what it was now, and in a few more years, no one would be left.

This planet that at one time had shown like a blue marble against a black background was now dark and lifeless.

Evil had taken everything, leaving nothing. This was the last chance to defeat evil, and now that it had passed, even the sun had dimmed, letting the earth become incased in ice.

Sometimes in the winters past when it was cold enough, the snow and ice would sparkle in the light…even moonlight…as it circled around the earth, but evil had even stopped that from happening. Like the people, this world was dead and lifeless.

Mary couldn't open her eyes, for what she saw scarred her soul. She had a fear that if she opened her eyes, all she would see was the darkness that covered the world.

Slowly, very slowly, her eye lids opened a small slit, letting in a little light, and Mary took a deep breath and opened her eyes all the way.

She was still standing in the studio. Was she having another dream—not of the past as before, but one of the future; one of blackness?

Someone called out to her.

"Madam President, we are almost ready for you." Then someone came up to her, trying to apply makeup to her face, but she put her hand up to stop them, saying, "I want the people of the world to see me this way."

As they started broadcasting, she wanted everyone to see the tears that streaked her face, the tears that had only a short time ago crept down her cheeks, and she needed for everyone see her tears and to hear the truth. There was no way she would let them cover these tears over with makeup; the people needed to see that even the president could cry, even if they had only come from another dream.

She stood in front of the camera, and clearing her throat, she counted three, two, one.

"I would like to thank this network, for, on such short notice, they let me speak to the people of not only this nation, but the entire world. I come to you not as the president of the United States, but as a person of our world."

Stopping for a second, as she tried to think of what to say to next, she continued.

"Our world, yes our world, for so long, we have only thought about the place that we live, to the point that when we don't agree. We turn to violence, harming others. The time has come when an outside threat has poised itself to take control of all of us. Even the world has turned another page, thinking that everything has become perfect, turning a blind eye to the fact that evil still exists.

She paused and then continued, "But evil does exist and it is ready to strike again. It lays silent, waiting for its moment. Our division is its strength and our weakness. I have seen what the future holds if we continue on this path.

"You may be asking how this can be. Look around at how you are living now. If someone asks for something, without hesitation, you would give it them, even if it left you with nothing. But there is a darkness lying in the silver linings of our lives. I have seen the future; again, you are thinking that it is true, that this lady has thrown a rod in her brain. I know that if someone told this to me, I wouldn't believe them. Look at what we've achieved—peace and well-being, which we didn't have before. We used to think of only ourselves and not others. It isn't that way now. But in the blink of an eye, all of this can be torn from our grasp. But I did in fact see into the future. You have to believe me."

Mary was shouting, "Believe me. Look around at what has happened, so if that can come to be, then what I am telling you right now is the reality of what is to come!"

She felt inside that her words were a mumbled jumble of confusion. If she hadn't seen it, she wouldn't believe it herself. Grabbing the podium to steady herself, she didn't know what else she could say or do.

Suddenly a figure appeared before Mary. Glancing around, she wondered if the others could see him.

From the expressions on their faces, she knew that they could see him too. Her security guards rushed forward. Mary lifted her hand signaling for them to stop, shouting at the same time, "All of you stop. He is a friend of ours!"

Mary turned back to look at the television staff, and she could hear sobs coming from them.

If it was true that the world had seen its future through Mary's eyes, then maybe all of them felt the pain and suffering that lie in the future, and if all did not become one ... had Lee helped the world to see through her eyes?

Mary wanted to thank Lee for his help but when she looked, he was gone; he was nowhere to be found. Where had he gone?

She asked one of her security guards closest to her, "Did you see the young boy that was standing here with me?"

There was a look of surprise on his face—more like confusion.

"Excuse me, Madam President but besides you, there was no one standing here." When Lee left everyone's remembrances of him ever being here were now gone.

"No, no. He came here to stand with me and show and explain to everyone that we are standing on the edge of destruction. Together we were going to try to unite all worlds," she said, still searching for him.

Another person came forward, asking, "Are you all right? I'm a doctor and if you want, I can check you over to make sure you are all right."

Then Larry came running over to her. Excitedly, his voice was almost shouting.

"You should see the telephone lines, fax machines, cell phones, anything that can be used to communicate with. They are coming in from the entire Council of United Nations and the leaders of all nations. So far as best we can determine, every one of them called to say they are fully behind you and will give control over to you—of all their forces and equipment and whatever civilian that wants to join with us."

Another assistant came forward; he was as excited as Larry.

"You should see it. Every capital and what seems to be every city—people have come together, pledging their willingness to join the fight. It's unbelievable," she said.

Mary searched around trying to find a window, any window. As she glanced through an open door she saw one. Mary had to see for herself what was happening outside on the streets. She went over to the window, but try as she might, she couldn't get the window to budge. Larry saw her struggling with it and came to her aide. Finally it opened, and she leaned out.

Looking out into the street, she could see thousands of people cheering and shouting, even though this far up; she could hear their voices and what they were shouting.

A feeling of hope raced through her. She thought maybe the struggle could end with the victory that she felt was now possible.

Once again Mary could hear Lee's voice, "*Mary, you have come far. There are many steps to be taken. The hope that you carry in your heart will be given to another.*"

She turned and looked for him, but it was only his voice that was with her, and what did his words mean: "They will be given to another?"

CHAPTER SIXTEEN

Leaving the bonds of earth, I knew that the sphere was now moving toward the moon. The stars looked like diamonds floating on a sea of black velvet. Most of the people who were lucky enough to leave the bonds of earth probably thought the same thing. It was as if the heavens had opened up and you could almost reach out and take one to keep forever in your heart, so that whenever you wanted to make a wish, all you had to do was place your hand over your heart, and when your wish came true, you could toss it back into the heavens.

The sphere began to slow as it drew closer to the moon. It started to swing around to the dark side. For a moment it was light, and then darkness spread over me. I was able to watch all of this happen, because the sphere I was traveling in was clear as glass. It had no seams, nothing to blur my view.

My eyes slowly adapted to the darkness. I could see two large objects lying suspended in the shadows of the moon. As I approached, I saw a few lights showing from them. These were the two Abiatharians ships that were stationed here to protect our world.

"Welcome to your first time in outer space," I said to myself as the sphere moved even closer to them. Near the bottom of one of the ships, an opening appeared. Light from it shone brightly against the black background, and from all my times of watching sci-fi movies, I knew this was where I would enter the ship.

Almost coming to a stop, the sphere inched closer toward the light. I could feel its pull, as if I was a fish being reeled out of a large body of water into a net.

The sphere inched into the light and through the opening that was the belly of the ship. Ahead I could make out what looked like a large chair, arms outstretched to take me in.

I felt the sphere settle into it. Touching down, there was almost no feeling of stopping. The sphere began to shrink around me as my body slowly settled lower. Holding my hand out, the sphere was now nothing but a blue, shiny marble that lay in my hand. Closing my fingers around it, I placed it carefully into my pocket, knowing that I would need the use of it again. Probably more than I could imagine.

Four people were coming toward me from the other end of what I would say is the landing bay. They were dressed in the blue outfits of the Abiatharians, all except for one.

Climbing down from the platform that I was on, I greeted them. Two looked to be in a high position of authority. Their faces were marked by the passing of time; many wrinkles covered their face.

"Thank you for letting me be a part of this," I said, reaching out my hand to them.

They stopped a few feet from me. Only one raised his hand to take mine and then lowered his head for a brief moment. Then as if I was in a higher position of authority, they briefly placed their hands to their foreheads in the form of a salute.

Looking at them, I didn't know what to make of this. But in my mind, there was something telling me that I had earned their respect and loyalty.

The one who was dressed differently reached out his hand to me as he said, "Welcome, Josaphat. It is a great honor to meet you. We have been waiting a very long time for you to come."

"Thank you," I said, shaking his hand, as I wondered if everyone that I would meet would say the same thing—that they have been waiting a long time for me to come.

He continued, "My name is Stephens. I am the commander of this ship, *The Temperance*."

Then he introduced me to the other three people.

"This is Commander Titus; he commands the other ship, *The Hornet*."

Then, turning to the other men, he said, "This is Captain Jonathan, my first in command, and this is Captain Demetrius, first in command of the *Hornet*."

Shaking each of their hands, I could feel their loyalty to me, yet I still had this strange feeling. I wondered why, because we had never met each other before this moment. I knew that, over time, my actions would gain the loyalty that was shown to me.

"Commander Titus, you need to return to your ship," Commander Stephens said.

"Yes, sir," Titus answered, as he left the bridge followed by Captain Demetrius. Probably to some type of fancy transport system like in the movies.

"We need to go to the control center," Commander Stephens said, moving toward a large set of doors off to one side of the landing bay.

Going over to the doors, he reached out and pressed a small button on the side of the door. It slid back, exposing what looked like an elevator.

Following him, the doors closed behind us. I could feel that we were moving up through the ship. As we went up, the lights and numbers flashed across a small screen over the door. I was right; it was an elevator—hard guess.

The elevator came to a stop and the door opened, exposing a long hallway that ran in two directions as we stepped out of the elevator, turning to the right, as we entered the hall. I was surprised to see that the walls and ceiling were made of glasslike material.

Going through the hall, I marveled at the sight of what I was seeing for the first time. Truly this was a gift given to all of us. What I saw above me was ... well, the only words to describe it were *unbelievably fantastic*. If everything could be this peaceful and evil was destroyed, it would truly be heaven.

Moving through another set of doors that automatically opened as we approached, and then down a short hall, one more set of doors opened, this was it—the heart and soul of the ship.

I looked around in awe. All the movies I had seen about this kind of thing were totally lacking in realism.

Inside, there were several dozen people working at their stations. Some came from different worlds and didn't look like me on the outside, yet I knew that on the inside, we were all the same, working for the good of each other. Maybe someday our world would be the same; if we were successful, then it could happen.

A voice brought me back to reality, as someone sitting in front of a large screen began to speak.

"Commander, the Gara fleet is starting to move."

Commander Stephens went over to the screen, asking, "Are they moving toward us or the earth?"

"They are moving in both directions, sir. Eight of their ships are moving toward earth; the others are coming our way," he answered, turning toward Stephens.

"Captain Jonathan, get all flight crews to the launch pad now!" he shouted. Turning to several others, he said, "Engage our protective shield. All laser weapons need to be online."

"Aye, aye, Commander," came the response.

Lights started to blink everywhere. I could see and sense people moving all over the ship, readying for a battle.

Reports came from different places throughout the ship. Shields were up; weapons ready; crews moving to their fighters. It was all a bit overwhelming.

Walking over to the commander, I asked, "What can I do?"

"In time you will know what you have to do," he answered.

"Sir," Captain Jonathan said. "There is a transmission trying to reach us."

"Don't block it. Let it through," he said, turning to the center of the room.

Amazingly, a figure appeared in the center of the room, but it wasn't a solid figure, but something that was projected there.

As quiet fell over the room, the figure became clear; it was a Gara. He started to speak.

"It's amusing to see your small force getting ready to die. You know that there is no chance that you can defeat us. We have twelve ships and you only have two, but we want to be fair."

He laughed.

"We'll let you decide if you want to live or die. You have thirty minutes. If you don't surrender, not only these two ships, but also all your forces on earth will be destroyed.

He slowly disappeared, but his words still hung in the air. We had thirty minutes to decide something that we already knew what the answer was: "*No.*"

"Commander Stephens, how many smaller fighters are there on your ships?" I asked, turning toward him.

"Each ship has one thousand fighters," he answered.

"We can't wait for them to attack us first. The fight has to be taken to them," I said, sounding like I knew it all, but I had to say it. *Why?* But no answer would come to me.

"What are your plans?" Captain Jonathan asked as he joined us.

"They will wait the full thirty minutes, expecting us to fight, before launching their attack. They know that these two battle cruisers will have to be destroyed first before they strike the earth. Let me explain my plan," I answered.

Our plans were laid out over the next few minutes.

"Five minutes before time is up, we will launch all two thousand fighters. One group of a thousand will be split in two. Half of those

JOSEPH A. LUNINI, SR.

will move to the right, and the other half will move to the left of the Gara battle cruisers that are moving toward us."

The remaining one thousand fighters will also be split. Five hundred sent toward the battle cruisers that are heading toward the earth. The last five hundred ships will be the bait. They will move toward the center of the Gara battle cruisers. This is way the Zulu fought their enemy; the center would draw the adversary toward them. The group on the left and the one on the right would act like the horns of a giant beast.

Once the Gara move toward the center, the outer groups will flank them from both sides, hopefully inflicting heavy losses.

Surprise has to work for us. Hopefully the first few minutes will catch the Gara off guard and in their confusion that may give us the chance we need. All this hinges on those priceless few minutes.

Time struggled to move forward. Sometimes when I looked at my watch I would begin to think that it was broken, only to see seconds slowly tick by. Then I realized that twenty-five minutes had gone by. Looking at Commander Stephens and Captain Jonathan, in conjunction with the other ship, the signal was given to move.

Watching on a large screen, the fighters moved out quickly into formation. The laser weapons on both of our battle cruisers fired at the Gara ships with all the power we had.

The blinding lights from the lasers helped hide the movement of our fighters. They were able to start the attacks.

The protective shields on the fighter, as well as the shields on our two main ships, were at full power. The fighters would be able to withstand several direct hits before the shields would fail, but the strength of the weapons on the Gara ships would determine how long our main shields would last.

Over time, the Abiatharians had learned that the Gara ships carried only half the fighters that our ships carried and that gave our fighters an even chance.

Space around the Gara ships became bright; it looked as if the sun's rays were mixed between the two forces.

The surprise attack had caught the Gara flat-footed in the first few minutes. Two of the Gara cruisers were destroyed, and another was heavily damaged.

That left only one of their ships able to attack us. This forced the Gara to call the eight ships that were heading toward the earth back, which brought their cruisers toward us as they joined the one remaining Gara ship.

Small fighters swarmed from the Gara ships, four thousand in all came from the eight cruisers that had turned back from the earth, moving through our five hundred fighters like a lawn mower cutting grass.

Our fighters fought bravely, but the overpowering strength of the Gara was too much. Fighter after fighter disappeared in a flash of light from the Garas' laser weapons.

Looking at the screen, it looked like a swarm of locusts moving toward our other fighters. At least two-thirds of their fighters had made it through.

Our remaining fighters were now fighting on two fronts. They were hammering at the one remaining Gara cruiser able to fight. It was being protected by only a handful of its fighters.

But an untold number of Gara fighters were coming up fast on them. Out of the two thousand fighters that we had launched, there were a little over a half of them left.

The Hornet turned toward the Gara fighters that were moving rapidly at our ships. Picking up speed, it dove into the Gara fighters; its laser cut them into pieces.

It may have stopped the Gara fighters from changing the outcome of this fight, but Commander Titus had overlooked the eight large Gara cruisers that were following the fighters.

As the *Hornet* broke through, it was met by the laser fire from the eight other ships. For a moment it looked as if time had come to a complete stop. Then the *Hornet* was gone. Only particles remained where it had once been.

We had tried to cut the odds down, but it hadn't been enough. I felt doubt starting to creep into my mind. Had we come this far only to be stopped? Shaking those thoughts from my mind, as I stood there, I looked around at the people who would fight to their last breath for the earth.

"Commander, the Gara are signaling. Should I let it through?" asked Captain Jonathan.

Stephen turned toward me. I could see the question in his eyes.

"Let it through," I said, turning to the center of the control room.

What appeared wasn't a Gara, but my own daughter, Marsha. There was an evil smile on her face.

Putting her hands on her hips, she started, "Well, oh great one, Father, you seem to learn the hard way. Lucky should be your middle name, because that is the only word that can describe you still being alive."

"Well it's good to see you too," I said, biting my tongue in anger.

"Come now, Father. Look around you. Most of your fighters are gone; this is the only ship you have left. There is no way that with this pitiful force you can stop us," she said, not moving.

"Marsha, you know that once I start something, I will finish it," I said, not moving either, as I watched her eyes.

"I know, Father," she said. For a brief moment, I almost sensed something else. But it faded away.

"This is your last chance to surrender, no more talk. So what is your choice? Surrender, or you choose to die." Turning, she was gone and the screen went to black.

There was something, but I couldn't put my finger on it. No matter what, we would not surrender. That would be the end of freedom, not only for our world, but the countless other worlds that had succumbed to the evil ways of the Gara that were waiting for us to free them from these shackles of evil and rebuild their worlds.

The command center was quiet. Nobody moved or said anything, and I could feel their eyes looking at me for the answer. In my mind I knew their fears. I had overcome my own fears; yet there were still lapses in faith, which I hoped one day I would have the chance to overcome.

"Commander, have the remaining fighters pull back and form a half circle between us and the Gara ships," I said, looking at the screen.

"Sir, the other ships are moving up to join in the attack," someone in the room said. I didn't know who.

Our one battle cruiser and about half of our fighters were all that stood between the Gara and the end of everything. Looking at the screen, nine Gara ships with thousands of fighters in front of them moved closer.

Who would strike first? I could feel the question coming from somewhere.

We had been given the chance to surrender, which wasn't an option. We had to be the first to strike. I hoped that by making them fight our way, it would possibly give us a better option, even if it was slim to none.

The Gara fleet started to move, very slowly, toward us. Even though the odds were in their favor, I knew that they still feared us. That fear was our signal.

"Now!" I shouted to Commander Stephens.

Turning, he gave the order. Our fighters hurtled themselves into the Garas.'

"Swing the end around," he shouted into the microphone.

He must have been an old history buff like me. What he was doing was what we had tried earlier. It was the same thing that one of the African tribes did to the British. As I had said before, move the center of fighters that we have left forward, and then hope we had enough to strike at their flanks.

It had worked before somewhat; maybe we still had a little luck left.

When our center of fighters moved close to them, the Gara directed all their fire power at them. This left the ends free to wrap around and strike, like the horns of a bull.

Their lack of brainpower enabled us to catch the Gara by surprise again. They tried to pull some of their fighters out to stop our assault on their flanks, but our fighters stayed close to the Gara ships. This left no opening for their larger cruisers to attack us with their laser weapons.

Our surprise tactics had caught them off guard; again this increased our odds. The Gara strength was cut down. They were now fighting on three fronts.

The Gara moved their largest ships, trying to do what we had done to their fighters—flank us. If they were successful, the battle would be lost.

Commander Stephens ordered the *Temperance* to pull hard to the left, as he tried to out maneuver the Gara.

Even in space when the ship moved that way, everyone in the control room was thrown to one side. I struggled to stand as I grabbed hold of a chair.

Regaining my footing, I watched the screen; our ship had banked hard and now came up fast on the Garas' flank.

"Fire all lasers!" he shouted. Bright flashes of light filled the space around us. Luck was still with us. Our lasers hit two of the Garas' battle cruisers. They were completely blown to pieces. The odds were still stacked against us, but even with that little bit of luck, the outcome was still in doubt.

Our fighters that were flanking the Gara struck them continuously. One of their battle cruisers was destroyed and another was disabled.

Our fighters had hit the Gara hard with good success, but the cost had been high. Only about five hundred were left fighting.

The *Temperance* turned hard, right into the Gara fighters which were being protected by several of their battle cruisers, with all its weapons still firing. Again Commander Stephens' move caused more damage to the Gara fleet. Another of their battle cruisers was blown into dust.

More of their fighters were also destroyed, not only by us, but in the confusion of battle, their cruisers had fired at the *Temperance* which was moving through the Gara fighters, destroying about half of their own fighters.

As the *Temperance* moved into this position our remaining fighters swarmed behind it. This saved most of them. They had moved so close to it that it was like they had become a part of the ship.

Our forces moved away from the Garas.' Then suddenly the *Temperance* turned back toward the Gara fleet. It was hit several times from laser blasts from the remaining Gara battle cruisers.

Alarms went off on all decks. We had suffered damage; no one was sure at that moment how bad it was. The command center was damaged. Several crew members were either dead or injured.

Those that had survived tried to help them, but it was only a limited effort. Their main concern was still the *Temperance*. This ship had to keep fighting, or there would be no help for any one.

Commander Stephens shouted, "Damage control, give me the status of our damage!"

Some of the communications were knocked out, and the rest of them that were still working reported that the ship had suffered major damage.

"Commander, we have lost most of our laser weapons on the starboard side. From decks four through nine, the shields in those areas are also down to sixty percent. If that section is struck again with that much force, the shields will fail and there will be a breach in the hull.

The command center had also suffered major damage. One of the officers gave Commander Stephens the bad news.

"Sir, our radar is out. We are flying blind, except for the communication screen, which only lets us see forward; also the main laser weapons control are damaged. They have to fire manually. The worst is that life support systems have been heavily damaged; it can only maintain the ship for a few more hours at most. Then everything will shut down."

Reality was finally beginning to set in. Surrender now and accept defeat, or continue to fight with our limited resources and power, which would mean certain death for everyone on the *Temperance* and possibly the earth; all the other worlds that rested their faith in us waited for our help to throw off their bonds of evil that controlled them.

Commander Stephens was in the process of answering that question. He had ordered that all shield power be directed to all sections of the ship, except the area that was damaged.

"What is he doing?" I asked Captain Jonathan. "If we are hit by the Gara laser in that section, the ship will be lost. You have to use the shield to protect that area."

Looking at Captain Jonathan, he said, "The shields aren't strong enough to protect the whole ship. It would be too weak to sustain any massive strikes, and that would knock the shields out, breaching the hull and destroying this ship instantly."

"What difference does it make then?" I asked.

"The difference is that like a wounded fighter keeps the injured side away from the attacker. We will fight, always keeping the vulnerable side away from the Gara," he answered.

The Garas' attack cruisers moved into attack formation with their four remaining ships that hadn't been damaged. The other two moved slowly away from us.

Keeping the damaged side of the *Temperance* away from the Gara was the most important part of our survival. Commander Stephen stationed several members of the crew at certain sections of the ship. They would become the eyes to replace the radar that the ship had lost. Using a communication transmitter, they would report to the command center the location of the Garas' ships.

The remaining fighters were now split into two groups. They were given the orders to fight on their own, since it was impossible for us to direct them during combat. Our fighters would have to choose what they thought were the best forms of attack.

The Gara battle cruisers opened fire on the *Temperance* with all the laser power they had. Their remaining fighters tried to move to our weak side, but one group of our fighters swung far to the right, trying to flank the Gara's four battle cruisers. It was a desperate chance. The group commander had seen that their fighters were trying to move around the *Temperance*, and the battle cruisers' attention was directed also at the ship.

Our fighters moved in, in three waves as they struck at the Garas' opened flank. The first wave landed a barrage of heavy laser fire, causing some damage to the ship. When the second and third waves struck, the Gara's ship imploded and then collapse in a blaze of fire. As our fighters flew past the other three, they turned to attack again, moving through the debris of the destroyed ship, firing until most lost laser power. Now with no weapons, they were helpless, but they continued to fight as they rammed their fighters into other Gara ships, as bright explosions lit up the blackness of space...

This was a fitting farewell to the brave crews that gave so much, so that others would have a chance of living without being chained to the darkness of evil.

The few fighters that still had power left fought till that was gone. Grouping together out of range of the three Garas' ships, and for one brief moment, everything stopped.

Then without a word of communication to each other, somehow they all knew what had to be done. They flew straight at one of the Gara's battle cruisers, destroying it, and themselves, in a gigantic explosion.

The word of their sacrifice was reported to the command center. For a brief moment, everyone stopped and looked at each other.

Laser beams striking the *Temperance* brought us back to what was at hand. Some place the names of those brave pilots would be read so that all the worlds could honor them. I knew deep inside that one day that would be so.

My attention was drawn back to this time. A loud explosion rocked the *Temperance*; I could feel death as I laid my hand on the walls as I tried not to fall.

The main power source of our weapons had been destroyed; there was no power to fight back with, our ship was at the mercy of the Gara. We still had power to move, but our life support system would stop in a matter of minutes.

Spotters on some of the other decks reported that the Gara's two still fully functioning battle cruisers out of the five that they had left deployed one on each side of the *Temperance*.

We could try to move from between them, but even using all the power that was left in the engines, it still wouldn't be enough to move us to safety.

Commander Stephens and Captain Jonathan came over to me. The other crew members that were there in the command center also came and stood with us.

Looking around at each other, a sense of pride could be seen on the faces of each person. They had fought the good fight, as best as it could have been done.

Commander Stephens stood at attention. Raising his arm, he saluted each one, saying, "It has been an honor and a great privilege to serve and fight beside each one of you."

A quiet stillness moved around us.

CHAPTER SEVENTEEN

Sue and Skylar watched in awe as the Rocky Mountains came into view. Far below their spheres, its peaks moved rapidly below them. Now for first time, they saw the blue of the Pacific Ocean. Sue could imagine what the early settlers must have felt when they first beheld the beauty of it. The ocean moved rapidly under them, but it wasn't the ocean that was moving. She knew that they were moving.

For that moment speed wasn't important. The spheres moved steadily over the water. In her thoughts her mind kept drifting back to Joe. How long before they all would be together again? Where was his battle being fought? *God keep us all safe,* she prayed.

Land now came into view, and she knew that this had to be the coast of China. The spheres started to move faster. Everything sped rapidly under them as everything became a blur. She wondered where they were headed.

What land was this? The spheres began to slow again. Sue watched as they moved over a low mountain range. They were heading to an area that appeared to be a desert. Moving lower, mountains came into view again.

With a jolt the spheres came to a sudden stop. They dropped rapidly toward the ground. Sue and Skylar braced for the crash. Then a few feet above the ground, the spheres stopped. Sue and Skylar barely felt it.

The spheres settled to the ground, and they started to disappear from around them. Sue and Skylar held out their hands as the spheres became marble size again. The marbles now lay in their hands. Knowing what to do next, Sue and Skylar took the marbles and placed them in their pockets.

"Where are we Grandma?" Skylar asked, looking around.

"I'm not sure," Sue answered. "I think we are somewhere in the Middle East. That was our destination."

There was nothing visible to tell them where they were. The only thing to do was to start walking.

Looking to see where the sun was, Sue pointed, saying, "We came from the east and before we landed, coming over the first set of hills, I didn't notice any large cities, so I think that we should head that way. Which I believe is northwest."

The two of them set out. A few palm trees dotted the landscape. She knew that water had to be near, and they turned in that direction. As they moved closer to the trees, they could hear a bird singing. It was strange—one bird, nothing else. No people, no signs that anyone had ever lived here. The sun was now high in the sky. The heat from it was starting to overpower them.

Thirst was becoming an issue.

"We have got to find water pretty soon," she said, wiping sweat from her face. She looked down at Skylar, knowing that her small legs couldn't walk much longer.

Suddenly a noise caught Sue's attention. Grabbing Skylar by the arm, they ran toward some low lying shrubs. Falling to the ground, she pulled Skylar down beside her.

Someone was coming up a small hill toward them. Sue squeezed Skylar's hand tighter, not knowing if it was friend or foe, shading her eyes from the glare of the sun, as she waited in fear, not for herself, but for Skylar. Sue could now make out the faint sound of bells. Watching, she saw sheep.

"Sheep," Sue said out loud in wonder. There was one lone man with them, guiding the sheep toward her and Skylar.

The sheep ambled slowly past them. When the man moved up to where they were hiding, he stopped. When he turned toward them, Sue could feel his eyes staring into hers.

Sue knew that they had been found. Standing up, she and Skylar didn't try to run; they stood their ground. Sue used her power to try and search his mind, but something was blocking her. Concentrating harder, she still couldn't penetrate his thoughts.

His body was covered by a long robe; but those eyes, they looked deep into her soul. A picture was starting to form around them and as they looked up at the sky, blue skies turned black. Stars shone in the background. Something horrible was moving across this vision.

People were fighting and dying in a battle between the Gara and the Abiatharians. Crafts on both sides were being destroyed. The fight went back and forth, even though the Gara had the superior forces. The Abiatharians were staging a heroic fight.

The picture slowed. There was one Abiatharians ship that looked like it was dying, sitting between two of the Gara ships.

Her eyes penetrated into the Abiatharians ship. Moving to the top of it, Sue watched as a man whom she didn't recognize stood in front of several people. He raised his arm, saluting the other people that were standing there in front of him. He was speaking, but she couldn't hear his words.

He moved from one person and then on to the next, as he saluted each and every one of them. Who was he? Her mind's eye tried to see around the first man. What kind of people would stand there knowing that your life was about to end? Only the bravest ones. Those who kept good in their hearts, for they knew they were going home. The man moved to the side. Sue could now see the other man's face.

"Oh my God!" she screamed, falling to her knees, holding her head in her hands as great sobs came from her, and she screamed again.

"No, this can't be true. Please, please don't let this happen. How does this follow what is written in *The Book of Forever*?"

Skylar moved closer to Sue, putting her arms around her, saying, "Grandma, remember what the book says. Do you remember?"

Sue tried to regain control of her emotions. Clearing her throat and wiping tears from her face, she looked at Skylar. Words were trying to form in her mind but when they did, she still couldn't speak. Sue looked from Skylar to the man, somehow hoping for some kind of answer, any answer.

Walking over to them, the man raised his hand and laid it gently on her shoulder.

"Joan is right, Susanna. You must cast the doubts from your heart and mind," he said, taking his other hand and removing the hood from off his head, exposing his face.

Looking at him, calmness flowed over her.

"Lee," she said, almost not believing what her eyes were telling her, for he was no longer a boy, but a man.

"Yes, my child. You must let faith become your support. For without it you are lost. You started on this path with the belief that what Josaphat had told you was the right thing to do," he said, as he looked at Joan. He continued, "This child's belief will be the tool that you will need, for her faith is far beyond anyone's."

Taking his hand from Sue's shoulder, he pulled the robe back over his head. Turning, he walked away from them. In one beat of Sue's heart, there was nothing where he had been standing; even the sand gave no signs that anyone had ever stood there.

Sue struggled to her feet. She took Skylar's hands in hers. Her heart and soul were determined to do what had to be done. Somewhere deep inside, she knew that she would be with Joe again. Lee had strengthened her faith with his words.

They started walking across this desolate land again. Sue could feel something guiding them; they were still looking for water. Their steps through the sand moved faster, almost to a point of running. The heat from the sun was lifted away from them.

Sue stopped pulling on Skylar's hand.

"Stay here. Someone is coming for us," she said.

Skylar looked at Sue.

"You're right, Grandma. I can feel it too."

Turning her head she could see a small road that ran toward them, Sue said, "That wasn't there a few minutes ago."

Standing there, they could hear the sounds of vehicles moving toward them. After several minutes, trucks could be seen moving closer. When the trucks were near them, they stopped.

The driver's door of the vehicle open; Sue recognized the man who was getting out. It was Gary.

He ran over to Sue and Skylar, throwing his arms around them, saying, "We were worried that you were lost. Your spheres landed in the wrong place."

"No, Gary," she said. "We landed right where we were supposed to."

He didn't know what to think of her answer, but he knew that whatever she said had a meaning in it. But this was not the time to question her, which meant that they needed to move fast. Time was against them, as it always was.

Pointing to the trucks, Gary said, "Come on, get in. We have to hurry."

After they were seated in the truck, Sue began to wonder how everything would turn out. She had to believe that in the end everything would be right.

The trucks traveled for several miles before heading into a small valley. What she saw surprised her, for as far as she could see, there were thousands upon thousands of military personnel from all over the world, along with thousands of Abiatharians and every kind of military weapon that existed. Looking closer, she also saw average people, men, women, and children holding anything that could be used as weapons. All races of people were gathered together as one. For the first time in history, all would stand shoulder to shoulder to fight the evil that had plagued man from the beginning of time.

In the next twenty-four hours, we would live or die together in the quest to be free from it.

The trucks drove through the masses of people, then it pulled up to a large tent, they stopped. Sue and Skylar got out of the truck. Turning around, they looked at all the people. What they saw was unbelievable.

"Susanna, will you and Joan please follow me," Gary said, heading into the tent. Inside, there were many military and civilians sitting in rows that faced a large stage.

They followed Gary onto the stage, and Sue wondered why they had been brought there. A noise behind Sue caused her to turn, and she was shocked by what she saw.

Skylar shouted, "Grandma, it's The Keeper!"

She ran over to him throwing her arms around him, at the same time jumping up and down. The child in her came out. If only for a brief moment, she could act her age. It was good for her to be released from the adult world she had been forced into, even if only for that brief time.

The Keeper turned to Susanna, saying, "I'm sorry for leaving you at the mercy of the Gara, but you had to strengthen your faith in preparation for what was to come into your life."

"It is hard to accept being left that way, but I understand the reason behind it," Sue said, feeling her faith rise higher.

Skylar had stopped jumping, as she returned to the role that had been chosen for her, she said, "My faith is also stronger; we will all have to be stronger, Grandma. I feel a darkness moving upon us. This will truly test our faith."

Sue looked at the child that stood beside her. Truly she was older and wiser than the number of years that she had lived.

Several men came up on the stage; The Keeper introduced them to Joan and Susanna. They were in charge of the military offense that was to make its final battle against the Gara on earth. Hopefully it would be successful.

Susanna and Joan's reputation of conflict against the Gara was now well-known to the masses that were gathered here. It was hoped that their being here would encourage the people to struggle and fight as hard as possible against the Gara.

As our plans of attack against the Gara were being discussed, a man ran into the tent, shouting, "The Gara is amassing their forces a few miles from us. There has to be hundreds of millions of them. They seem to stretch for thousands of miles in all directions. Sir, there are too many of them!"

"Everyone, please calm down!" The Keeper said, trying to shout above the fear that was spreading through our people. "They may have the numbers, but we have the faith. That is our strength."

Somehow his words calmed the fears that had overcome every-one. People stopped and stood quietly, listening to his words.

"Nothing is ever accomplished by letting fear overcome your spirit. We are one now. Side by side, we will walk into the valley of shadows, and we will fear no evil. For the Creator of all will be with us," he said, raising his arms above his head.

Loud cheers erupted from the mass of people. It was so deafen-ing that Sue's ears hurt. It was a good kind of hurt. We would make a good fight of it, and then our final plans were laid out. Now was the time.

Skylar and Sue followed The Keeper and the others out of the tent. As they moved to the front of our forces, you could hear and see the movement of the Gara. The ground under our feet began to tremble from the massive number of them. Even at this distance that separated us, it still felt like as earthquake.

Looking across at the Gara as they moved toward us, Sue couldn't see anything else. It was as if during a storm, the surge of the ocean rose up higher and higher, stopping a brief second before it crashed onto the land, destroying everything in its path.

Noise coming from behind them caused Sue to turn; she could see a massive force of all kinds of aircraft moving toward the Gara. They were from nations throughout the world. The aircraft cast a dark shadow over the land, as if a giant hand had removed the sun from it.

Something behind them caused her to turn back toward the Gara. They had launched a response to our aircraft. The sky above Sue took on the image of locust descending on a field of wheat, ready to devour everything in its path.

Like two caged animals facing each other, both sides were ready for the ultimate confrontation; fangs were bared, with snarls coming from someplace deep inside. All that had to be done was for the cage doors to be opened, releasing the savages to tear into each other.

The Gara movement forward suddenly stopped. Our aircrafts were given the orders to prepare for their attack.

Sue could feel the fear in everyone around her; most had never been in a battle before. Killing someone wasn't what they wanted to do, but it had come down it. To save the world this was not an option. Now it was kill or be killed. Never before in the history of the world had this been so important.

Everything became deathly quiet, and then it was shattered by the sound of explosions. The Gara fighters streaked toward our lines. Flashes of light preceded each explosion, ripping large holes in the ground, moving closer to our people.

The signal was given. Our aircraft streaked toward their fighters. Two giants crashed together. For a brief time, both sides came to a stop, but the advance power of the Gara's weapons started to tear apart our forces.

For every one of their crafts that we destroyed, at least ten of ours were gone. The Gara were winning the struggle between good and evil.

The land forces moved together. It was the same thing. The Gara's weapons were far superior to ours, but we didn't stop fighting. Even the people that only carried rocks and sticks fought on.

Red color now covered some of the ground. Everywhere, our planes and people still tried to move forward. But it had now become apparent that we couldn't even hold onto the ground we had started on.

We were slowly being pushed back, even as more people and planes arrived. All nations were sending everything they had into this fight. Nothing was being held back.

But there was nothing that could be done that could stem the tide. The Gara were too strong—not their soldiers, but the weapons they possessed.

Minute by minute, all our steps were backward. Even though none turned to run, each step we were pushed back only made our people fight harder. The Gara were winning, but they were paying a heavy price for it.

Sue knew that it was only a matter of time before our resolve began to fail. People could only give so much before they stopped struggling and gave up.

The color of the ground was now a deeper scarlet, and the smell of death brought the struggle closer to an end. Evil's grip was starting to strangle the life from us.

Large sections of our people were destroyed; where hundreds of thousands of people had once stood, there was nothing, only blood.

The sun had been blocked out by the massive amount of our planes, but it was now beginning to shine through. Thousands of them now lay scattered over the red sand. Our forces were now cut to less than half of what we had started with.

In only a few hours, what we had hoped would be victory—defeat was now staring into our eyes. Those evil eyes were those of the Gara.

Something had to happen to stop it. Skylar ran out from behind Sue, toward the Gara. Words came from her as she moved.

"*CARO-FI-TE-VIRS, LY-SA-TE-OWE-O-RO-KI!*" (Creator of the universe, bring forth the power to destroy them!)

Lights brighter than the sun began to come from her. It was so strong Sue had to shade her eyes from it. She could barely see Skylar.

Wind moved around Skylar. Her body lifted up from the ground. Again, bright lights flashed out from her. They moved faster and faster away from her. Skylar's body started to spin; wind and light tore through the Gara.

Their screams filled the air as she continued to move forward. She also directed her power toward the Gara's fighters that moved above her. In an instant, a vast section of them were gone. Hope began to move through our people. They started to hold their positions. Some even moved forward. Maybe our defeat wasn't going to happen.

Armored vehicles on both sides had been locked in a gigantic struggle, but the same problem beset our armor. Its weapons were not equal to the Gara

Massive destruction had pushed the armored vehicles back into themselves, causing total confusion among the ranks.

As Skylar's power swept through the Gara, Sue saw a chance to use her power of mind blending against them. Standing at the front-line of our people, moving forward, she faded from sight. With every-one occupied with the battle, no one noticed that she was no longer with them.

As she moved invisibly through the air, she spotted what appeared to be a Gara armored vehicle. It was the vehicle that was directing the attack against us. More vehicles spread out behind it.

"*This is the one,*" she said to herself. There was no time to ponder what she must do. Rapidly, she moved toward the vehicle.

A strange feeling moved through her body as she felt herself slipping into the material that was the vehicle's skin. Her eyes adjusted to the new surrounding that had now become the home of her being.

Once she had become the skin of the vehicle, Sue could see the Gara that was directing the attack. A feeling of hate rose up in her soul. It was a feeling she didn't have the power to control, so she let that hatred become the dominating factor in her plans of destruction against the Gara.

Moving swiftly, she took control of the vehicle. She turned it back toward the others that were following. The vehicle that she was driving launched fire at the Gara vehicles, ripping some of them apart. This threw them into mass confusion. They didn't know why their own vehicle was firing on them. Their thoughts were controlled by the one Gara, and it was the vehicle that Sue had become and was controlling.

Watching the lead vehicle firing at them and without directions of what to do, they followed suit. Firing on anything—Gara or Abiatharians—it didn't matter.

Armored vehicle after armored vehicle erupted into flames. Sue knew the tide of the battle was turning back in our favor. Our armor moved ahead with new courage, smashing into the Gara, driving them back on to their heels.

Some of the Gara even abandoned their vehicles, fleeing in fear—something they had never felt before. Fear was what they had always instilled in others. Now it was shoved deep inside them.

On all fronts of the battle, good was flowing over the land. Victory was now within our grasp. The Gara were losing their will to continue on. The evil that had plagued the world was losing its hold on us, and good was rapidly rising over it.

Suddenly the skies turned dark. Lightning flashed from the darkness, striking the ground as it moved over the field of battle. Winds with the strength of a hurricane moved from the sea across the area, ripping apart everything in its path.

Fear spread like a plague over the land. What had once been a victory was now once again returning to despair. People were throwing down their weapons, trying to flee from the fear, but it moved with them. There was no place to run.

Sue was tossed from the vehicle that she had been driving. Some power stronger than her was taking control of the battle.

When Sue tried to stand, she could see in the distance hundreds of lightning bolts that were being hurled at Skylar, striking her with millions of volts of electricity. She was thrown hundreds of feet, landing hard against rocks that protruded from the ground. Lying there, she didn't move.

Fear ran rampant over Sue. She could hear screams coming from somewhere. She then realized that they were coming from her. Sue felt her soul being torn into fragments. The will to go on started to die a slow, agonizing death. For that moment all feelings had deserted her, leaving her soul a blank canvas that no painter could find the colors to bring life back to.

Stillness settled over the battlefield. Everyone had become like statues. Nothing moved. No sounds could be heard. Only the movement of the wind over the dead and dying could be detected.

Sue somehow found a spark of inner life in her heart, willing her to go on. Looking down, she saw her legs move forward but not by her own will. Something else was moving them. Who or what it was, she didn't know, only that it was taking her to Skylar.

Reaching Skylar, Sue knelt down beside her. Lifting Skylar into her arms, Sue pulled her close to her chest and prayed that it was true, that they couldn't be killed. She gently laid Skylar down on the ground and rested her head on Skylar's chest. Listening, she could hear a faint heartbeat.

But there was no time to rejoice; again Sue felt the ground shake. This time it was different.

"*Something horrible is about to happen,*" a voice whispered to her. One that was familiar to her but yet strange. Could it be the Creator?

Again everything shook. No one could stand. The force was too much; even the sky trembled.

Sue raised her head as a sound floated over the ground. Wiping tears and dirt from her eyes, she was met by a sight that was unbelievable. Were her eyes playing tricks on her, or could what she saw be true?

From the water on her left, a creature rose, rising at least one hundred feet tall. The creature had several heads connected to the body by long necks. Each head snarled, and evil sounds came from somewhere deep inside. Fire flowed from its mouths. The flames reached out, burning everything that it came close to.

The ground again shook from something buried deep. Large cracks appeared; they moved out from one spot. The ground again shook, but this time it was a hundred times stronger.

Smoke rose above the rocks that boiled out of the crevice. In the smoke that had risen, something else could be seen. Another creature had crawled out of the bowels of the earth. It was exactly the same as the creature that had risen from the water.

It was the devil himself, and it looked as if it had split into two creatures and now stood before everyone. Had Gara made an alliance with the devil, or in reality were they also the devil? At this moment the answer was yes.

Sue could hear someone calling her name. She tried to stand up to see who it was, but she couldn't, for there was no way that she would let go of Skylar.

The voice drew nearer; she could feel someone kneeling next to her. Again she wiped her eyes.

"Gary." The word spilled from her lips. It was all she could say.

"Susanna, are you all right?" he asked, trying to lift her up, but she wouldn't let go of Skylar.

"No, no. I can't leave her," she said, holding her as close as possible.

Other hands moved around them. They took her arms from around Skylar.

"Please, Susanna. They will take care of her. We need your help. The Gara are signaling that they want to talk," Gary said.

Those words brought her back to reality and with Gary's help, Sue stood. Her knees felt like rubber, but with an inner strength and the help of others, she moved back to the center of the camp where it had all started.

Arriving, they found several of the Gara waiting for them. Sue counted ten of the ugly evil beings standing there, looking like they were ready to feast on the remains of our forces.

"At this moment, they probably could," she thought.

Wasting no time, the Gara laid out the facts as they saw them.

"You must be Susanna, one of the three great ones," he said, a laugh sliding up from deep within him.

Turning, this thing pointed to where Sue had recently come from, saying, "You are the only one left of the three. The young one is no more, and the other who ventured into outer space was also destroyed. That only leaves you."

Anger filled her, but she wouldn't let them see it. "They are still alive. You haven't won. We will still fight until we have destroyed you," she said, standing straight, with pride inside her.

"Such great words come from you, but there is no substance to back them up," he said, taking a step toward Sue. But she didn't back up, instead she moved forward. They were face-to-face.

"Give it your best shot," her voice challenged him.

"This is the end of our talk," he said. "We will give you one hour to surrender. If you do not, the beasts you see before you will be unleashed to finish what we have started ... your destruction."

Suddenly a large pole came hurtling from the sky, landing a few yards from where they stood. The Gara moved over to the pole. Standing beside it, he turned back to face Sue, saying, "You can use this to give us your answer."

Another Gara came over and stood beside the pole. He carried something in his arms. Raising his arms, he dropped it.

"In one hour, if you surrender, raise this flag, so there will be no doubts. If not you will be destroyed," he said. Now both of them joined the others and walked away.

Sue stood there, watching the Gara move away. Gary touched her shoulder. "We will leave the decision up to you," he said.

For a brief time, Sue didn't know what the answer would be. Hearing a small voice coming from behind her, she turned around. Standing there in front of her was a young girl; she looked to be about the same age as Skylar.

"Excuse me," she said, holding something out to Sue.

"What's this?" Sue asked, turning it over trying to figure out what it could be.

"It's a flag my family made. Please open it," she said. Sue unfolded it. All that was written on it was the word: *Freedom*. Sue turned and looked at Gary, and they both smiled.

CHAPTER EIGHTEEN

As Commander Stephens lowered his hand, a voice came over the intercom.

"Sir, this is crewman Edwards. You won't believe what is happening," he almost screamed. His voice was like that of a child who had received something that they had wanted forever.

"Calm down, Edwards. Tell me what you mean," Commander Stephens said back to him; his voice showing no sign of change.

"Sir, go to the glass walkway. You won't believe it," Edwards said again, his voice still growing more excited.

Commander Stephens looked at me then turned and walked over to the door that led out to the glass walkway. As he went out, the rest of us followed, not knowing what to expect.

Once out, we were greeted by the blackness of space dotted with stars. Looking around, that was all that could be seen. Looking down, you could see the earth floating through a field of blackness with stars as a beautiful background.

"Wait," my mind said. Something was missing. Edwards came running toward us.

"See? I told you," he said.

"Told us what?" Commander Stephens asked, his eyes searching the blackness that surrounded us. Only the stars could be seen.

My eyes also searched along with his.

"That's it," I heard my own voice saying. "They're gone."

"Who's gone?" he asked.

"The Gara," Edwards interrupted. "They left. I was watching and waiting for them to finish us off, and then they turned away from us and doggone it, they left. I couldn't believe my eyes, but here, you take a look and see if you can find anything. They're not anywhere to be seen. None of the other crew that was watching has seen them either. They're gone."

He was right. There was no sign of the Gara any place. We stood there. A kind of disbelief was shared by each one of us.

"Why didn't they finish us off? We couldn't fight. Our lives were at their mercy?"

"Sir," Edwards said. "It's kind of strange."

"What is?" Commander Stephens asked.

"We received a message from them right before they left," he answered.

"What message?" I asked, feeling something close to me.

"It was very short. Only three words: *one more time*," Edwards answered, with a questioning look on his face.

One more time? my mind asked. I hadn't heard those words for a long time. A smile formed on my lips.

Commander Stephens looked at me, asking, "You're smiling; do those words mean something to you?"

"I think they do, but it has been years since they were said to me. They came from someone who I loved very much," I answered, still looking at the emptiness of space. The stars were shining like diamonds. They radiated a soft blue color.

He came up to me and asked, "Who?"

For seconds, I said nothing, then, "We need to get this ship repaired. Our help is needed on earth."

He didn't push any further for the answer to his question. Turning to Edwards, he said, "Let me use your communicator."

Edwards handed it over to him. Taking it, he started, "All crew members aboard this ship. We need to head for earth. It needs our help. We have a few hours to repair the damage, so let's get going."

As he headed back to the command center, I headed to my quarters. Repairs weren't what I could help with. I needed time to think; inside of me, questions had to be answered. Could it really be the person I thought it was? Could they be one who turned the Gara ships away from us? Only time would tell.

Entering my quarters I knew it was selfish, but my mind, not my body, needed to rest. Lying down, I tried to reach Sue with my thoughts. She needed to hang on and to know that I would come to help her. Time was the hinging factor that everything rested on. If only my powers of stopping time were strong enough to work now, but I knew they weren't.

I could feel the *Temperance* start to heal as the repairs continued. Some would say the ship was an inanimate object, but I felt that it was somehow alive. Everything that was created had life in it. Everything we hold or touch should be cherished.

Closing down my mind, I rested for a couple of hours, and when I woke, a picture appeared in front of me. It was earth. My eyes moved as if I was in an airplane moving through the atmosphere. Closer I flew. Ahead, I could see a great battle taking place.

The picture switched to a different scene, not of the battle, but of a faraway place lost somewhere in space. A figure appeared, yet I wasn't close enough to make out who it was. A feeling inside told me I would meet this person in the future. I wasn't sure of what this meant.

Someone knocked at my cabin door, and this brought my mind back to this place and time. Getting up, I went to the door. Opening it, I found Captain Jonathan standing there.

"Josaphat, you are needed in the command center. Would you please come with me?" he said.

"How are the repairs coming on the ship?" I asked.

"You know it's funny, but some of the repairs we knew we had to do. Well, when we got there to start working on them, it was as if the ship had somehow repaired itself… strange isn't it?" he said.

I didn't say anything back to him. A small smile crossed my face. I knew how the ship had been repaired. As I said before, I simply believe that everything has life in it.

"It repaired itself…"

He turned his head back to me. "Huh?" he asked.

"Never mind. I was just thinking out loud. It's not important," I said.

"We should be ready to head for earth in about an hour," he said.

Following him to the control center, the *Temperance* felt healed. As we walked my hand slid along the flesh of the ship. It was warm, not cold. There was a connection between myself and it. The ship seemed to have a pulse moving through its being. I tried to understand the bond between the two of us.

The ship was made of materials that hands had formed; the pulse had been made by hands that had never been seen.

We arrived at the command center and as we entered, Commander Stephens was giving out orders. Standing there, I marveled at his ability. He was always two steps ahead of what was happening.

Seeing me enter, he turned to greet me.

"I hope you rested well. We will need all of your abilities once we reach earth. Our long range communications are back in full operations, and news from earth is not good."

"Are there any reports on my wife, Susanna, and our Granddaughter Joan?" I asked, with concern in my voice.

"Not much," he answered. "Our forces are on the verge of being destroyed. The Gara have offered them a chance to surrender. The time given to them will expire in thirty more minutes."

"Sir," Captain Jonathan said. "The *Temperance* is ready to move. All repairs have been completed."

"Good," Commander Stephens answered. "It's time to go and kick some Gara butt."

I could feel the power of the engines as they revved up, bringing full life back to the *Temperance*. A glow formed a halo around every part of the ship. Movement could be seen as the stars started to fade away.

As we turned the ship, looking on the projection screen, a small object appeared. I knew it was earth as we moved closer to it. I was amazed by the beautiful appearance of the earth. Nothing had ever looked as wonderful as this blue marble, which floated through the blackness of space.

Something else caught my eye—millions of pieces of debris from the mass destruction of thousands of ships, from both sides. It was devastating to know the amount of lives that were destroyed in this battle.

I felt sick to my stomach at what I was seeing. Hopefully, at no time now or in the future would anyone ever paint as horrible a picture as this again.

All the conflicts that had been happening for millions of years and grew with each additional conflict that occurred had been between beings who thought that what they were doing was right and justified. In this struggle, only one side was fighting for the good of all beings over the entire universe. This had come to be the greatest struggle of all—good versus evil. Could this be the final battle?

Could this be Armageddon, the final battle? If one thought that way, then yes it could. For those who thought differently, yes it also could.

Bringing my thoughts back, I could hear everyone in the command center as the excitement grew. They were all in their dress uniforms; pride shone on each of their faces.

Coming from the dark side of the moon, Commander Stephens looked at his watch.

"Five minutes before our people on earth have to give their answer to the Gara. Josaphat, you will need to go first and join your wife and granddaughter," he said, coming over to me. Shaking my hand, he said, "Good luck, my friend. We will see each other very soon."

"Yes, we will, but I believe that a time will come when that will be different," I said.

It was time. Closing my eyes, I felt my body rise up and then disappear as it moved through the blackness of space and then dropped rapidly through the atmosphere of the earth, down between a few clouds that floated over the land. This time I didn't use the sphere. My powers had grown again, and I had matured enough to make a difference, I hoped.

When I opened my eyes, I was behind Sue and some other people I didn't recognize. I could see that they were talking. Slowly, I walked up behind her, putting my hand on her shoulder.

She turned around; her face had a look of surprise on it. Throwing her arms around me, shouting, "Thank God you're alive! I love you so much!" was all she could say before a soft cry came from her. Taking my hands, I held her face, lightly wiping away the tears that ran down her cheeks. Her arms gripped me tighter, and I could feel the love she held in her heart for me. I knew she felt the love I held in my heart for her.

We stood there for a few seconds, holding onto each other. Then a familiar voice broke the quiet.

"Can I be a part of the group hug?"

Looking around, we saw Skylar standing there. Again the tears started to flow, but now from all three of us.

Skylar ran into our arms.

"Yes," Sue said. "You complete this group hug."

This was a hug we had shared millions of times. This was our moment together.

"Are you all right?" Sue asked, holding Skylar close. "When I left, I thought you were badly hurt, but you're all right now."

"Yes, silly Grandma," she said, once again a child for a second. "But he helped me," she said, pointing to a figure walking toward us. The sun was causing us to shade our eyes; we couldn't see who it was at first.

"John!" Sue shouted as he joined us. "We need to have a bigger group hug!" But to truly complete it, we needed Nancy and, well, Marsha too.

Our hug was interrupted by a voice. "Susanna, the time is up. Is this the flag you want to raise?" Gary asked.

"What flag?" I asked.

"This one," Sue said, as she held up a small section, enough for me to get a glimpse of what the flag looked like. I could see the word *Freedom* painted on it.

"Yes, Gary. Let's all raise it together," she said. Walking over, we all took the flag, connecting it to a rope. We pulled together. The flag rose to the top of the pole and in the next moment, a gust of wind snapped the flag, unfurling it so that all could read the word *Freedom* painted on it and somehow, we would make that a reality.

The command was given to our people. We wouldn't surrender ourselves to the Gara. The unified world, what was left of it, would fight.

Someone handed Gary a note. As he read it, he looked at us, saying, "Every nation has sent all the reserves of people and materials that they have. Nothing is being held back, but I don't think it will be enough to defeat the Gara."

Leaning over to him, I said, "Don't underestimate the power we have. There is a surprise waiting for the Gara, one they don't have any idea is coming."

He looked at me. I could see a question on his face. Taking my arm, I pointed up, saying, "You have got to learn to keep your faith. Sometimes it can take a long time. I know it did for me." A smile was on my face.

Gary turned, saying, "Good luck to you," as he went to join our forces.

Another voice came from behind us, saying, "Now it is complete. This is when the Promise will be completed. All will overcome one."

Turning, we saw The Keeper walking over to us. He took each of our hands, one at a time, leaning over, saying something to Skylar that we couldn't hear. Then he looked at us, saying, "My time with you is almost over. You have come a long way, learning with each step you took. The three of you have given up so much, but those losses will remain a part of your heart forever. Today you will turn another page in *The Book of Forever*. Many more pages you will still have to turn." And then he turned to Skylar once more.

"You, child, will be the building block that will move far beyond the bounds of heaven and earth. Greatness will become a part of your name. All beings, whatever they are, will know of you, even before you appear to them. Remember what I whispered to you earlier."

Then he turned to us.

"Today is your day, for the people of this world will cast off the bonds of evil. But you will not completely destroy it, only drive it from this world. Evil will wait for you out there," he said, pointing to the heavens.

Then he lowered his head briefly, then turned and walked away, disappearing into the crowd of people that stood behind and to the side of us.

Explosions tore into our forces, too many to count. They came from the sky and ground. But the most powerful ones came from the two beasts that had arisen, one from the sea and the other from the bowels of the earth.

Signals were given, and everything of power that we had was hurtled toward the Gara. We were David, and the Gara was Goliath. All that was needed was the rock and the slingshot.

Darkness again tried to come over the earth. Lightning flashed, and the wind hurtled toward us, driving an icy rain deep into us, but our forces continued to move forward.

The Gara now unleashed the beasts to destroy us.

At that moment our forces slowed but then moved forward again, fighting and dying as bravely as anyone had ever done before.

The two beasts grew angrier. Fire erupted from their mouths, burning large swatches through our forces, both on the ground and in the air. Over and over massive amounts of destruction ripped through our people.

Our advance came to a stop; it looked like a person walking on a tightrope, moving ahead, then slipping now and then, slowly going back then forward.

This was the time. Moving across space, my mind sent a message to the *Temperance*.

You are the straw that is needed to break the back of the Gara.

The darkness of the sky was torn apart as the light of the sun broke through, followed by the whiteness of the *Temperance*, bringing down destruction upon the Gara as it moved over them, destroying the whole of their might, as if something was moving with unknown power; a power that had never been felt before. Our forces moved forward again with a new strength in their souls. They were cutting through the Gara's forces like a hot knife through butter.

Sue, Skylar, and I mind-jumped to the center of the attack, and with our powers we destroyed large sections of the Gara's forces. The beast that had risen from the earth spewed fire in our direction.

Skylar rose into the air. Bright light swirled around her as she called on the Creator.

"*TS-S-I, CARO, O-DE-HS-LATI. LY-SA-OR-OWE-O-RO-KI.*" (It is time, Creator, to end this evil. Bring forth your power to destroy them.)

As the last of those words moved through the air, a great and powerful flash struck the beast that had risen from the earth, and it was no more.

Skylar turned and moved to meet the other beast that had risen from the sea; again she spoke those words, calling upon the Creator to bring strong power to destroy it, and as before in that moment, this beast was also destroyed. There was a great fear moving through Gara. Mass confusion started to tear into their souls, and great wails of pain rose from them.

The *Temperance* had destroyed all of their ships that were in the air, cutting off their only route of escape.

Our forces were destroying the Gara that were fighting us on the ground. We moved like a machine. The Gara sensed that the battle was lost, but true to the very end, evil would not let go.

Moving toward the center of the remaining Gara, Skylar, Sue, and I were looking for the cell that contained the head of the evil. It had to be destroyed.

Our power cut a wide path through them. It had become quiet. Looking around and finding that nothing remained of the Gara, all that was found was the head with its long snake-like arms that had controlled the evil, as it tried to hide in its life-support pod.

As we walked over to it, a voice came from inside the pod that sustained its life.

"Please don't harm me. My power is gone. All evil that once controlled your world has been destroyed. I beg you for my life. How can you call yourself good and at the same time destroy something that is begging for its life?"

Looking at each other, we didn't have the answer to this question. Could you destroy something that had begged for mercy, even if it was pure evil?

And if that evil was left to live, knowing that it could come to grow and flourish once more, could you or would you be able to decide?

I had no answer to this question.

Something greater than us had to make that decision.

Groups of people moved around us, saying not a word; but having heard the question, they also had no answer.

Turning to face them, we said nothing. At that moment a bright light flashed behind us. Without turning, we knew the question had been taken from our hands. Was it life or death? We would never know, for it was gone.

The crowd erupted into a loud cheer. Evil was removed from all our souls, and a giant weight was lifted from the earth.

Walking through the masses of people, we could feel great love, not only for us, but for each other. Holding Skylar and Sue's hands, we found the command tent. As we entered, we were met by leaders from all over the world.

Mary was the first to greet us, saying, "You three have secured the future of this world. A lot is owed to you. Only ask and it will be yours."

The rest echoed what Mary had said to us.

"Give us a few minutes alone," I said. "We need to decide, please."

A soldier came over and led us to a small room that was away from everyone.

John also joined us. For a few minutes no one said a word. Could we wipe away all the memories of what we had been through and return home? But I knew that was impossible. The loss to our family was small in comparison to what the earth had lost.

Finally Skylar stood up; she slowly looked at each of us before saying a word. She was trying to see into our hearts, and a smile came to her lips.

Each one of us would probably like go home and not remember what had happened. We are only human, and as humans, we only want our own corner of the world left to do our own thing. As the saying goes, "We have paid our dues, now leave us alone."

"Skylar, I know we have done more than most, but can we just walk away?" John asked.

"He's right. We had our chance to let this pass from our hands, but we chose not to let go," Sue said, a look of concern on her face. Sue turned to me, asking, "Joe, what are your feelings?"

Taking a few minutes before answering, I said, "I'm the one who started us on this path, and yet, I would like to go home and forget all about it, yet there is something inside of me that makes that impossible. There are questions that we have no answers for. Part of our family is not with us. There has to be an answer to where or what has happened to them."

"You mean Marsha and Nancy?" John asked.

"Yes," I answered. "They are part of us; we can't let them go without knowing what has happened to them."

"So you are saying that our answer to that question is that we want to continue on with this struggle between good and evil?" John said.

"Yes, John," I answered. "No matter where it takes us, we will go on until we find the rest of our family. Hopefully with them we will be able to throw off the chains of evil that binds all of us."

Walking together, we silently went back into the large tent.

There was a surprise waiting for us: Commander Stephens and Captain Jonathan.

"Great ending, wasn't it?" Captain Jonathan said, throwing his arms around me in a bear hug. He was a large man, and it felt like a real bear was hugging me. I felt something dark pass over my soul. I tried to block it. I only knew that at some time in the future I would understand this feeling.

Everyone started to laugh. I introduced them to my family; it felt like our family had gained new members.

The tent was full. Groups of people sat around quietly outside the tent. A public address system was set up so everyone could hear what we were going to say.

As we stepped on stage, the four of us stood behind the president as she introduced us.

"It is my great honor and personal privilege to introduce these heroes. For without their sacrifice, our world would still be held by the chains of evil that has controlled us for thousands of years. Because of them, our world is in the process of great healing. We have come together as one—no more separate nations. This day is the beginning of a great new era for this world. Thanks to these people, who have made it possible."

A thunderous applause erupted from the people. I thought it would go on forever, and then it finally it stopped.

Taking hold of the microphone, my mind was swirling. What could I say? I felt a warm, invisible hand touch my heart, giving me the courage to speak. Looking out over the room, I could see where the warmth was coming from. At the back of the tent, I could see Lee standing there, a smile on his face. I could feel his words in my mind.

You have pleased me by your deeds and by your decision to go on. More pages will be turned in The Book of Forever. *Your handprint will be on the pages, and it will be written in the book about the greatness you will accomplish. Remember to always keep your faith, no matter what you encounter. The mountains will be high, and the valleys will be low, but you three will never be alone. Let hope and goodness be your guide.*

Closing my eyes for a second, I let his words sink deep into my soul. But when I opened my eyes he was gone. "*Who was this young boy who spoke words that could touch your soul?*" I wondered.

"Joe, what's wrong?" Sue whispered, leaning close to me.

Looking at her face, I was struck by her beauty. It was as if I were seeing her for the first time. Moving my eyes to Skylar, and then finally to John, it was as if I was also seeing them for the first time. The whole world had taken on a different look. Even the people who were there had a new light around each of them. Standing there, I had changed—not on the outside, but on the inside. It felt as if I had been reborn.

Turning back to Sue, I answered, "Nothing's wrong, Sue."

I believe for the first time everything was right. We would travel far from this planet, destroying evil wherever it hides.

In my heart I knew we would find Marsha and Nancy, with the help of Lee and Daniel.

Bringing my thoughts back, I started to speak. "One more time…"

The End…Maybe